TRUNKED BY A SPIRIT

TRUNKED BY A SPIRIT

Text Copyright ©2022 by Mary Cecilia Freeman

Illustrations Copyright ©2022 by Tanya Maneki

Printed in the United States of America.
Published by MCF Publishing Company

The following is a work of fiction. Any names, characters, places,and incidents are the product of the author's imagination. Any resemblance to persons, living or dead, is entirely coincidental.

ISBN 979-8-9857145-1-7 (hardcover)

ISBN 979-8-9857145-0-0 (paperback)

All rights reserved. No part of this publication may be reproduced, scanned, or transmitted in any form, digital or printed, without the written permission of the author.

Cover Design & Formatting: Stone Ridge Books

Website:

www.writewithcecilia.com

TRUNKED BY A SPIRIT

LILY'S GUIDE TO RELEASING ANTIQUE SPIRITS BOOK 1

M C F

This book is dedicated to all Catholic teenagers in the world, especially to the teens in my own family. Life isn't easy, especially for us Catholics. But, who said being a Catholic has to be boring and dull?

To my family, especially those who have always believed in me. Encouraging me to grow as an author. I love you all so much!

To a few amazing co-workers who have hearts of gold and have supported my author journey from day one.

To my editor, Donna, who worked tirelessly through the million spelling and grammar mistakes. You're a true blessing.

To my illustrator, Tanya, who has been the creator collaborator of both my books so far. Thank you for turning my sketches into amazing works of art! You are one brilliant and skilled artist!

CONTENTS

From the Author

Hey there Reader! My name is Lily Shels. I would say life is peachy, but that would be a lie. Life kind of sucks for me right now. Everything was going fine until I turned 13 years old. I found out that I can feel the presence of spirits in random antique objects. Which is really confusing and hard for me to process because does that mean I am possessed or doing something majorly wrong here? Being a Catholic and all, makes this very, how should I put it, bad? I'm not even sure why it would be bad but it just seems like it would be. I've never heard of any Catholic saints having spirit freeing powers before, so hopefully I'm just breaking new ground here.

If Mom or Dad ever found out or the priests…I'm not sure what would happen to me, maybe an exorcism or something. I love my parents and they love me, but this weird spirit thing might be something I can never talk to them about. Sometimes, being a Catholic is hard, and not what I would consider fun at all.

I've done a pretty excellent job at keeping my curse/power a secret from almost everyone, so far. There have been many close calls. Which, the last spirit I helped free, landed my butt in therapy for a few weeks. Thanks alot, Isaac

 # Chapter 1 

Despite the sweltering heat Lily's arms broke out in goose-bumps from the jolt, shivers she usually gets when she recalls the spirit Isaac.

Looking around as Lily quickly walked past stores, she spotted her fast becoming favorite store in the entire small town. The antique store where her school crush, Patrick, worked.

Before heading inside the store to escape the humid air, Lily checked her social media account, adding the antique store location to her latest story. Then checked her hat, skirt and overall appearance.

She looked hot…and sweaty. This is why she takes pictures of her cute outfits before going outside in the summer heat.

It's so bloody hot--not dry heat, but a soaking-wet, humid, everything--sticks--to--you kind of heat. Lily yanked on her skirt that had glued itself to her upper thigh somehow. *Stupid skirt!*

Lily opened the door, basking in the cool air whispering over her skin.

Once inside, Lily stopped in front of the first thing that caught her eye.

I don't think I've seen this before. Lily thought. It was a big trunk, remade into a dresser/bookshelf thing. It was pretty cool looking. Feeling the smooth paint, her finger barely made contact before a familiar jolt surged through her body. "Oh man." she jerked her hand back, away from the trunk. It was happening again. Another spirit was trapped by some random, older item that Lily always found. No one else could see or connect with them, except for her. She didn't actually see them, only felt their presence and despair.

That one touch was all it took for Lily's week to go down the drain. Taking a deep breath, Lily placed her hand firmly on the trunk and closed her eyes. Once connected, skin to trunk, she whispered to the spirits' presence. "I accept your spirit and story. Show me your path."

Lily surrendered her planned week of adventure, settling for her new mission. No point of complaining, it is what it is. The trapped spirit needed her help, even if she had plans. Plans to visit her best friend Doris, plans for a fun photoshoot, even plans to hang out, doing nothing. They were gone like smoke in the wind. *Poof, swept away as if they never existed.* Lily pictured herself standing in front of the spirit, spewing a good long lecture. But, in the end, it wouldn't matter.

Lily felt her shoulders drop. She remembered from the previous missions that she would lose every ounce of energy dealing with this spirit. It wouldn't matter if she had more time and a thousand plans, she wouldn't have energy left to do anything except sleep.

Only Lily could see and feel the spirit dwelling inside this trunk. *This one is restless, wanting to be released, to be free. Which means I need to work fast.* Accepting her weird little talent, there is no going back after making contact with the spirit.

Lily made up that "I accept" speech, when these spirit incidents happened more often than she liked. Like superheroes have iconic last words or a great quote. That one is hers. *Sounds kind of cool, I think. Sometimes I need something to get me in the mood--to solve these things. Le sighhhhhhhhhhhh. It was her favorite expression, but It wasn't working. I wish I never came into this store or that my hands had an on/off switch.*

The temptation to ignore it and walk away was always there. *Trust me I've tried. Nothing works.* Lily couldn't ignore a spirit no matter how far away she was from the object. Once contact was made, Lily was bound by some invisible contract with the spirit.

It's like the spirit had a rope wrapped around me, that they tugged on, every day, all day--until I had their story finished and they were free.

"First things first, how much is this trunk?" She muttered to herself.

Looking for the price tag, Lily caught the attention of an employee working at the front desk nearby. It was Patrick, her long-time crush coming toward her.

"Hello there, Miss? Can I help you?"

Lily pushed her large hat back, revealing her face. "Hey Patrick. It's just me."

"Oh, I didn't recognize you with that large hat on. Very vintage."

That right there. Ladies and gents, is why I dress up. To hear those words "Very vintage" from my long-time crush...although he doesn't know it. And there goes my face--is it just me or is it hot in here? If she was being honest, Lily only dressed up today because she had discovered Patrick worked at the antique store, from a friend. *Get it together Lily! Cool off before you start smelling like sweat. Le sighhhhhhhhh...*

Patrick offered a friendly smile, tapping the trunk. "Do you need help with this?"

That smile-- I could only stare for a split second. It was the very one I dreamed about hoping he would focus it on me.

"ummm? Uh yes! How much for the dresser--I mean trunk thing?" Lily grimaced, realizing how stupid she sounded.

Patrick looked for the price tag. It wasn't there. "Sorry, I'm not sure. Let me ask the manager. Be right back.`` He turned, heading toward the back.

He'll think you're a weirdo, if you don't cool it, missy. Lily waved both hands, trying to cool her flushed cheeks, watching for Patrick to return.

She stopped waving the second Patrick walked toward her. Lily noticed immediately from Patricks clenched jaw and fists that it wasn't good news. "Hey Lily. Sorry, I think this is just for display. The manager said the family that donated it didn't say it could be sold. So we have to wait for their approval before giving it a price. There are a few others in the back I can show you, if this is the style you are looking for." He waved his arm towards the back, smiling while he led the way.

As Lily walked away from the trunk, her gut sank. *Nope, this is not going to be a fun one.* The hair on her arms stood up, covering her skin with goosebumps. The spirit trapped in this trunk was going to give her trouble if she wasn't careful. From past experience with them, they won't do anything to the object or people around them, but with each step away Lily felt the connection yanking her back. The spirit made contact with Lily and will pester her until she completed the mission. Their connection is through their collective emotions and thoughts. She could see their memories but couldn't see the physical spirit- -only feel their emotions and thoughts. Before they died. They communicate by sharing their memories. In collecting these memories, Lily pieced together a story line until it revealed the regret or reason the spirit was still trapped. From there she finishes writing their story in order to free them.

"Is there any way I could speak with the trunk's owner? I know it's a little strange, but this trunk truly caught my eye."

Staling while she decided on an evasive reason, Lily fiddled with the brim of her hat. "Ummm I'm doing a photoshoot and *this* trunk is perfect!" *Sheesh, nothing like overselling it.* Her voice cracked at the end sounding way too loud--causing Patrick to give her "the pity look". *You know, that look, "I knew she was nuts" one.*

Patrick chuckled, "You must really want that trunk." He smiled, trying to placate Lily. "I can ask Zoe for the owner's number?"

"Oh my gosh, thank you. That would be awesome, *please*! Do you need my cell or social media info to reach me?" *Perfectly executed there Lily.* She had rehearsed that 'reach me' spiel for an hour this morning--Polite-yet direct.

"No, I'm good." Patrick replied, clearly uncomfortable. He rubbed the back of his neck while waving away Lily's suggestion.

POP!! Annnnnd there goes that dream. Not only did Patick say no, but he even frowned when he said it. Lily could feel her heart falling, smashing into a million tiny pieces. *Why wouldn't you want someone's info? Even if just to check them out.*

"The Manager, Zoe, can call you once she speaks to the owners. Zoe knows your sister, so she has your home number." Patrick finished as new customers came into the store.

Patrick stilted, evasion–trailed off when new customers entered. Pasting a smile on her face, to hide her frustration, as they finished with a quick "See ya", Patrick hurried to greet his customers.

Stupid spirit! Stupid skirt! Stupid, dumb trunk...Not only did they ruin my week, But now Patrick HATES ME!

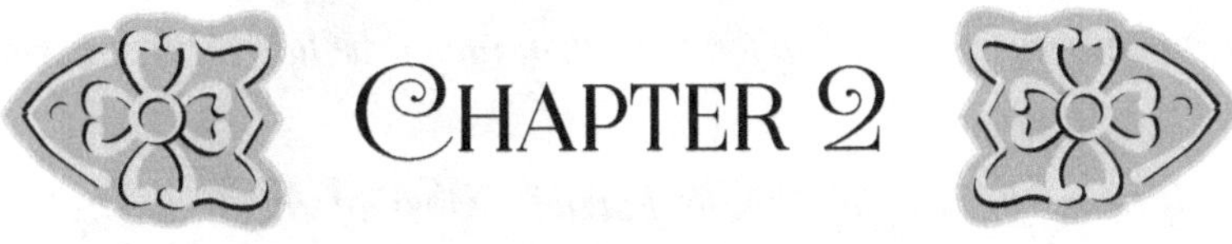 Chapter 2

Once safely in her own bedroom, Lily threw herself on the bed, princess style. Closing her eyes, she laid her arm across her face. *I swear, it's like an invisible force field surrounds me when I'm near boys. Like my freakiness is felt by all boys, the second they get close to her. Once they sense it, they run! LE SIGHHHHHHhhhhhh* An overly dramatic groan escaped Lily. *Why does this always happen to meeeeeeeeeeee?* Smacking down her skirt, Lily's frown deepened. *Stupid skirt…I look better in pants. I thought, if I wore something modest and cute, like Mom keeps insisting I do, he would notice me more. But noooo! One more reason I hate these stupid skirts!*

Lily turned over, rolling up in the blanket. *That's better, my nice, cozy, blanket burrito.* Thinking back to when she first noticed Patrick, her mind grabbed onto those amazing possibilities. *He was the only boy who noticed me. Once, I was left alone at school.*

Ok... I actually had stupid math tutoring after school, and my mom was late for pickup. Patrick was waiting for his parents to pick him up, too. He walked over and we talked about school the entire five minutes--until my mom, with her bad timing, drove up, and honked. Parents always show up when you wish they'd be late, or in my case a little bit later.

It was so nice talking to Patrick. Most of the time, we stood awkwardly, watching everyone else leave. I always feel so alone and embarrassed. I'm not allowed to have my cell with me at school--Which is totally not fair. I barely got a cell phone in the first place, it's another one of those strict catholic parent rule things. **No cell phones until you're old enough to have a job.**

Other kids at my school are allowed to have them without a job. Heck, I even saw a first grader with one.

Anyway, Patrick is so smart. He did most of the talking. He told me he is good at math, and that he really likes sports–like football. Except this year he might not make the team.

He had said "My parents want me to focus on getting my grade average higher for college." Patrick said with a slight smile.

That smile. The one I have been dreaming he would beam my way! Man, is he cute. Le Sighhhhh.

Wow, where was I? Unraveling from the blanket, Lily felt the humiliation all over again. "No, I'm good" his response circled through her thoughts and mind like a fidget spinner.

Painful and blunt. His blunt response reminded Lily of her older sister, Mina. Mina would have said "OUCH! That stings." teasing me, out of my self pity party, like always.

Mina enjoyed letting Lily humiliate herself, especially with strangers. Mina always got a kick out of Lily's most embarrassing moments.

The absurdity of it caused Lily to suddenly giggle. Recalling Mina chasing her through the house, trying to get the tv remote back. When Mina tripped over her own two feet, falling flat on her face, the face-plant was hilarious! Like a slapstick scene right out of Lily's anime shows. When Mina tripped, she tried to save herself, but failed. *SMACK!* Lily Laughed so hard she ended up with hiccups, while Mina groaned from the floor.

Feeling slightly happier, Lily realized she wasn't the only person to make mistakes. *Take that Mina! MUAHAHAHHAAAAA! Lily added a raspberry to top it off.*

Lily's mind turned to her spirit curse. *Is this some sort of punishment from God? Had I done something so bad that deserves this?* Lily wondered, *trying to recall every bad thing she had done in the past few years.*

Her list was interrupted when Mina's voice came up the stairs, loud and clear. "Lily, supper is ready."

"K" Lily replied. Pausing for a second... *You know what, maybe Patrick was just having a really bad day and that's why he said that? Yeah! Like maybe his parents told him not to take anyone's number or info because he was supposed to be focused. I heard a few girls say his parents are super strict on things like cell phones. So he had refused, in order to not get himself in trouble. Yep. That's it! That makes sense. That Patrick would snub me for his parents' rules.*

With a better attitude, Lily strolled into the kitchen to find out that her bad day was not over yet--Her nose bristled at the odor wafting out of the kitchen. *Ughhhhh. Stew again with mashed potatoes, again!?! Lily* hoped dessert would be worth gagging dinner down. *Le Sighhhhhh...*

The kitchen was crowded, her two brothers, Theo and Max were carrying plates into the dining room while Mom finished the cooking. "HHEHEHEHe" Lily snickered, as one brother walked past. Max had mouthed off yesterday. Now, he has to do Lily's chores, plus the floors, this weekend.

You might think that I am being mean, but 99.9% of the time when "the brothers" do anything. **It-is-always-stupid.** *Plus, it usually gets them into a ton of trouble. So in My personal, sisterly opinion…*

HE-- *<clap>*DE-- *<clap>* SERVED-- *<clap>* IT *<clap>*!

Shooting her an evil glare, her brother hurried past, shoving Lily into the door frame. Lily's smile morphed into a sneer before she stuck her tongue out.

Mom's admonishment was totally expected. "Lily, leave your brother alone--otherwise I'll make **you** do someone else's chores."

Lily immediately dropped her smile. Mom's threats were never taken lightly.

Spotting the dessert on the kitchen island, Lily felt joy and peace flood her body, *There it is.* The dessert that will make the awful meal tolerable. *Box brownies!!! Soft and warm in the middle, while still chewy around the edges…..Oh man, I need to be fast or the boys will get all the best pieces.*

As Lily's mouth watered at the thought of enjoying the lushious brownie, she could hear her Mom's words echoing through her memory. "You could make a sacrifice." The constant reminder about being Catholic and the graces you can receive from little sacrifices was always there. Sometimes Lily found the reminder annoying. Little sacrifice? As if giving up the best part of the brownie dessert, to two little impish brothers, was just a little sacrifice.

Lily recalled a rather long conversion she had with her mom not too long ago about sacrifice and what it meant for her.

"What's the point of these 'sacrifices' anyway? From what you just said a sacrifice is something you can give up in thanksgiving to God or as an atonement for a sin against God. So, unless I'm making up for a sin, I technically don't have to unless I want to right?"

Mrs. Shels smiled, shaking her head slowly at her daughter's clever remark. "True, God only wants you to make sacrifices, whether that be in thanksgiving or in repentance, on your own accord. But, before you decide that all small sacrifices are not worth your time, just remember, a sacrifice offered up to God of any size, earns you a special grace. And graces are opportunities to obtain favors for yourself and others. Think of them like brownie points." Mrs. Shels grinned. Lily could tell she was proud of her analogy. Brownie points, now her Mom was speaking her language. If only graces were really brownies points that you could eat every time you earned one.

At least her Mom took the time to explain some of these Catholic practices. Now that Lily was older she had more questions about her Faith and did not feel comfortable asking some of her teachers since their answers were always "the answer is in your catechism book.". Which does not help. Why was she asking more questions? Curiosity? Maybe it was because of the spirits? Or was she just more curious about it all since she was growing up? Lily shrugged, realizing the long tangent she had taken was distracting her from the real problem at hand. To beat Max and Theo for the brownie? Or to go at a normal eating pace and let the brownies pieces fall where they may?

Lily decided to eat dinner and let the chips fall where they may. If she beat her brothers then she did. If Max and Theo finished first then Lily would accept her defeat and offer up not getting the best brownie piece.

Usually no one rushes to finish dinner quickly, however when Brownies are included, the forks flew faster than the speed of light. Lily wondered if this was something mothers did on purpose--choosing a hated meal together with the best dessert--ensuring that they ate the dreaded vegetables?? In the end, gagging down the stew and mashed potatoes would be totally worth the chocolatey gooey goodness.

Cutting a generous brownie, Lily placed it on her plate. *I'm going to enjoy every last crumb of this brownie. Magnifique, or whatever French people say.* She beat her brothers and didn't have to sacrifice anything after all. *Ha! Take that you bane of my existence!*

After cleaning up, Lily grabbed her pen. It felt like it weighed about 50 pounds. Clearing the kitchen counter, Lily began her homework, which ensured more doodling. Opening one notebook, she flipped through to see how many doodles she added to each page. *I don't understand how anyone can get through all their homework without a single sketch or doodle. Non-doodlers puzzle me. My notebooks are filled with notes, scribbles and sketches. But, some of my teachers insist on checking our notebooks. Why? They instruct us to complete assignments in our notebooks just so they can riffle through them? Let me tell you. I use up an entire white-out® pen before handing in my notebooks. I've had a few who find my sketches amusing, but most don't. They knock down the grade points for every scribble found.* Feeling slightly peeved, Lily stuck her tongue out, imagining her teachers. *Some of them have no imagination and are boring.*

With that thought, Lily touched pen to paper. With that simple motion, the trapped spirit's thoughts rushed forward. "F....Fr something.." Lily closed her eyes, trying to connect to the spirit. "Fredrick, Ahh that's it!" Lily quickly wrote the name in her notebook.

When she recalled touching the trunk, the rush of memories flooded her mind. Those memories were as clear as day--as if Lily was present when they were created--only through the eyes of Fredrick.

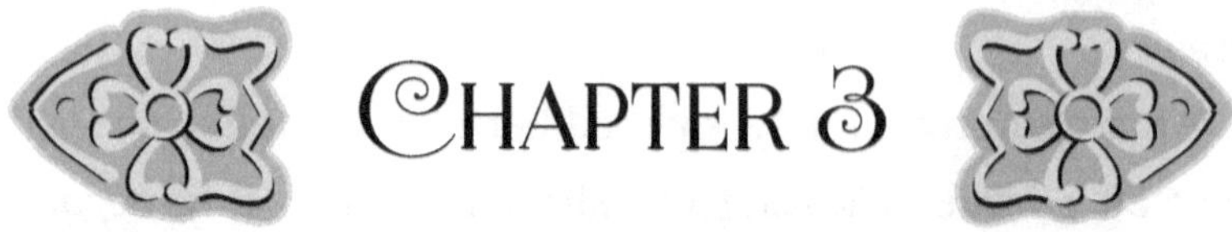

Chapter 3

The old stuff or antiques, have more soul due to them not being mass produced. Made a few at a time, they were made to last for years. Which is why I think antiques have more spiritual possibilities and I've noticed, over the past three years, I find more missions in antique stores than any other place. I can freely touch anything in a drug store or other modern shop, but in an antique store, I feel like I'm playing some kind of russian roulette, where trapped spirits can grab me and not let go.

Lily's mind wandered as she sketched out details about her newest Spirit stalker. Fredrick is an older man who died suddenly for some reason a few years ago.

According to the memories Fredrick shared with Lily, life was peachy until around the 50 years old mark.

His memories were really blurry and indistinct during

that time. Lily felt Fredrick's pain. Her whole body felt heavy, exhausted, like his intense thoughts were too much. She worried what was to come next as she continued to sketch out his story.

Looking down at her notebook, she tried to link some of the details together.

What the heck does this bird mean?

In the past, when a spirit shared memories with Lily, they came in a specific order. First, a hint of where they are from-- a country or a state. Then, a little about themselves-- name, age and random things that made them happy. After that, comes bad memories, things that they regret, depression, illness. Then, the broken memories, like a canvas splattered with unwanted feelings. *Those are fun.* Most of the time, listening to music helps Lily deal with that rollercoaster of emotions.

The last spirit was a bad one. So much pain and depression- he nearly committed suicide. Sometimes the feelings overwhelm her, making Lily's life miserable. Being a teen was an emotional journey already, adding this to her life was another level of misery.

Lily's trial with the last spirit, Isaac, scared her best friend.

Doris recounted the horrible semester to her occasionally. "You randomly disappear after school and then found later in the woods by yourself, you'd burst into tears periodically throughout the day, and in the saddest voice ever, you once told me –*A gunshot marks the start for some, but the end for others.*"

I don't remember saying that. Which is slightly concerning. I can't forget that feeling though--complete despair. That was a rough month.

Thankfully her sister thought Lily was having a rough time at school--bullies and such. She took her out to dinner and rollerblading twice that month to pull her out of her funk.

My sister can be a real pain, but she's awesome just the same.

Slapping her hand on the counter, Lily yanked her thoughts back to Fredrick's story.

The bird is a little weird looking...

Her sketch showed a long neck and fat body. It reminded Lily of a short, fat turkey. Maybe a baby turkey?

Do turkeys have white feathers? This makes my head hurt.

It's interesting that these headaches happen right after she receives a new mission. Which probably indicates hard core spiritual energy flowing from someone else's memories and forcing their way into Lily's brain.

Quite an intrusion, if you ask me. Lily dramatically mimicked an old fashioned Lady of high class. Her right hand resting on her heart as the left hand gently touched her forehead.

Making sure none of her siblings were spying on her, Lily pulled out her phone. She is allowed a phone, but her mom doesn't want her distracted while there's homework to do. "You won't get any homework done when it's on".

It's a distraction, but no one likes homework. Not even our teachers. But mom's rules are non-negotiable. *Cell phones, pants, so much is limited. Such a pain sometimes.*

If I scan this image to my phone will it figure out what kind of bird this is? Snapping a picture of the sketch Lily tried to upload it into a reverse image search.

Searching…

The wheel of death spins on her screen... Nothing!

 Searching again.

Finally...Images of fat little birds that look nothing like her sketch. *Maybe this has nothing to do with where Fred is from.* Lily tried to concentrate on Fred's memory of the bird.

Hunting or bird watching?

In one memory Fred watches the birds through some kind of scope. There are a few of them walking around, but his vision is slightly blurry. *A faded memory?* One of those moments when you are looking at something but your brain is focused somewhere else.

"How's the homework coming along?" Mom's voice entered the room thirty seconds ahead of her. Good thing too. Lily slipped her phone into her pocket as quick as lightning.

"It's coming...very slowly." Lily pretended to still be immersed in her homework. *Man, it's scary how moms can sneak up on you without a sound.* Another real pain, many good songs have been interrupted by mom's sneakiness.

"It must be super slow, hun. You haven't even opened your books." Mom raised one eyebrow with that *tsking* noise. "I received an email from your homeroom teacher today."

Lily tried to gauge if this was a good thing or bad thing while her stomach fell to the floor.

Then the smallest grin lit Mom's face. *Oh good, not bad news.* Lily's shoulders dropped as the tension left her body. Like a balloon being deflated, the air escaped between her pursed lips.

"He said your grades have improved and you seem more cheerful lately. I'm glad to hear it." She paused a second too long for Lily's comfort. "I know school, especially at this private High School, is not easy. Remember, I was in high school once upon a time. I really want you to *try* these next few years--maybe get a scholarship. Your art skills are improving and we are very proud of our little artist." Mrs. Shels wrapped her arms around Lily. "I know we don't say it enough, but we are very proud of you, Lily. Oh and I bought you a little something today. Here you go." Mrs. Shels handed a paper magazine to Lily.

"Vintage Teen Magazine? Cuz looking like a prairie girl is coming back or something?" Lily browsed through the first few pages of the magazine. Feeling the continuous modesty lecture coming.

"I read through it and thought it was pretty darn neat! Just give it a chance. Ok?" Giving one more hug, Mrs. Shels left the room.

Just like that, Lily's mood lifted about 1000%. *Encouragement and a magazine. Not bad Mom.*

Mom has a way of doing that. She will pop in to yell at you or so you think, then ends up saying something that makes you feel important. The funny thing is, she didn't before. This is a new thing she has been doing lately. As if she's trying to...encourage us somehow? The magazine upon further inspection didn't look too awful. Even saw a page about fashion and makeup.

Who knows really. Maybe Doris is right when she says, "It's all a plot parents use to make us work harder. I don't trust it."

I don't care if it is all a plot. I like it.

Good old Doris, my best friend that is only a year older than me. She is in 9th grade, just like me. We started out as art buddies, our art teacher asked everyone to pair up and I noticed her notebook was covered with this super cool looking anime picture. A young girl and boy wearing elaborate japanese garments. After they were told to pair up Lily turned to Doris and asked if she wanted to pair up with her. Doris eagerly nodded her head. That project earned them both high scores and it taught them both that they worked well together. Lily recalled how Doris invited her to work together at her house. Lily was impressed to find out that Doris liked working with plenty of snacks to munch on. "What's wrong?" Doris asked her, Lily had stopped just inside Doris's room. "Your room is so *cool!*" The two girls giggled as Doris showed Lily around her room. Stuffed animals and pillows overflowed from her bed to the floor. Her walls were covered in banners, posters and printed pictures of anything Doris was interested in. Lily remembered how almost magical Doris's room was. Even now she is never bored seeing the newest updates to her room. There's always something to see in her room. They both found out they enjoyed anime and kpop. After their project was done they ended up attempting to learn a new dance they saw online. Which failed but they had fun trying it out. *Gotta get with the trends.*

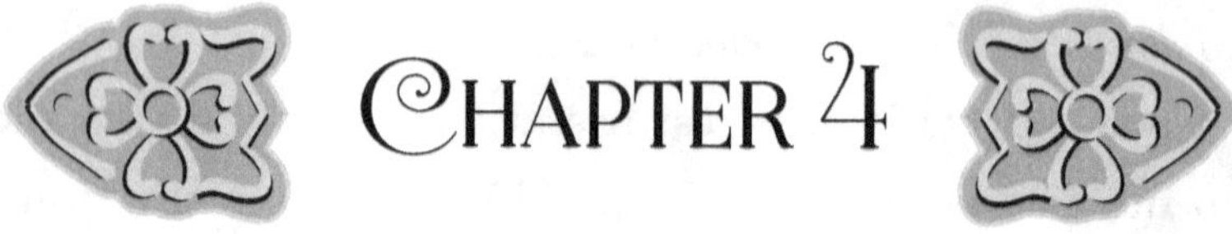

CHAPTER 4

Once Mom is gone Lily pulls out her phone.

Mina, the oldest sister, snuck up behind Lily, snatching the phone. "AHA!"

After getting over the small heart attack Lily hissed "Give it back, Mina!"

Mina dodged Lily's attempts to get the cell phone back. "Aren't you supposed to be doing your homework? Being such a bad little girl, Lily." Mina dangled the phone like bait, just out of Lily's reach.

"Give it back." Lily took one final swipe, barely missing the phone. "I *am* doing homework. I needed a short break is all."

Mina tossed the phone to Lily. "Fine, I have to get ready for work anyway."

Catching it, Lily tucked the phone safely in her pocket. *That was too close. Mina is just jealous, because when she was in high school, she wasn't allowed a cell phone at all. While we younger siblings got lucky, and were given cell phones when we turned 13 yrs old.*

"How's the spirit stories coming along?" After glancing at the magazine and open math notebook, Mina walked to the cupboards. "Are you working on a new story right now?"

"Yes, right now I'm working on a spirit who's trapped in a trunk. His name is Fredrick." Lily tapped on her math notebook.

Mina gave her a reassuring grin. "Let me know if you need anything then."

Pulling out a large bag from the cupboard, Mina asked. "Hey, where did these chips come from?"

"I think Brandon bought them. Is there a name on it?" Lily shrugged, continuing to doodle in her notebook.

Lily could hear the crinkling bag as Mina searched for a name.

In our house, one must be thorough when name searching. In the Shel household one rule stands fast and hard: **No Name, Fair game.**

This mainly applies to food. Which is why Mina and Lily checked before they helped themselves to the yummy chips. In fairness, we always look before taking. If there is no name we can help ourselves. The Shel girls have a better sense of fairness than the Shel boys. The sisters will take some, but the brothers will eat the entire bag without thinking.

Mina paused,"No name on the bag!" she whispered with a mischievous grin. Shaking the bag she headed to the counter for a baggie.

Lily watched as MIa opened the big bag, pouring a smaller portion of chips into two baggies.

These chips, Gardettos®, were a rare treat. If the second bag of chips was meant for Lily, then she would take back every mean thing about her sister being annoying.

Please, please, please, be for me…Yes it is! YUM!!!

Lily happily munched on her snack while she flipped through her Math book. Once she found her assignment, she completed her homework. Moving onto Science, she read through her notes, stopping every once in a while to sketch or add a random memory from Fred, the needy spirit.

I wrote all his info in the back of my History notebook, right? Shuffling through her notebooks, Lily frantically searched for Fred's memories. *Nope, wrong notebook.* She flipped to the back of her Art notebook and found nothing again. *Which notebook did I put it in? Dang it!!* Banging her forehead on the counter she tried to dislodge the location of Fred's notes.

Lily checked all her sticky note tabs, accidentally pulling a few loose. She noticed that these particular sticky notes were cute but useless because they didn't hold their place. Lily decided to move on without replacing the tabs. *Waste of time if they don't stick, anyway.*

Her search finally ended in the back of her Math notebook. *Go figure.*

Everyday, all day, all school year long, Math and Lily don't mix well. Not even a bit. Math was the class that Lily was the most hopeless in. So her notebook was always in her book bag, which made it convenient for important stuff. *Note to self. The subject you despise is where you will find your notes on Fred.*

Sticky note that...oh, I already did. See, it doesn't work. Le sighhhh...

Now that her homework was completed she turned all her energy toward Fredrick. In the back of her Math notebook she added the following notes.

Frederick is too long, I'll just call you Fred instead.

Haha! See I am a poet!

An older man when he died.

You didn't die from old age, did ya?

Under the cause of death Lily wrote:

Unknown.

The trunk either belonged to Fred or to someone he was very attached to.

There is that strong spiritual presence to the trunk.

The weird turkey bird

Which is possibly a fluke that leads nowhere. Maybe it will make sense later.

Bird might be a pet, of sorts.

Lily set her pen down, closed her eyes and dropped her shoulders. Sometimes when she relaxed and concentrated on the spirit, their memories flowed easier into her mind.

'Ok Fred, let's see what memories you have about that trunk. What about your family?'

After the fourth interruption from her siblings, Lily decided to change location. Their snack breaks were killing her focus. The kitchen worked better for homework, being out in nature creates a stronger connection sometimes, thus helping her relax. Plus she kinda liked being outside during the cooler evenings.

Pffft. Lily packed up her books, pens and assignments, placing her book bag where she wouldn't miss it in the morning. Then she finished off the last few chips, before heading upstairs. This change of venue seemed to work well when Lily wanted to connect with her spirit stalkers. Their memories were easier to draw out when she was outside in the open air.

Just like the magazine said. Nature is the best way to relax and boost energy. Which was in the nature and God section.

Lily made a quick stop in the bathroom, then grabbed a

smaller, travel-size bag. It was her memory-collecting kit. It contained her favorite colored ink pens, a few 7hb mechanical pencils and a white square eraser with a pink heart in the middle, a simple jade ring, along with four of her 12 crystals. Which she got for Christmas.

Lily chuckled remembering how confused she was when she got these crystals. She wanted a set of crystals from ebay that helps boost focus and school grades. And her Moms bought her the Catholic version of the crystals. The 12 crystals that the high priest Aaron wore to represent the twelve tribes of Israel. Along with a reminder that praying and working hard was a stronger solution than some stones. She did get the amethyst and emerald stones she wanted so she figured that was close enough.

Lily tucked the rest of her supplies into her bag: chapstick, tissue, hair ties, gum and rosary ring. A granola bar for a snack. Each item in her kit was carefully vetted. Either because they were recommended through research or selected based on her personal experience.

She detoured to the kitchen before heading outside, grabbing her math notebook and a bottle of water. Lily's plan was to sit on the trampoline, in the warm breeze, and think. She enjoyed the cooler nights, Summer was almost here, and the heat forecast was looking intense.

CHAPTER 5

Until Lily finished the spirit's story, it was like an itch--irritating, yet insistent. In many ways it felt like a curse. Only lifted when the spirit's story is told, and they are ready to move on to their eternal resting place: Heaven or Hell. Lily found herself praying that they trapped time as a spirit was their Purgatory penance so when they are free they can go straight to Heaven. Prayer. Another subject her parents tend to harp on. Sometimes she wondered what was the point of praying? Does it really do anything?

Lily knew her frustrating situation was getting to her. She being the lucky conduit, Lily had the charming task to uncover their unwritten chapters, and whatever was attaching them to this world.

Once contact is made with the spirit-object, the persistent

itch begins. Any plans to do anything, go anywhere are thrown out the window. Lily's brain won't stop until she reveals the spirit's problem and releases them. Her mind is obsessed with the person and their story--what happened to them, did they do something wrong to deserve this? Why or how can she help them and not anyone else? Which is why it's a rollercoaster of emotions.

When the spirit's story becomes sad or even depressing, Lily experiences all of those emotions at once. Over time, if the story is not finished quickly, the concentrated emotions overwhelm her.

It hurts.

It is weird to feel the emotions of someone you have never met. Unsettling to know what they feel in the darkest parts of their mind. Frustrating to be unable to help them. Depressing to know they suffer yet unable to change the final outcome.

Overall, it just sucks. Major Le sighhhh

Lily selected one from many mood playlists on her phone. "I think this one will do." *Some uplifting music with positive vibes.* Earphones in, music playing softly, she sprawled across the trampoline letting the breeze kiss her skin.

After a few bliss filled moments, Lily jerked upright. Her mind was swamped with memories from Fred's life. She grabbed her notebook and pen then began to write.

Fred did own the trunk.

Wherever he packed it to go made him very sad.

Lily tried separating Fred's emotions from the details connecting him to the trunk. The memory played inside her head like a movie, but everything was a bit out of focus. There was something missing--one minute Fred was packing, then the room would fade to black. Back and forth, fuzzy to black, black to blurry once again. When it finally cleared his trunk was packed. The blurry moments felt like skips in Fred's memories.

Lily had a few ideas why Fred had those memory skips.

He's blocking something. This happened before with the suicidal guy. He had some horrible pain and blocked out two specific people from his memories. They were the two who pushed him to suicide. It took his entire story for me to figure that out. His blurred memories were because he was blocking them from his mind.

Lily felt like she was close to figuring out Fred's last name. "Ok, Fred. Give me a clue, what's your last name?"

Returning to Fred's memory, Lily was in a new room. *Is that a telephone?* It was a really old telephone--a big, black box that hung on the wall. It had one of those dialing circles and a hand-held black thing that you talk into. Fred walks into the kitchen, and Lily notices someone else is in the room, standing near the island. Papers are stacked neatly on the island that Fred begins to sign. He's frustrated, angry even. The papers are hard to read--blurry to the point that Lily cannot make out what they say. It's strange to watch Fred feeling for the papers or the other person's hand guiding him to where he should sign his name. This other person has long hair, a female, maybe his wife or daughter? Or so Lily guesses. Before she can figure it out the memory is gone.

Possible wife or daughter helping Fred with paperwork?

Old dial phone on the wall.

Maybe that will help me figure out what year he was alive. Unless Fred just lives in a really old house--which would be my luck.

Lily tried to concentrate on anything else that popped out from that one memory?

Feelings.

Feelings of frustration, bordering on anger. That anger spiked when he began signing the stacks of papers.

Still no last name.

I need to go back and inspect the trunk. Maybe it's engraved somewhere. I've seen a few engraved trunks at other antique stores, so maybe Fred's is too.

Tomorrow would be hard because it's Sunday and the store would be closed. Lily would have to wait until Monday when she could talk to the store manager about the trunk's current owner, and if she could look inside of it. Patrick obviously forgot to have the manager contact Lily about the owners. It had already been an entire day, yet Lily still hadn't heard from anyone.

Things were starting out with as much frustration as the last spirit. Leee Sighhhh

Trying to connect the details of the trunk to Fred was difficult because it had been remodeled.

Maybe the internet would have images of how Fred's trunk looked before it was remodeled.

"That will mean researching, where is my phone?"

Lily typed 'OLD TRUNKS'. No results. Making it more specific, she typed. 'Old trunks for travel'. "There we go, tada." Images and info on old travel trunks filled her screen. The trunks were usually very large and quite heavy. They were made for extended long-distance travel. Mostly made from wood and metal, the exterior was ornate, depending on how old or expensive it was. The interior varied depending on the manufacturer. Some had compartments for hanging clothes, with small boxed off areas for jewelry, stockings and such. Others had drawers built into the sides of the trunk. Some were square in design while others had rounded tops. *Not round, Oval.* The small compartments were not attached to the trunk itself, but literally an extra piece placed inside the trunk once it was filled.

Fred's trunk was one of the larger, old, wooden ones. Sturdy with an oval top lid.

Oh, with metal on the side. I remember, now. The metal was pretty rusty in Fred's memory, but the store buffed it to shiny again. *I don't know if that is important, but I guess I will find out.*

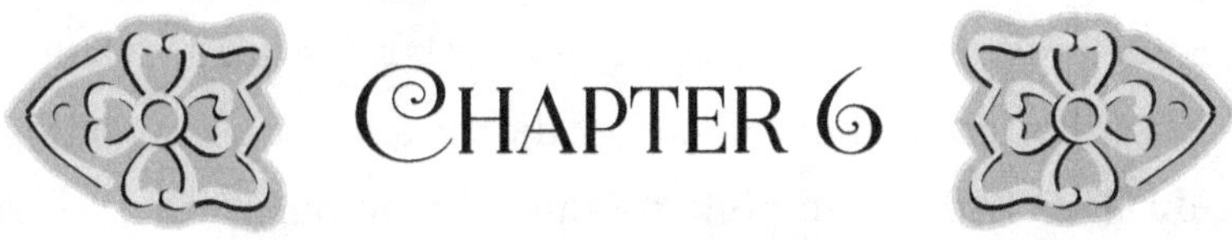

Chapter 6

Each spirit is a new mission every time. Which meant Lily could never be 100% sure what would be significant in the end.

Notes for Monday:

Go to the antique shop to inspect the trunk.

Ask about the owners and how much the trunk is.

Pray it is cheap enough for me or convince the owners to give it to me for free.

Homework and history quiz for Tuesday.

"Please be free, please be free, PLEASE BE FREE!" It really sucked when her missions led to buying a spirit infested item instead of something cute or pretty. Having to buy an old ugly doll, or some random toy that made no sense and used up all her money, was frustrating. Explaining them to Mom and Dad sometimes proved very difficult. Especially when they always asked: "Why did you buy that ugly thing, Lily?" *And I didn't have a good answer. Trying to convince them with this response, "Oh, it's just an ugly doll" doesn't work well. Usually I follow that up with "it's for art class.", or " I like the clothes on it".* Something, anything to make them think Lily actually wanted it.

That thought reminded Lily of the vacation to Texas with her family. That trip tipped off her sister Mina to her spirit problems and resulting emotional fallout. After returning home, Lily searched high and low for the two spirit-trapped antiques, when Mina cornered her with the strange purchases. Presenting Lily with the razor and cigarette case that she bought at an antique shop. "Lily, what is going on here?" Mina demanded. She stood blocking the entrance to Lily's bedroom, and clearly wouldn't be moved until she got an answer.

Lily was speechless, she couldn't tell Mina the real reason. She would never believe the truth, even if she told her. Who in their right mind would? Lily felt sick with worry. How could she explain the spirits' attraction to her, to Mina? *Great...This would happen with these two spirits arguing over who's story goes first.*

"First you bought that ugly doll. Then a random book about economics. *You don't read anything without pictures!* Now these?" Shoving the two questionable items closer to Lily's face. "You can't expect me to believe *these* are for art class. They must be important, especially since you searched the entire house for them. So, if you want these back..." Mina crossed her arms, leaning closer to Lily, "...you need to explain what's going on."

Lily stood frozen while her brain scrambled to form a believable answer. She can't tell Mina the truth...she might tell

Mom and Dad. And who knows what would happen then. She can't tell Mina.

The razor and cigarette case were only a few inches away from her. She could lunge and maybe knock Mina down to grab them and lock herself in her bedroom. Unfortunately, that plan would not work because even though Mina was slender, she couldn't be knocked down easily.

Mina waited, watching Lily's every move like a hawk on the hunt.

At that moment, one of the spirits interrupted Lily's argument with Mina. 'We'll help you get them back, just knock her down.' Lily felt their energy surging, overriding her own will. Without a better option, Lily decided to try rushing Mina anyway.

Pushing into her sister, Mina countered by grabbing Lily's arm in one swift move, then pinning it behind her back. Gently Mina slammed Lily into the wall before letting her fall to the floor.

In my own personal experience, don't ever try to take down my older sister, Mina. She is a Judo Master! If that dumb spirit hadn't tried to control me, I wouldn't be in pain right now.

Lily's face was smushed into the floor while Mina sat on her. "Get off me, you *cow*!!" Lily shrieked.

Mina rubbed her nails on her shirt then blew off invisible dust. "No way." She laughed, "Not until you tell me why these things are so important."

Lily was now convinced that nothing short of a full confession would move Mina. Once she made up her mind Mina was impossible to budge.

Lily reviewed the last few weeks in her head. She has spent the entire trip home sleeping because the spirits' emotions and memories had overwhelmed her. Their stories weren't the worst emotionally she had ever dealt with, but stressful with two at the same time.

She would experience a handful of memories, then sketch out the bones of their story.

She couldn't release the two spirits before she had to return home, something Lily never had to do before--not finishing a mission in the location where she made contact. This time, she would have to be several hundred miles away to complete the mission. Something she never thought could happen. Lily was certain if she waited too long, the distance and time would sever her

connection to the two objects and their trapped spirits. *Who knows what would happen to me and the spirits if that connection was severed?*

Lily felt the tears run down her face. "I can't tell you!" She would love to confide in her sister-- with anyone really--but nothing she could tell Mina wouldn't sound insane. A Catholic teenager who can feel and free spirits...no way would Mina believe her.

Hearing Lily's sniffling and heavy breathing, Mina slid to the hardwood floor. She needed answers and Lily had been lying and secretive for too long. "What do you mean Lily? Why can't you tell me?" Mina huffed, "You just don't *want* to tell me!" Mina paused, "You can tell me anything, I'm your *sister*. I want to help you."

Lily shook her head "no".

"You have to tell me, *something* is wrong and it's more than just normal teenage crap." Taking a deep breath, Mina tried to regain the calm that she had when she began this conversation.

"Look at you...crying over some old razor and cigarette case. Why?"

Again, Lily refused to give Mina an answer, violently whipping her head side to side. "I *can't* tell you.." She sniffed loudly. "...you won't believe me anyway."

Letting Lily calm down for a minute, Mina considered a different approach. She spoke in her calmest, soothest, most sisterly voice. "Lily, I don't care why, I just need to know you're ok.

That nothing serious or dangerous is causing this. I promise, I'll listen.Just tell me what's going on, *pleease.*"

Finally Lily decided she couldn't get away without giving Mina some explanation. Lily wanted to tell her the truth "Ok, I'll tell you, if you give me my stuff."

Lily waited for Mina to turn toward her bedroom door before picking up the two antique items. The second her fingers touched the cool metal, her anger blocking the spirit's bad advice dissipated and she reconnected with them.

Taking the time to grab a tissue, Lily began preparing herself for a long conversation with her sister. "Mina, first promise you will believe me and not tell anyone. Not a single soul. Not Mom or Dad or the priests."

Mina agreed with a quick nod of her head. Her eyebrow raised for an instant.

"This will be hard to explain…" Lily released a puff of air. "… and I doubt you will believe me. But I'll try to tell you anyway."

Mina squinted her eyes and waited. When Lily didn't continue, she finally said, "I promise. Whatever it is, I'll try to understand." She tapped the razor and cigarette case sitting on the bedspread. "Why are these so important to you?"

Lily gritted her teeth and forced herself to reveal her greatest secret. "I feel spirits that are trapped inside random, antique objects."

Mina stiffened, her eyes tracking around the room for the drugs she was now sure were influencing her sister. Her suspicions confirmed, she considered how she would handle getting Lily the help she obviously needed. "Oh... tell me more about these *spirits*?" Mina wanted Lily to keep talking while she decided what her next move would be.

Lily was completely unaware of her sister's true concern and continued with her explanation. "Once I make contact with the trapped spirit, I'm able to feel and see their memories. Which I collect, organize and complete their story. That frees them from the earthly object. I am their only way to move on, I think." Avoiding eye contact, Lily raised her eyes from the floor when she heard a snort from Mina. Her sister tried covering the noise up with a cough, but it didn't work. Lily felt the anger boiling up from inside her body. Her fury over her sister's snort fueled Lily to jump off the bed and grab the razor and cigarette case.

Lily turned to Mina. " I *knew* you wouldn't believe me!" She hissed through gritted teeth. "Are you going to tease me about this now? Tell everyone I'm nuts and need some sort of exorcism?" Stomping her foot, she demanded. "Stop laughing at me. This isn't funny!"

Mina immediately stopped, losing all trace of a smile. She was stunned, this was worse than she imagined. Lily's sudden anger had caught her off guard. Clearly this trapped spirit delusion was important to her sister.

Mina caught Lily's arm as she tried to leave the bedroom. "You're right Lily, I don't believe you..yet. Maybe, if I could see whatever it is you see, I could understand. Could you get the spirits to talk to me too?"

After wiping her tears, Lily scrunched her forehead in concentration. "I don't know, I guess I can ask, but I don't think that's how it works."

Lily asked, *Spirit's, can you do that? My sister thinks I'm crazy-insane, lost my marbles and ready for the padded room! I could really use some help here!*

Lily was disappointed when the spirits responded. *No, we can't do that. Once we make contact we can't communicate with anyone else. Sorry, tough luck.*

Great, what other proof do I have? What can I show Mina that will convince her that I'm not lying? How do I convince her that my connection to the spirits is real? This is why I never talked about it.

Mina squared her shoulders with her arms crossed to ask. "Well?" Realizing her mistake in challenging Lily, she softened her harsh stare and let her arms fall to bed.

"The spirits say they can't do that and I don't know what else *will* prove it to you." Lily tossed up her now empty hands in frustration. "You can't feel them or the connection, so it's impossible for you to understand."

Mina shrugged her shoulders. "Well, then I'm not sure wha..."

Lily interrupted mid-sentence, practically yelling. "*WAIT!* I know, I can't prove it now, but once I get their story I will be able to show you something then."

Mina crossed her arms wrinkling her forehead in confusion.

"What do you mean *get their story?*"

Before Lily could answer her, Max, one of their younger brothers, yelled up the stairs.

"HEY!! Time for the movie!"

Lily jumped in surprise and Mina gasped slightly. Both just now felt how tense they had become during this entire conversation.

§

Lily felt tense every time she recalled that unexpected confrontation. The entire awkward situation was worth it because Mina was willing to believe her. Listening to crazy stories and asking how the missions were coming along. Offering help if she needed anything or wanted to talk about them--it really made a difference for Lily having someone else to talk to. Bouncing ideas about the spirits off her sister made Lily's emotional rollercoaster ride less confusing. Lily felt she could process their stories clearer and faster, minimizing their negative effects.

Mina now says, "I may not know what you are feeling, but you can always tell me anything. That's what big sisters are for." Before drawing her in for a huge, bear hug.

Even if Mina is only doing those things to make me feel better I appreciated it. I know she isn't 100% convinced that I'm telling the truth about the spirits but she's helped me all the same.

Lily liked having Mina's help with the missions. Together, the two sisters solved the two missions about the razor and cigarette case. Mina proved to be good at solving mysteries, and Lily proved she was not taking drugs. Eventually Lily found a way to show her sister that the trapped spirits were real and needed their help. To Lily's further surprise Mina didn't think there was anything wrong with Lily's spirit releasing power.

"I still think you should talk to a priest about it but until you feel comfortable doing that I'll help keep an eye on you. And if you do anything weird and out of character again I'm coming to get you.

Like a movie ending, the credits rolled through Lily's memory. The background music was so familiar she finally realized it was the music coming through her earphones. It jolted her back to the present, and she noticed the sun had dropped in the sky. Her soft bedspread had been replaced with the harsh trampoline mesh. She needed to get back to the mission--the trapped spirit, Frederick, and his trunk.

Lily knew she could connect better with the spirits if she was near the object, even more so if she was touching it. The trunk in the antique store was her next problem. How would she afford the trunk? It was by far the largest antique she had to acquire and she knew it would be expensive. Much more expensive than a razor or cigarette case. How would she convince the trunk's owners to give it to her for free? *Please, Fred, ask your relatives to give it to me.*

If not, Lily would have to use her own money. Her parents were like most parents, if she was old enough to make her own money she could pay for her own things. Babysitting, doing extra cleaning jobs or getting A's were how she earned the extra cash she needed. Quickly searching on her phone, she typed in: **Antique trunks prices**.

Her mouth gaped while she scanned the probable bid prices for antique trunks. The prices were all over the place but still ridiculously expensive. Small trunks are between 50 to 75 dollars and larger trunks, like the one in the store, were from one-hundred dollars to thousands of dollars. Making a mental tally of how much she had earned the last two months, Lily figured she had about 150 dollars total saved. She also had a 20 dollar IOU from Theo that she could collect. But even then, she was still short, and couldn't afford Fred's trunk. Judging by what Lily remembered, it probably fell more into the thousands rather than the hundreds, with all the polished metal trim, hinges and scroll work.

Maybe I will get lucky and the owners will give me the trunk for free. Otherwise, I am in a crud ton of problems if Freddie-boy costs me more than 150 dollars.

Another thought occurred to Lily, *Mom?...What will she say when I bring this trunk home? Will she make me take it back? Where can I hide it?*

Lily thought long and hard about this issue with her mom. She could ask or say it's part of her room's new retro upgrade. Even though the trunk looked old and dumpy, with a bit of paint and imagination Lily was sure she could convince her mom. Or maybe, Mina was the answer. She buys anything she wants, and Mom and Dad don't care. If she asked her sister to buy the trunk, Lily wouldn't need any explanation--no one would ask anything.

I'm a genius! On a roll, Come at me problems! Feeling empowered Lily bounced around shadow-boxing the invisible problems away.

In case Mina won't help, Lily decided not to spend another penny until her sister agreed. Nodding with determination, Lily had a plan she would put into action on Monday--unless Mina was willing to help. *I should call the antique store...Oh crud! I forgot to ask Mina if the store manager contacted her yet?*

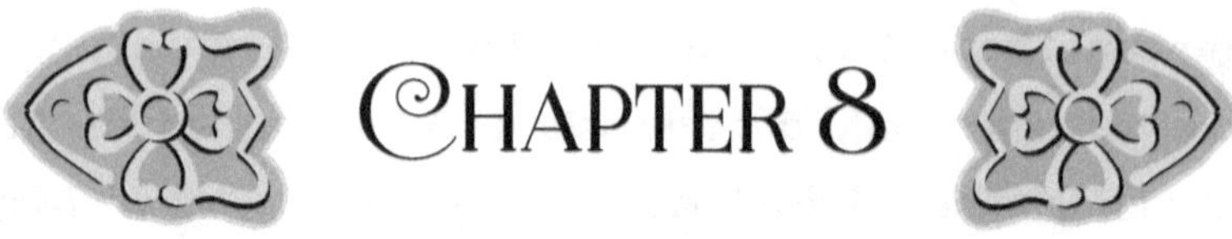

CHAPTER 8

The weekend came and went like normal. A quick call to the antique store and their hours for Monday, was followed with plans for Lily and Doris to meet there after school. Sunday after Mass, spending the day outside and watching movies with the family, Lily impatiently waited for the antique store to contact Mina.

What would she do if she couldn't get the trunk? This has never happened before, if she can't get the trunk would she be able to free Fred? Or would she just go insane? How would Mina save me then? Maybe splashing some holy water would work? Lily's head started to throb with the possible bad outcome of the future.

Adding to the uneasiness of the day, Fred, her spirit stalker, was unusually quiet. Lily found herself wandering around her room trying to coax Fred into sharing something new. So far, no luck. *Was Fred ignoring her or was Lily losing the connection?* Lily felt the panic building inside her body. Pacing faster and faster in a circle, chewing on one thumbnail, she tried to reverse the process--jumping into Fred's mind like he did hers.

What's going on Fred? Where are you?? Did you break the connection? Why aren't you answering me? Frederick, can you hear me!?!

Lily woke up Monday, to a dark and gloomy morning. Usually the sun peeked into her room, shining through her curtain. But not today. The wind was blowing against her window, the sunlight replaced with darkness. *Monday, Le sigh...* the weather matched her mood after she failed to reconnect with Fred. The last thought she had before passing out at 1am was begging Fred or any other spirit still trapped to help her. *Did I really offer to find and free all of them?*

Lily wished she could go back to sleep but the end of school was coming soon. She couldn't afford to miss any more days or fail her math class. After last night, her problems with algebra seemed small compared to going insane. Monday's were usually the perfect day for her to be late. The rest of the family scrambled to get back into the groove so no one cared if she was later than usual. Mondays suck and she was pretty sure 99.9% of the world would agree with her. Except today Lily couldn't afford to upset her mom, resulting in not being able to meet Doris after school. She had to touch that trunk and reconnect with Fred.

Before she knew it, Lily and her brothers were packed inside the van and arriving for her first class of the day. At her locker, Lily removed the books and notebooks for her later classes, then hurried to her English class. Once seated, she opened her notebook and found the sticky note.

Remind Doris that we are walking to the antique store.

Ask about the trunk price.

To make sure she saw the note, Lily used her brightest highlighter--neon-pink. Going the extra mile, she drew stars and hearts all around it with the neon-yellow highlighter.

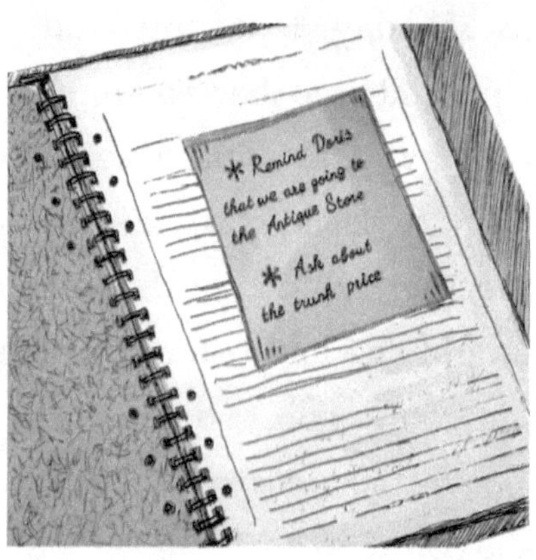

Lily asked her parents on Sunday if she could walk around town with Doris after school. *Of course, not knowing exactly what I wanted to do, they said, "yes".*

Lily noticed Max, her younger brother, giving her the evil eye. Half-eye-roll, half-side-eye glare, shooting icy daggers at Lily when she walked out of the living room. She knew he was upset because he had also asked to go out, but was told, "no". *He's so stupid, trying to sneak out then get caught, before deciding to ask. He'll never learn and deserves what he gets.* Her brothers never listened to the simple rules in the Shel household: Always. Ask. First! It's not hard, but they insist on making their lives difficult. *Dumb brothers.*

Doris walked into class, late as usual. From her wrinkled uniform and the pillow marks still on her face, Doris was having a rough Monday. More evidence that people benefit from a later start on Monday mornings.

Class started off normally, but toward the end Lily felt panic gripping her. Fred had been quiet all Sunday, but as soon as she entered the building his emotions overwhelmed her. She tried putting Fred's memories aside, so she could focus on her class. But he was persistent. As a last resort, she pulled out her Math notebook in the middle of her English assignment. Hiding it under her class book, she wrote a few memories currently invading her thoughts. One memory throbbed like an open sore, oozing with pain and panic. Fred was reliving a horrific change with terrifying consequences.

Come on, Fred! This is not the best place for me to have an emotional breakdown.

Lily felt anxious, aggravated, and that something bad was about to happen. The feeling crept along her skin with Goosebumps slowly rising on her legs and arms.

Nooo, keep it together, Lily! You can't have another meltdown at school. You already have 'that crazy girl' reputation from last semester to live down.

Lily was yanked out of the emotional tsunami by the teacher--calling on Lily to answer a question. She was already embarrassed when she stood up, completely unaware exactly what the question was, let alone what her answer should be. Her English teacher simply shook his head and told her to pay more attention in class. Returning to her seat she took a deep breath and tried pushing Fred's memories out of her mind. *Let's try making it through the school day without having any emotional meltdowns or embarrassing moments. I don't need this to become a thing for me.*

Memory sharing invokes the same emotional responses as living through the actual event--a not so lovely side effect of her missions. Lily tried to describe how it felt to Mina. It felt like having a second period without the mess but with triple the emotional rollercoaster--sometimes lasting for weeks. Lily noticed that not being in direct contact with the spirit object, this time, had a few perks as well. Two days with little to no memory invasion and Lily could relax, enjoying a normal day. At least once she got past the anxiety of not knowing what was going on with Fred.

The bell rang, loud and clear, lunch at last. The surge of high school students heading toward the cafeteria made it difficult for Lily to find Doris. They were meeting for lunch to discuss their after school trek to the antique store. Although Doris didn't know Lily's secrets, she was always up for an adventure. Even though Doris is her best friend, Lily worried what Doris would say or do if she knew the truth about the spirits. She could almost hear Doris saying, 'Are you for real or Is this some social media stunt? Are you recording me?' This was exactly the reason Doris didn't need to know *why* they were going to the antique store.

As soon as Lily sat down at the table, Doris shrugged with a sheepish smile on her face.

"Change in plans, don't kill me. I can't come with--after school. Dad is taking us out for dinner before the lil twerps' soccer game. Maybe next time?"

Lily was annoyed until she noticed a twinkle in Doris' eyes, again. *A boy! Whatever happened to besties over crushes?*

"That's alright, next time for sure...sooooooo will *He* be there?" There it is, that slow smile spreading across her face. Lily knew when Doris changed her plans to go to any sporting event, it was usually to see her crush, Derek. Doris hadn't shown much enthusiasm for sports until she met Derek-one huge soccer fan. He used to play in high school, until one year during a game when he broke his ankle and knee cap. It was bad and it ended his soccer career dreams. Now he is a former player training as a coach. Doris met him after he graduated, at one of her brother's soccer practices. She only went to the practices to spend time with her dad, which was ironic since now she went to meet her boyfriend. *Le Sighhhhh...boys, making girls do crazy things.*

"Of course!" Doris didn't hide the pink rushing onto her cheeks. "I was thinking, should I wear the normal, cute, tee-shirt or something extra special this time? I will be wearing these cute open toe sandals with a light, blue-jean skirt." Her smile grew every time she mentioned *Derek*, like a secret she couldn't wait to share. Lily noticed every time she flashed her pearly white teeth. They were mostly straight except her canine teeth; that protruded more than the others. It was considered cute in Japan, so Doris didn't care if they stuck out or not.

One more thing Lily and Doris connected about, their love of Japanese trends and culture.

"You should really support your little brother's team more." Lily thought for a minute before asking Doris. "Do you have one of their tee shirts?"

Lily continued eating her lunch waiting for her friend to get it. Still Doris didn't catch onto Lily's suggestion, so she added. "Derek really likes soccer, and if he sees how supportive you are, especially with your little brother, he might actually notice you." She tried winking at the end of her message. It took a full minute before Doris understood, then winked back. Grinning, the two friends spent the rest of lunch period deciding what Doris would wear to the soccer game to catch Derek's eye.

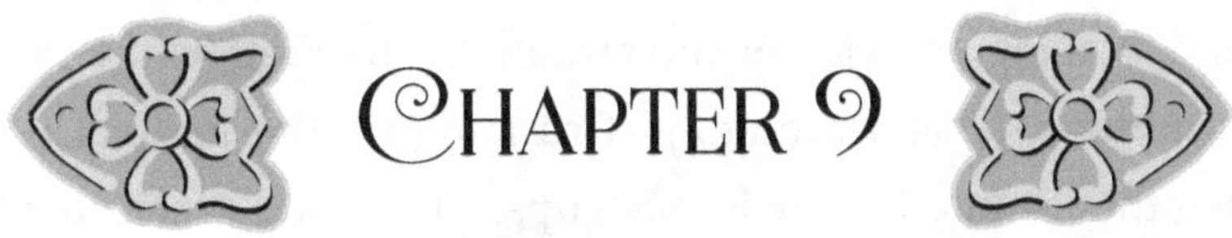

CHAPTER 9

The rest of the day breezed by for the two girls. Doris was distracted by daydreams of her soccer-coach-love-Derek, and Lily worried what her mom would say when she picked her up without Doris. Lily could already hear the argument inside her head without a way to avoid it.

If she waited another day, she risked losing all connection to the trunk and maybe even Fred? Which would cause her to go insane and it wouldn't matter what her mom was upset about.

Lily considered not telling her mom for a few minutes, then decided against it. She would be in more trouble if she didn't tell her mom. *When in doubt don't do what the boys do.* She giggled at that thought. Lily decided to text her mom later and ask if she can still go without Doris.

Classes continued--a pop quiz in Science, which Lily felt

she did excellent on. *Thank you, note taking skills.* --a compliment from her music teacher, which was a huge accomplishment since the music teacher was known for being strict with high standards; the day ended with P.E. aka physical torture in Lily's mind. Forcing us to jog or run around the football field without warming up? No warning, just running on the football field! Then they wanted us to do push ups, squats and other horrible contortions in knee long skirts!! *By the end of class my face is so flushed and covered in sweat. With hair sticking up randomly all over the place. I look like a swamp creature and I feel like one. NASTY! If I didn't get to go home afterwards, some people might swear they saw the missing link walking around town.*

When the bell rings and school is finally over Lily is ready to escape. Feeling more refreshed after switching clothes and washing her face with cold water, Lily pulled out her phone. Texting her mom, she anxiously waited for an answer all alone-- because Doris abandoned her for a soccer game and *Derek!*

Waiting for her mom, time seemed to move as fast as those cold molasses in January she's always talking about. When the text popped up 'Yes' on her screen, Lily released a sigh of relief then headed to the antique store.

Maybe this was for the best. Now Lily could spend the entire time at the antique store, but more importantly, focusing on the trunk and Fred, without worrying about her friend.

Jamming the cheap earphones in, Lily began the ten minute walk from her school to the antique store. Glad that she remembered her earphones, she got lost in the music and found herself steps away from the antique store before she knew it.

How would I survive without the ipods, mp3's and cell phones. I don't know how my parents lived without them back when they were teens. Talk about glad we were born in this modern day and age. Cell phones with music all the way!

Lily checked her reflection before entering the store, making sure she looked good. Patrick might be working today.. *Hair, check. Clothes, check, I guess. Still looking damp from her P.E. class and now her walk. Lily smoothed her skirt. Again pants would have been nicer. I hope he's not in today. I look awful.* Taking a deep annoyed breath, Lily headed inside the store.

Patrick wasn't at the front desk to watch her grand entrance, thank-goodness. Instead, a middle-aged woman sat behind the counter, reading a magazine. *It must be Patrick's day off.* Her shoulders slumped leaving her feeling like a deflated balloon. *All that effort for nothing.* Even though she wished him to not be there today, she still wished she could have saw him.

Lily finally noticed that the store was empty. Her stomach jumped when she passed the trunk. Fred's spirit was calling out to her, but Lily decided to inquire about the price and owners before reconnecting with him. She didn't know why, but she felt bad asking the employees about the trunk without at least looking through the store once. Ignoring the guilt, she headed up to the front desk, avoiding the trunk in case Fred's emotions got the better of her.

"Excuse me, Do you know if that trunk is still for sale?" Lily offered her a friendly smile.

Looking up from her reading the woman glanced at what Lily was pointing at then back at Lily. "That trunk isn't for sale.

The owners loaned it for display only." Her eyes dropped back to her reading, immediately dismissing Lily as no one important.

"Do you know the name of the people who own it?" Lily could tell her persistence was starting to annoy the lady.

After tossing the magazine across the desk, the clerk crossed her arms and replied. "Brookes. They live in the next town over. Why?" She huffed.

"I really like it. Plus I wanted to learn more about the history behind it. I'm sort of a history buff when it comes to old antiques." Lily's smile brightened, hoping to sell the story. In some ways what she said was true. She did like history--or at least she learned to like history more since connecting with her antique-trapped spirits. Having to research every object is a pain, but after their story is completed. Lily can look back and see how much she learned about their history, and the object itself. With the stress of writing their story over, it is really cool to know more about the objects she now owns.

The lady took a deep breath trying to remain calm. A longing glance at her abandoned magazine letting Lily know she didn't want to deal with Lily or her questions.

Maybe if I look really interested and come back later, she'll give me more information on the trunk. "I'll just go see if there's a craftsman's mark still on it, if you don't mind?" Lily walked over, placing her hand cautiously on the trunk so she could reconnect with Fred.

Nothing happened.

Lily placed both hands on the trunk, closing her eyes she tried calling to Fred inside her mind.

Fred...Fred? Please say something. FREDRICK! I'm here! All you have to do is say something.

Fred did not answer Lily's pleas.

Sweat beaded on her forehead as she wondered. *Am I... too late?* Her hands trembled at the thought she had lost all connection to Fred. *Is this the beginning of my insanity?* Not knowing what happened or was going on with Fredrick made her feel insane. Like slowly being driven mad by the millions of unanswered questions. Her nerves snapped like cheap thread pulled too tight, she was unable to think of anything except reconnecting with Fred.

Lily knelt down next to the trunk trying desperately to make a connection. She called out to Fred's spirit with her panicked thoughts. Pleading with him to reconnect or at least answer her. Nothing seemed to work. None of her previous spirits were silent for more than a few hours. Three days had passed and even now touching the trunk didn't help. Out of options, Lily prayed to God for help. A habit her parents drilled into her from a young age. 'If you need help, ask God.' Mrs. Shels would say. Right now Lily needed all the help she could get, because nothing else was working. So she prayed...and prayed...and prayed some more--desperately hoping God was listening.

Lily's thoughts swung between prayers to God and threats to Fred.

God please help me find Fred, Please...

...Fred, so help me if you don't answer soon I'll kick your bony spirit butt to the pearly gates and back!

Before her knees ached from kneeling, Lily felt Fred's spirit break through. Her mix of prayers and threats had worked its magic. Or maybe that was the power of prayer her Mom was always telling about. Her fingers tingled with the reemergence of Fred, goosebumps raced up and down her arms as his spirit fully reconnected. After such a long absence, the slow stream of thoughts and memories filling her mind was disorienting. Frederick was back! To her great relief, his memories were normal and on track. Not as distorted or chaotic as she thought they would be. Picking right back up from when they had stopped.

Lily folded her hands together in a thankful prayer.

Thank you God!

Fred please don't ever do this again...my nerves can't take anymore.

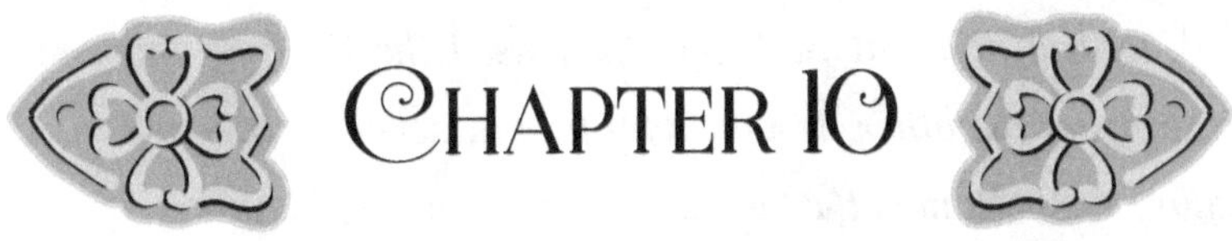

CHAPTER 10

One memory pushed forward in Lily's head. *Finally something I recognize.* Fred sat in a chair while someone in a white or light gray nursing uniform unpacked his trunk. *This isn't what I remember, this is something new. Where is he? A hospital? Why is there a nurse unpacking his stuff? Wait a minute...that isn't the same trunk, either. It looks completely different, the lid is flat, not rounded like the one beside me. Why is this trunk different, does he have two of them? Great...do I have to track it down too? How much is that going to cost me?*

Fred...why did you switch? If this trunk isn't yours, then why are you attached to it? Please tell me there aren't two trunks.

After the vision passed, Lily tried to imagine how the trunk in Fred's memory became the trunk in front of her. Maybe she didn't recognize it since the trunk had been taken apart and made into a bookshelf.

Lily circled the trunk-bookcase, noticing the major differences between the two. Besides the lid shape, they looked similar. The same size, metal ornamentation and wood. *Maybe it is the same trunk with a different lid? Like they used the lid from one and the bottom from the other. Is that why he's attached to this one instead? Because the bottom is the bigger half of the original trunk?*

Lily ran her hands over the wood to see if she could feel any difference between the top and bottom pieces. She must have pushed a little too hard because the makeshift bookcase top began to wobble dangerously. A book fell from the top shelf, making a loud *Smack* against the floor. Lily picked up the book and gently returned it to the top shelf. When the top wobbled again, she inspected the space between the top and bottom pieces. They were not attached to each other, simply balancing one on top of the other. New wallpaper had been added since Fred's hospital memory, and some shelves had been added as well. Altogether, the trunk was in good condition.

She searched the metal pieces for any seal from the craftsman. Those would tell her whether these were from two different trunks, or if this one was completely different from the one in Fred's memory. The trunk was covered with random knick knacks added by the antique store. It appeared a fresh coat of paint was added too. Lily couldn't inspect every inch while it was still a display piece, she would have to wait until she had it in her room. There she could take it apart and check every millimeter. *By the time I am done, I'll be an expert on antique trunks.*

Nothing new was discovered by her search. No special

carvings, metal craftsman marks or writing of any kind. Lily decided to snap some pictures to study later. Just in case she couldn't negotiate the price today, she could at least study the pictures. And, if there was a second trunk, she had these pictures to help her find it.

Fred was slowly re-connecting her to more memories. Lily turned to assess the clerk's current mood. The cranky clerk was re-reading her magazine leaning back in her chair. *Perfect! Let's make this quick.* Striding to the desk, determined to get the owner's information, Lily flashed her most convincing smile.

"That trunk," Lily nodded toward the bookcase, "...looks great. But I couldn't find a signature or a craftsman seal. Could you ask the owners If they would be willing to lend it or sell it to me?"

The clerk looked up, furrowed eyebrows practically meeting in the middle. Before she could dismiss her request, Lily interrupted.

"Couldn't you just call them and have them email me?" Lily dropped her eyes purposely to the open magazine. "Sounds easy-peasy to me." She set the paper with her email written on it on the counter. "If I can't buy it, I would love to use it for my photoshoot. They can contact me here. Thank you, and have a nice day!"

Lily sailed out of the antique store like she had places to go and people to see. She almost snapped her fingers for her invisible assistant to really sell the idea, but thought that was overkill. Acting like an adult was fun.

The clerk looked at the paper and shook her head. Just out

of view, Lily waited to see what she would do. When the clerk picked up the phone to dial, Lily fist pumped and hurried to the corner to text her mom.

Patrick must have totally forgotten I asked him to do that. Or maybe there is another reason. Lily's heart fluttered as she pictured Patrick apologizing to her. *His smile beamed like sunshine. "I'm so sorry, Lily. Will you still go out with me? Even if I messed up so bad?" He knelt at Lily's feet with her favorite flowers and chocolates.* She returned to the present moment with a giddy squirm, shaking her head while trying not to blush. This daydream was one she would love to come true. It left her grinning from ear to ear, as she imagined their perfect date together. Le Sighhhhhhhhhhh.

Lily happily daydreamed about Patrick, while keeping tabs on Fred, and waiting for her mom. She abruptly snapped from her dizzying teen love when Fred shouted the name 'Cummens'. Repeating it to the point that Lily's stomach cramped.

Stop it, Fred. That hurt! I'll do some research when I get home. So please, back off with the stomach cramps.

But Fred continued shouting Cummens' name, so the

cramps grew worse.

Were the cramps because she was disconnected from his spirit for a few days? Or maybe she was close to finishing his story. With her past spirits, when she was close to releasing them, physical pain manifested as if their spirit was being ripped away.

Lily's mom picked her up shortly afterward. *Thank Goodness,* was all Lily could think in that moment. She did try to search on her phone for anyone named Cummens--on different social media platforms--but couldn't find any connection to Fred or the trunk. Once she was buckled up, Lily and her mom headed home.

"Mom, when we get home can I use the computer? I have research to do."

"Sure honey, what are you looking up?" Her mom asked.

"I'm trying to find someone named Cummens or Brookes." Lily realized this was the perfect way to bring up the trunk. "I found a really cool, retro-looking, trunk in that antique store. I asked to borrow it for this photoshoot Doris and I are doing."

"You're planning another photoshoot? I didn't know that." Mrs. Shels raised eyebrows filled the rearview mirror.

"We sure are. We are going for a retro-antique-vibe for this one. Which is why the trunk is perfect!" Lily glanced at her mom's reflection. *Does that sound convincing?*

"Do you know anyone by the name Cummens or Brookes?"

"Cummens, Brookes? No, I'm not familiar with either of them, but maybe you should ask your older siblings. They work in the grocery store, they might know who they are. Why do you have two names? Is it their trunk?" Mrs. Shels asked, sounding truly interested for the first time since they began the conversation.

"Yes and no. The Brookes own the trunk, but the clerk said it's not for sale...exactly. Which is why I asked to borrow it. And Cummens might be a relative of the Brookes, in case one doesn't know I can ask the other." Lily felt pretty proud of herself. She was sort of telling the truth, and so far, her mom was not against the photoshoot. *Maybe this mission will be easier if her mom thinks the trunk is part of a photoshoot. No sneaking around after all.* Lily chuckled to herself. *All that panic and stress thinking Mom was going to flip and be completely against everything. Le sigh. Stressing for nothing…hopefully.*

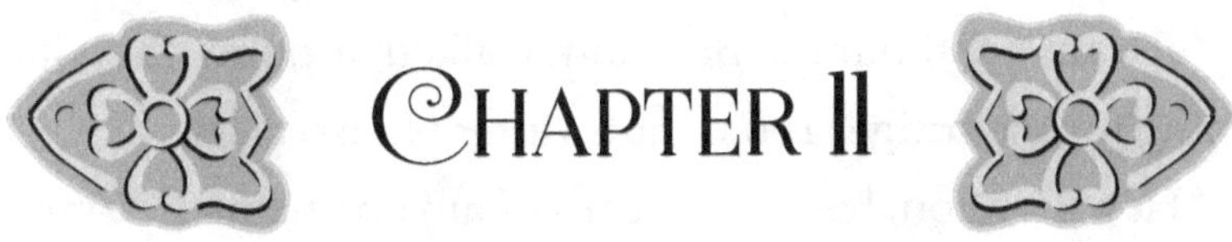

Chapter II

In the kitchen Lily finished her homework and waited for Mina and Brandon, her oldest brother, to come home. Both worked at the grocery store until 9pm. If she wanted to ask them a few questions, the best place to wait was the kitchen. Both Brandon and Mina stopped here for late night snacks before heading to their own rooms.

Brandon would lock his room and not let anyone in after he was inside. Which meant Lily would have to catch him before he headed to his lair. It occurred to her that her older brother spent less time with the family and it only became worse the older he got. He spent more time working or playing video games than anything else.

Mina was the same, with a few exceptions. She didn't lock her door but spent her spare time working on college assignments.

Plus she was helping Lily with her spirit stories. Once again Lily felt an instant relief knowing Mina believed her and listened when she had a story to dissect.

The kitchen door squealed when it swung open, interrupting Lily's train of thought. Brandon walked around the island, aiming for the fridge. Ten minutes after Nine o'clock.

"Hey Brandon, have you heard of anyone named Cummens or Brookes?" Lily rushed to ask before he could head upstairs.

Brandon kept his head buried in the fridge while answering. "Nope. What's for supper?"

Lily knew he didn't think about her question, his stomach overriding his brain. "We had fried chicken with mashed potatoes...and leftover brownies."

His head popped out at the mention of brownies.

She added with a chuckle. "But...we ate them all." Feeling impish, Lily couldn't help snicker at his disappointed and annoyed look.

"Really..." He raised an eyebrow. "...you had to get my hopes up?"

"YEP." She replied with a sinister grin. "You better believe It!" Brandon did his fair share of teasing Lily. *Revenge is sweet!*

Plus he didn't get into as much trouble as she thought he should, especially when he purposely tried to mess up her sketching. Or made fun of her school uniform--*even if she hated it.* Poking her when she was doing homework. Or the worst was when he took over tv time. No matter who was watching, he would take the remote and kick them out. But he wasn't always a pest--sometimes they talked for hours about cool stuff. Big brothers are "ok" sometimes. Lily concluded that Brandon was normal for a big brother.

Weird. Usually Mina followed Brandon into the kitchen since they drove together. "Where's Mina?"

Brandon piled a plate with snacks, mumbling as he left the kitchen. "She's in her room."

Surprised by that information, Lily put her books away before heading upstairs. She needed to ask Mina about the Cummens. *Lights off. Good.* 'Lights are to be turned off when leaving a room empty', Mrs. Shel would remind her children, 'We are not made of money'. *Le Sighhh.*

Knocking softly on Mina's closed door, "It's me." Lily whispered. She entered when she heard, 'Come in'.

"What's up?" Mina spun around in her chair. "More spirit stuff?" She had her books, a bag of chips, and a sandwich from the grocery store, laying half eaten on her desk.

"Yep...I'm looking for a family named Brookes so I can borrow or buy their antique trunk. And Cummens is somehow related to them. It's important somehow." With one sentence Lily could relax, knowing Mina would understand that it was about another trapped spirit.

"So Brookes and Cummens? Which one is the spirit's last name?" Spinning back to her desk she grabbed the sandwich before facing Lily.

"Last. His full name is Fredrick Cummens. But the family that owns the trunk are called Brookes." Lily replied after climbing on her sister's bed. Taking a look around the room, Lily was confused but slightly impressed. Mina's Bright lighting, tall plants, and simple decor was clean and cozy. Mina had been working since she was in 9th grade. She had been saving money and lately redecorating her room into this new, simpler modern-style. The only place in her sister's room that was messy was the desk. Books, notebooks, pencils, random pieces of paper and now food. Mina was working on top of earning a college degree in massage therapy. There was a large pile of books next to her desk. The largest one read, *Therapeutic Massage*.

"I'm glad you came up, today's been so busy I forgot to show you the email I got from Zoe." Mina opened her emails to show Lily the message. "By the way, next time give me a warning when you give my email to strangers. I almost deleted it."

"Sorry, I forgot I gave them yours." Lily grabbed one of the large fluffy pillows, snuggling against it.

"So tell me…" Mina kept her eyes on Lily, "…who's Patrick?" She waited to see what Lily's reaction would be.

Mina knew she had a crush on some boy, had she guessed it was Patrick? Lily smothered her face with the pillow after Mina gave her another questioning look. *He didn't forget after all!*

"Oh? Is Patrick the boy you've had a crush on all school year?"

Slowly Lily looked over the pillow. *Were her feelings so obvious? Does everyone know about Patrick??*

For the next several minutes, Lily talked Mina's ear off. She told her everything about Patrick. Complete details--from the way he looked to his dancing skills. "Last fourth of July at the town party, Patrick was on the dance floor with another girl. He was so great, twirling *her* around, then dipped *her*."

Another girlish squeal of glee escaped Lily just imagining if she was that girl.

"Earth. To. Lily. Earth to Lily!" Mina waved her hand in front of Lily's face bringing her attention back to the moment. "Sorry to interrupt your moment of teen love, but I wonder why you gave Patrick my email instead of your cell number? You missed a perfect opportunity there." Mina pulled the pillow away from Lily's face, teasing her. "So, what did happen? Did he ask for your number then your face got so red that you ran out before you could give it to him?"

"No. That's not at all what happened." Lily knew she was as red as a tomato while she explained what Patrick said. *Even remembering it was as painful as the first time. How could Patrick do that to me? If only he knew how perfect we would be together!*

"Ouch. Dang that's rough. You've had a crush on that boy for a while now." Mina caught Lily's shoulders pulling her into a bear hug. "AHHHHH my poor lil sister had her feelings crushed by her long-time crush…..Don't you worry!!" Mina's voice flexed between loud and obnoxious to soft and mocking care. " Mina, your favorite and bestest sister ever, will help you through this heart-breaking moment!!" She continued in that annoying voice while squishing Lily in the tightest hug possible.

"STOP IT!!! You're so annoying!" Lily pushed against Mina until she was free. While Mina kept teasing her and trying to wrestle her into another suffocating hug. Lily appreciated how her sister was. *She is so annoying...but at the same time it's how she shows she cares.*

"Feel better now?" Mina asked Lily as she smoothed down her wrinkled tee shirt.

"I suppose so."

"Good now tell me what's going on with this trunk. I could use a nice break from all this studying." Mina closed her books and retrieved a hidden bag of candy.

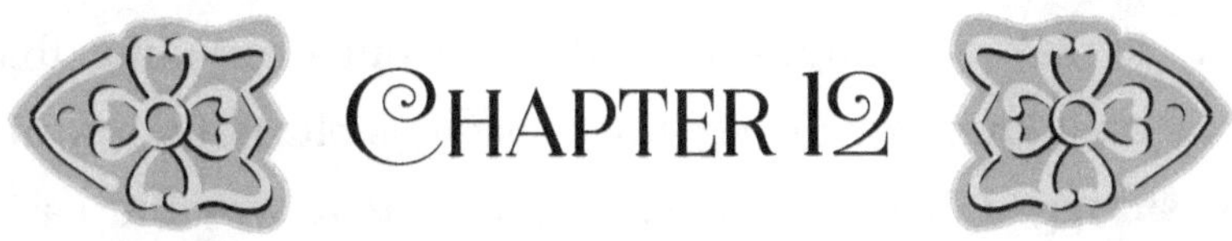

CHAPTER 12

Mina spent the next half-hour researching anyone named Cummens, while Lily filled her in on the most recent memories and new information about Fred and the trunk. *Possibly now two trunks.* At the thought of having to find another trunk, Lily felt a small moan bubble up. Distracting her brain from that awful possibility, she rummaged around the tray of snacks that they brought up from the kitchen. Their deduction skills worked that much better with junk food.

"It's really weird. Most of Fred's memories, in the beginning, were clearer with an occasional blurriness. They started out a little hazy, but now every new memory he shares feels like I'm watching the world through the bottom of a glass. Almost as if he's crying all the time."

"Why do you think it's tears or crying? Because your version of the memory is fuzzy?" Mina asked, tapping away on her keyboard.

"That's the only thing that makes sense to me." Lily scooped another handful of popcorn. "His memories are so blurry right now, it makes it impossible to figure out everything that's going on. I know when I cry my eyesight is blurry for a while." She shrugged her shoulders."I figured that was the easiest explanation, since he's sad all the time."

"Sure." Spinning around in her chair to face Lily. "But maybe there's another reason for his blurred vision. Did any of the other spirits have the same thing?"

"Nope." Lily shook her head. "Fred's the first one I've met with this vision problem."

"If that's true, then maybe there is something else going on here. Unless this guy is really depressed, he wouldn't be crying all day. Which doesn't sound like a grown man at all, and according to what you have already told me, he seems like a normal old man."

Lily shrugged her shoulders again. "What else is it?"

"Without knowing about Fred or his family, it's hard to tell. There could be many reasons for blurry vision. How old was Fred when he died?" Mina handed the popcorn bowl to Lily.

"I don't know. Old, ancient geezer, I guess. I think I remember seeing possibly a grown daughter in one of the first memories. I'm not sure who she was, but she looked at least mom's age. And Fred's a whole heck of alot older so I highly doubt she was his wife. But I couldn't see very well either."

Mina stopped eating her popcorn. "You know, just hearing

you describe what you can't see, and how each newer one gets worse, maybe…" Her eyebrows arched, "…his eyesight is fading? You did just say, he's really old."

Is Frederick going blind? Of course, that makes perfect sense. Lily was shocked how quickly Mina landed on something obvious that she couldn't. Thank Goodness for Mina! Lily had no idea if she would have figured that out without her sister's help. *Oh no! Wait, what if I can't see enough of Fred's memories to finish his story?? I'll go insane for sure if that happens. Is that why he keeps disappearing? Is he trying to hide his blindness or just unwilling to accept it?*

"How will I know for sure if he's going blind?"

"Think about it." Mina held up her hand as she made her point. "His memories are becoming progressively blurrier. Plus didn't you say he signed papers in the beginning. What you saw might have been his doctor's office."

Lily nodded in agreement as her sister pointed out more reasons going blind made sense in Fred's case.

"You indicated that he was frustrated and angry. It was probably his eyesight fading or having to get checked by a doctor. Maybe he was hoping for an easy fix. Do you know what year this doctor appointment happened?"

Lily clutched the pillow, letting herself melt into the mattress. *Great! Way to be mean to a dead person. I hope he doesn't report me to the Spirit-Council.* "Poor Fred. How awful it must have been losing his eyesight like that. No wonder his emotions were all over the place." Recalling some of the memories and how painful they were, she wondered how Fred survived that kind of hell. "I don't really know. I can guess, but I can't tell the difference between 1962 and 1978."

Mina's face scrunched up with obvious confusion. "What do you mean you don't know? Can't you just ask him?"

Laughing Lily replied. "I wish! But that's not how it works. There are rules for these spirits, their story has to come from the memories. They can't answer specific questions."

"Well that's not helpful! How do you figure this out? Do they expect you to be a mind reader or dream interpreter?"

"Not quite, more like a cryptologist." Lily had been waiting to use that word for a while. *Cryptologist. She liked calling herself a code breaker.*

Mina snorted at the cryptologist remark.

" But there's more to Fred's story than that. Why is his spirit attached to that trunk? What's the link? On top of that, there might be two different trunks now!??" Lily's frustration grew as more questions than answers piled up in her mind.

Mina paced around the room, her eyes glassy and her thoughts far away. Lily knew that look.

Mina was pondering those questions as she walked around the room. Both girls realized they had more questions but very few answers. Lily was so grateful that she now confided in Mina because her insight proved to be invaluable. Having two minds is always better than one, when it comes to figuring out the spirit world. At least that was the conclusion Lily had reached. Watching Mina pace, Lily could tell her mind had snagged on some important point. *What did she figure out?* Lily bounced on the bed impatiently waiting for Mina's answer.

Mina stopped pacing just long enough to grab some popcorn. "How many memories involve the trunk?"

Lily's excited smile dropped. "Just two. Fred packing a trunk. I couldn't see the lid to tell if it's the same one as in the antique store or not. Then, Fred is at a new place with a nurse, unpacking a trunk that is different. So I'm not sure if there are two trunks or not. Or why Fred is attached to one I found in Zoe's store."

"Maybe the trunk isn't that important to Fred's story? Let's forget about the trunk and focus on the common thread. From your past experiences with spirits, there has been a pattern in each story. What is the pattern for Fred?"

"You mean, is there anything that all of the memories have in common?" Lily asked, her eyebrows dropping toward her nose.

"No, not exactly. Think more about how you freed each spirit. When the third spirit arrived, did you notice any common need to finish their story?" Watching the confusion chase across Lily's face, Mina tried another way.

"Ok, Lily. How do the spirits find you?" Mina pointed to the email. "Where do you connect with the objects? They've all been the same, right? With you touching it."

Lily nodded.

"Ok, so then you start receiving memories from that spirit. You put their memories together and learn about their family history. Then, you find what connects the spirit to the object so you can release the spirit."

"Yeeeesssss." Lily draws the word out slowly as if unsure of her answer.

"That's a pattern, right there. You have already completed step one, now it's time to dig into his family history. That should lead you to whatever the connection is between Fred and the trunk." She watched Lily's eyes glaze over. Mina waited for the lights to come on in sister's brain. Somehow it seemed as if she was out to lunch at the moment.

She fluttered her eyelashes at Mina. "What are you doing tomorrow?" Lily used her sweetest, most innocent, child-like voice. "I could use a ride to that address in the email?" Pressing her palms together in a prayer-like pose, she tilted her head to one side. "Plllleeeeeaaassse???"

"Ahh, I see. Since it's my day off I should get the honor of driving you all over the place?" Mina crossed her arms over her chest with a mocking chuckle. She continued to glare at her sister.

"But I will love you forever." Lily batted her lashes ever faster.

Letting her arms and shoulders drop, Mina admitted defeat "Fine. I'll drive you there after school--if mom says it's alright. But...you need a plan for what you are going to ask--without creeping everyone out."

Lily responded with two thumbs way up.

"After all, you are a stranger asking about a deceased person's trunk and family history." Picking up the pillow that had fallen on the floor, Mina chucked it at Lily's head playfully. "Now get out! I have studying to do and you have school." Ushering Lily from her room, Mina said good night as she started to close the door. "Hey, you are still feeling ok even with this new spirit mission right? Nothing funky going on?" Mina's voice lost most of its playfulness. Meaning she wanted a serious answer.

"Yes, so far it's been emotional but nothing too weird. Thanks for checking." Leaving the room, Lily waited till the door was closed before pressing her lips against Mina's door. "Good night, Memes. Thank you!!" Just short of a yell. She could hear grumbling through the door as she walked toward her room.

CHAPTER 13

The next afternoon Mina asked Lily. "How much homework do you have tonight?"

Lily pondered as they drove to the next town in her sister's nice clean car. The air freshener, *Hawaiian Vacation*, smelled really good--like sweet, fresh fruit. "For once, I don't have a lot of homework." Lily's smile dropped slightly, wondering what Mina would ask next. "Why?"

"I was thinking about going to the library to do research for school. So we'll be stopping there first, really quick." Mina noticed Lily's frown. "Is that a problem?"

Lily's heart raced. "Please. Let's go to the Brookes house, first. I really want to just get this done and over with." She whined. The entire day has been stressful enough--thinking about what she would say and what she would do when they said no. Both Fred's and Lily's future depended on the outcome of this intervention. "We can go to the library afterward."

Mina took a slow, deep breath. "Fine, but make it snappy. If they are friendly they'll want to talk for hours. Remember we have a deal."

Turning the corner, the GPS showed the Brookes house at the end of the block.

"This is it. Looks like a normal neighborhood so far. No overgrown yards here. Everything looks organized and well-kept. Not a creepy, broken down house in sight." Mina observed trying to calm a hyperventilating Lily.

The Brookes' house was plain-jane, tan with white trimmed windows. A two story house with a small front porch. The front yard had a very small flower section, with a swing off to the right side of the front porch.

"Ok. Do you have your list of questions ready?" Mina asked as she parked along the side of the road.

"Yes, right here in my pocket. I have my notebook and pen too." Lily tapped the pen on the small hand-sized notebook.

"Guess you're ready then. Better get going, I'll wait here and study." Mina watched her sister walk up to the house. When Lily rang the doorbell, Mina opened her book to read.

Once Lily reached the front door, she poked the yellow doorbell. A few seconds later, she heard noise from inside the house. The front door opened slowly.

An older woman opened the door, spotting Lily, she smiled. "Hello, can I help you? Are you selling something, hun?"

Releasing a nervous laugh, Lily shook her hands. "No

I'm not. I am looking for the Brookes family. I was told this is where they live." Smiling her sweetest and most friendly smile, she watched the old woman's facial expression shadow with concern.

"Yes, I am Mrs. Brookes. Can I help you with something?" Mrs. Brooke's smile wavered when her lips pursed together.

Lily took a deep breath, calming herself before answering with an even friendlier smile. "Hi, Mrs. Brookes. My name is Lily Shels. That is my older sister in the car over there.`` She pointed quickly in the direction of the parked car. "I got your name from the antique store when I asked about the trunk on display. I was wondering if I could borrow it for a retro-themed photoshoot?"

Mrs. Brookes looked nervously over her shoulder as she leaned away.

Shoot, she doesn't believe me. Probably thinks I'm a nut! Lily gritted her teeth, "We just want to borrow it for a week or so for the photoshoot."

Mrs. Brookes stepped back, reaching for the door.

NOooooooooooo!! It's all over if she leaves! My life is over, my family will disown me and Fred will haunt my drooling body forever! Don't. Let. Her. Leave! Say something, stupid! "I promise I will take good care of it. I will return it in perfect condition. If you allow me to borrow it, I promise no one else will be allowed to touch it." Lily felt hopeful seeing Mrs. Brookes let go of the door and folded her hands together.

"I will see to it that Lily does take care of the trunk, Mrs. Brookes." Mina chimed in, surprising Lily when she placed her hand on her sister's shoulder. She had decided to help, just in case Lily needed any extra support. Mina knew that Lily often got lost in her thoughts and didn't make sense. "Hi, I'm Mina, Lily's older sister."

Mrs. Brooke's forehead wrinkled as her smile faded. "A trunk? What trunk are you talking about? Where is this antique store? Are you sure you have the right family?"

A young man walked up behind Mrs. Brookes. "Hey mom, who's this?" The man stood taller than his Mom, leaning over Mrs. Brooke's shoulder. Besides his sandy blonde hair, the mother and son looked like two peas in a pod.

"Honey, maybe you would know what these young ladies here are talking about. This one wants to borrow a trunk from an antique store. Did we give away a trunk?" Mrs. Brookes turned to ask the young man.

Rubbing the back of his head, he fidgeted. "Ahh yeah, Mom. I'll deal with them. Go on and start dinner without me. I'll be there shortly" He ushered his mother back into the house, smiling as he waved her away. "That was close. Hi, my name's Carter Brookes. My mom doesn't know we donated her old trunk. She has a hard time letting go of family junk. Are you asking about the trunk in Zoe's store?"

"Yes, sir. That's the one." Lily replied, her confidence returning.

"Did I hear you say something about a photoshoot?" Carter leaned against the door frame, keeping the door open with one hand.

"Yes, my friend and I want to use the trunk in our Retro

photoshoot." Lily replied, noticing for the first time that his pants were stained with neon-green paint.

"Sounds fun. I will let Zoe know I said you can borrow it. How long do you need it?"

"Awesome! Maybe a week or two? Thank you so much!" *EEEEEEEEeeek! Keep it together till you get to the car, Lily.*

"Two weeks?" A puzzled expression crossed his face.

"Yes please, I will need two weeks for all the locations we are filming in."

Carter's smile quickly returned. "Sure, you can keep it for the two weeks. It's an old trunk, just be careful and return it safely when you are done." He reached for the door.

"Real quick, out of curiosity. Did the trunk belong to your Father, by any chance?" Mina asked before he could close the door.

Carter replied. "No, It belonged to my mom's grandfather before he died--before she was even born. It's just an old piece of junk taking up space. A sad reminder of a horrible person. My mom doesn't need to memorialize a man she's never met and wouldn't like if she had. She's the only reason I haven't taken it to the dump!"

Lily stiffened as she struggled with the emotional surge from Fred. He was going nuts inside her head, yelling:

"That's a lie!"

"How would he know!"

"I'm not a horrible person!"

"He's never met me!"

Lily was prepared to clamp a hand over her mouth and run

for the car. Fred's anger was overtaking her common sense. He really wanted her to yell at Carter, and wasn't afraid to hijack Lily's voice. Lily's mumbled "Thank you.", was barely audible as she escaped.

She could feel Fred's anger breaking through her emotional barrier as she ducked into the safety of the car. *Frederick! Stop it, right now. I...We cannot afford to lose this trunk now. If I yell at Carter like a crazy nut, any chance of releasing you is over because people don't like dealing with insane teenagers!*

Her stern warning calmed Fred just enough that Lily regained full control of her own emotions.

When the two sisters were buckling up, it occurred to Lily that Carter had not asked why they were inquiring about the trunk's history. *Maybe he just doesn't care?*

"Smart thinking there--asking who the trunk belonged to. I totally forgot to even ask that." Lily praised her sister once Fred's anger cooled down.

"What was with abandoning me back there?" Mina asked as they pulled away.

"Fred was going nuts and trying to take over my body, I had to get him out of there. I'm sensing some family problems. Major problems."

"A spirit can take over your body? How??" Mina asked, sounding intrigued and a bit concerned.

"It's weird, but yes. Spirits can take over if I'm not careful--the spirit can overtake my mind and force me to say and do things I don't want to. They overwhelm my emotions with their own to the point that I lose control. It's really intense and freaky. I don't like it."

"Do the spirits do that often?" Mina signaled to change lanes.

"Only twice so far. Just now and when you stole the razor and cigar case."

"You mean you had help when you tried to take me down? Is that the best they can do, because that was pretty lame."

"Well that's not a good example. They did force me to lunge at you, but then they ran out of energy. I guess they weren't as powerful as they thought they were." Lily shrugged her shoulders.

"So, do I need to have a budget-friendly exorcist on speed dial from now on?" Mina's laugh died when she noticed the fear in Lily's facial expression. "I'm joking Lily. Sorry, I guess it's stressful enough as it is without me making fun of it."

"It's alright, I know you can't understand unless it's happening to you and plus, if I wasn't so worried about the religious side of things the exorcist joke would be funny." Lily folded her hands, tightening them as she considered how different life would be if she had never found any of the spirits.

This is a curse.

Mina grinned softly. "Hey at least now we can work things out together. I can't see how you figured out the other spirits all by yourself. I mean you stink at math majorly."

"What does math have to do with solving spirit cases?"

"Nothing really, just pointing out to Fred that if he needs you to do any math, he's stuck."

The two sisters simultaneously stuck their tongues out at each other.

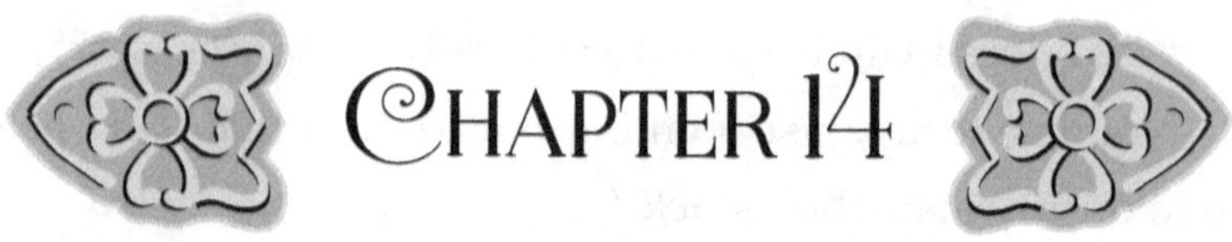

CHAPTER 14

After a short trip, the sisters parked near the public library. Once inside, Mina veered off for the books about therapy while Lily headed straight to the computers. Pulling out the chair, Lily sat down and began her research. On the drive over, she decided it was time to figure out what era Fred lived in before he died.

Like searching for a folder in her own memory cabinet, Lily tried to recall the first memories from Fred. *Let's see. There was a large, black, wall-mounted telephone. The phone looked old, like back in the days with dailing and cords.*

Lily typed into the computer.

Old black dial telephones.

After looking through several images with old telephones, she finally found one that matched the one in Fred's memory.

So these are from the early 1940's to late 1970's, called rotary phones.

"R-o-t-a-ry" Lily whispered while studying the images of the old telephones. *How did they use these ancient machines?* Pulling up Youtube, she searched for anything on rotary phones or how to use them. All she kept thinking as she watched., 'How to dial a Rotary phone' video was...*I am so glad I live in the cell phone age.*

She watched a few videos before Mina tapped her with a book on her shoulder.

"You ready to go? I'm all checked out." Mina Lifted the pile of books she was borrowing for Lily to see.

"One second, then I'm ready to go." Lily snapped a picture of the dial phone that looked like Fred's. One minute later, she was relaxing in her sister's Hawaian smelling car, headed to the antique store.

Familiar bells chimed as they walked into the antique store. Immediately the store clerk's head swiveled toward them.

"We will be closing soon, please be quick." Zoe's dismissive tone caught Lilly's attention.

"Closing? It's only 5:45pm. The sign says they close at 6:30pm." Lily whispered as she tried to catch up with Mina.

"Someone's in a bad mood." Mina muttered as they wandered through a few aisles.

After walking aimlessly, Lily wondered. *What the heck was Mina doing? We should be getting the trunk! But I'll wait, maybe there's a method to her madness.*

After several more minutes passed, Lily's impatience morphed into worry. They were running out of time or even worse,they risked annoying Zoe. She could kick them out of the store, without the trunk. No matter how many glaring looks she sent Mina, her sister walked even slower. *How is that even possible?? How slow can she go?* Lily held in a laugh at her accidental rhyme. "If you are trying to annoy Zoe--it's working." Lily hissed under her breath. "That's the third time she cleared her voice while glaring at us. Can we get the trunk already?"

Mina pursed her lips, failing to hide the mischievous grin. "Really? It's only 5:55, we have plenty of time. What's the rush?"

Lily exhaled, feeling as if all her patience had died. Fred's thoughts had become more active since they entered the antique store. Between her sister and Fred's constant nudging, her stress had reached the end of its tether. Grabbing Mina's arm, she pulled her toward the counter. Mina's evil smile widened.

"Ok, ok. Sheesh. Apparently there are two cranky people in this store." Mina laughed. "Hey, Zoe. How are yo--..." Mina didn't get a chance to finish her question before Zoe interrupted.

"Yes, yes. Got the email and here's the hand truck for you." With that Zoe maneuvered the cart beside the trunk. Between the three girls, the trunk was cleared then the two pieces were placed on the dolly. Moving it to the back of Mina's car, they loaded the trunk lid into the back seat and the trunk base into the back.

Zoe took the cart and left the girls without so much as a wave. After entering the store, she flipped the open sign to closed, then disappeared.

"See, everything worked out." Mina waved away Lily's worries.

Lily shook her head, rolling her eyes at her sister's mischief. "You're a real pain, you know that?"

"Of course, It's my one mission in life."

As they headed home. Lily remembered to thank Mina for helping her today. "Even so, thank you for your help today. I would have been screwed without you."

"Yeah, you better say thank you." Mina shoved Lily's shoulder playfully. "It's my day off and I spent it helping my sister with her weird spirit problem. It was a nice change of pace."

Cranking up the music, they jammed all the way home.

§

Once home, the girls brought one piece at a time up to Lily's room.

"What's that?" Max, their little brother, asked. Following behind as they brought the lid upstairs, he commented, "It looks like a piece of junk?" Max kicked the side of the lid once they put it on the floor.

"Hey! Don't do that. Get out of my room!" Lily's anger spiked before Mina intervened.

"Max, beat it before I use you as my acupuncture dummy." Mina held her ink pen like a syringe then chased Max out of the room.

One more trip to the car and the trunk sat in two pieces on Lily's bedroom floor. Lily felt Fred's presence become stronger. No more long distance communications. Now she could physically and mentally connect to him whenever she needed.

"Alrighty, I'm off to some well deserved tv time. Do me a favor and keep me in the loop about Fred. You know, in case he tries to overtake your body or something." Mina winked before leaving Lily's room. She stopped suddenly, looking at the trunk with a frown. "Let's not repeat last semester's near death experience--shall we?"

"Absolutely! Thanks again for all your help, Sis!" Mina winked back. "You're the best sister ever!" Mina's serious expression faded with Lily's reassuring smile and wink.

Lily remembered last semester. That was too close a call for comfort. That one spirit, Isaac...his sorrow and pain ran so deep it nearly caused her to end her life--if it weren't for Ava. Ava... was the one to follow her onto the roof of the school building. She stopped Lily. Stopped her from--Lily didn't want to remember the rest.

Forcing herself to switch her thoughts away from the pain and the horrible, heartbreaking sorrow that could still overwhelm her. Worse still, Fred connected to the emotions that Lily was feeling, as if he knew that very same pain. Something clicked between the two spirits, causing Lily to feel suddenly overwhelmed and dizzy. Swaying left then right, her hands grasped the bookshelf just in time. Steading herself the best she could while holding onto the bookshelf, Lily convinced herself that laying down would fix the problem.

"Man Fred. Give me a minute before hitting me with the hard emotions like that." Groaning softly, she held her throbbing head in her hands.

Stumbling to the bed, Lily rested her throbbing head on the pillow before she threw up. Closing her eyes for a moment to stop the room from spinning around her, Lily swallowed hard. Pushing the bile back down into her stomach, she forced her thoughts toward a perfect date with Patrick. Before she knew it, Lily and Patrick were at the park. She was dreaming. She knew it but didn't have the strength to pull herself away from the fantastic date.

Upon opening her eyes a few hours later, she noticed things were different. Her room was dark. The house seemed to be abandoned. Lily had not moved an inch from where she passed out on her bed. *How long have I been asleep?* She rubbed her eyes, rolling over to check her alarm clock.

"8:30PM!!" Taking a deep breath, Lily realized she slept

through dinner and homework time, and was now missing family movie time. At fifteen-years-old, Lily was allowed to watch movies with her older siblings once her homework was completed. *No way I'd get away with sneaking down and doing my homework later.* "Thanks a lot, Fred…."

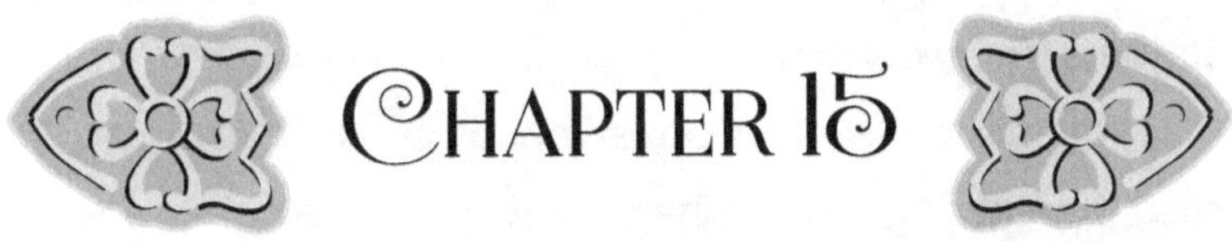

CHAPTER 15

Leaving her room she headed downstairs to the kitchen. Most of the family was in the living room watching a movie. She could hear the clashing swords echo in the hallway. Lily gave up trying to guess which movie. She was too exhausted and wobbled to the fridge. *Need food.* She held her stomach when it emitted a rumbling growl.

Mrs. Shels carried a few dishes to the sink. "Hey honey, are you feeling better?"

Lily continued rummaging through the fridge. "Yeah, just really hungry." Lily replied, unsure if her mom had checked on her earlier.

"I called you for dinner, then sent your brother to get you. But, he said you were sleeping." Mrs. Shel crossed her arms leaning against the counter.

*Uh oh...*Lily thought, *Mom thinks I was trying to get out of homework. Better to distract her now.* "Which brother?" Scanning the fridge, Lily asked, "What was for supper? I don't see any leftovers." Nothing new or different was in the tupperware containers. *It must have been a good dinner and I missed it.*

"Homemade pizza." Mom swept at invisible crumbs. "You missed a really good dinner." She shrugged one shoulder. "Sorry, but pizza doesn't last. There might be pizza pockets in the freezer downstairs or there's always leftovers." Mrs. Shels left the kitchen. "Did you like the magazine I got you? It's becoming a new monthly addition at that fancy store downtown so if you do like it, I could always pick you up next month's magazine?"

"I like it." Lily was going to say she hadn't actually looked at it since Fred came along. But she knew her Mom wouldn't understand so she kept the answer short.

Mrs. Shels smiled and nodded before leaving the kitchen.

I knew it.....This has Max written all over it. He probably knocked once, whispered 'dinner time', then left. Out of all her brothers, Mom had to send Max...Why couldn't she ask Mina? Max probably volunteered to get back at me. Lily grumbled the entire way to the basement and back. *That dumb, pesky, lil brother. I'll beat the snot out of him next time I see him. Pizza! Homemade pizza! A treat that we don't get often. Max knew this was a perfect opportunity for him to get extra. All because I yelled at him for kicking the trunk lid. Wait till I get him alone, I'll teach him--EATING MY PIZZA!!*

Still muttering threats and complaints, Lily slammed the Pizza pockets in the microwave.

Pizza pockets were no comparison to her Mom's homemade

pizza. *Brothers...the bane of my existence--next to the spirits.* Suddenly it dawned on Lily--she was cursed. Almost every single spirit she has freed up to this point, were male. *Are all of them out to ruin my life? Both the living and the dead?? I'm totally cursed! But I'll win in the end--just you wait and see.* She imagined the curse standing in front of her and threw a few good punches. *TKO!* Lily danced around the bloody corpse of the curse on the floor.

Lily's vengeful thoughts occupied her while the pizza rolls cooked. She pulled out her bookbag, to see how much homework she had to complete before bed. The Vintage Teen Magazine slid out from between two of her books falling onto the table.

Lily laid it flat, off to the side of her other homework. *I'll take a look at that later. I don't even know why I'm resisting. Maybe it's because Mom wants me to love it. It probably has a bunch of prayer stuff in it.* That seemed to crush her interest in the magazine. Lily pulled out the books she muttered, "Math, hate. Science, meh. And...history, meh--at least that teacher is good." The entire class was more enjoyable when the teacher actually liked what they were teaching. "I have a quiz tomorrow so I need to be in bed by 11." Sighing heavily, Lily prepared for the long night ahead of her. Usually 11 wasn't that late for her, especially when doodling, sketching or enjoying music. Time flew by. However when homework needed to be done, time slowed to where every five minutes felt like an hour. By 11, Lily was about to tape her eyelids open. *Homework just plain sucked.*

"You've got this." Fist pumping the air above her head, Lily tried to cheer herself into the fighting spirit. She was sure she'd have all her homework done and in bed way before 11pm.

10PM Update.

Lily sang made up lyrics to the tune in her head, losing all interest in her History notes again. "...I love doodles and I cannot lie. I'll show you how to draw that eye... With a line right here--and one over there, you will get that Look! Just wait and see. I'm a doodly!!" Catching herself repeating this song for the twentieth time, Lily slowly banged her head on the counter trying to dislodge it from her brain.

11pm Update.

Mrs. Shels poked her head into the kitchen. "Lily, how much longer?"

"Not too long, Mom. I'm almost done and headed to bed soon." Lily slipped the doodle pages under her notebook.

"Good girl." Mrs. Shels opened Lily's math book, flipping through a few pages then shutting it. "Math, huh? Just do your best." She shook her head mournfully.

Lily smirked as her mom pushed the book away. "Were you good at math, Mom?"

"Honey, Math was a subject I struggled with. I was hoping you would get your dad's math-gene. But alas, looks like you got mine instead. The math-strugglers bus is filling up fast with this family" Mom chuckled at her own bus joke.

"So...since we both stink at math? Is it ok if I don't pass, right?" Lily grinned so wide every tooth was exposed. Mainly, she was trying to be funny, but half hoping her mom would agree.

"Oh no you don't. Math sucks, I will admit that. However,

you are a bright, smart, young lady and with a little hard work, you can pass too. Just ask your father for help, not me." She returned the toothy grin before leaving the room with a wave 'goodnight'.

Sighing, Lily accepted her tragic fate. Looks like her new deadline was Midnight. The pizza pockets finally kicked in with a boost of energy. Lily finished her homework before 12am, and also had time to jot down memory details from Fred. She tucked the magazine back into her book bag.

Once in her room, Lily quickly said her night time prayers. Flopping onto the bed, she stretched out, closing her eyes. *I hope I get some peaceful sleep tonight.* She thought before drifting off to sleep. Which felt weird, since she usually didn't worry about it.

Lily slowly woke, shoving off the pile of sweaty, heavy blankets. Un-twisting herself from the tangled mess, she pushed herself upright against the pillows. The sudden movement caused her head to spin like a kite without a tail. Lily massaged her temples and groaned. She remembered from the last time, thankfully the fever only lasted a few hours. By her calculations this fever was right on time. Lily knew when she woke up, feeling sick from fighting a fever all night, that it was because the trunk was in her immediate space. When the spirit infested object was in close proximity, the first twenty-four hours, the spirits, memories and emotions overwhelmed her. Usually causing a fever. Thankfully, it didn't last. Unfortunately, she would be well enough to still go to school. *Stupid school...why can't I be sick during school hours?* She tested her forehead, almost wishing the fever would return.

All day, Lily wrote down every memory from the night's sweaty delirium. Once the object was in her possession, the spirit's memories flowed into her like a broken dam. During History, she almost failed the pop-quiz when she wrote *Fred Cummens* as the 16th President of the United States. Thankfully, she checked her answers before handing the paper in.

"Yoooo, Earth to Lily?" Doris waved one hand in front of Lily's face several times. "Hey, there." Doris sat in front of her staring, one eyebrow arched. She pressed nose to nose, peering into Lily's eyes. "Are you in there?" Doris waited a few seconds. "Who is *Fred*?" Doris pointed to Lily's notes with one finger, tapping impatiently while waiting for Lily's response.

"Fred?" Lily checked around her desk. "Who are *you* talking about?" Lily asked as her mind returned to the present. Blinking a few times, she realized Doris was only inches from her face. Lily jolted away from her best friend.

"This," Doris tapped the paper again. "It says...Fred saw doctors--got bad news...and is going blind." She shoved the papers at Lily, then leaned back, crossing her arms. "Who. Is.

Fred? I won't ask nicely again."

"Oh that...Ummm." Lily hesitated. Should she tell Doris about the spirits? She already read some of her notes. *What the heck was she supposed to say?* The whole situation was too complicated to explain. Thankfully, Lily had been writing short stories for a few years before the first spirit mission. To avoid explaining, Lily told Doris these stories were made up. Stories that Lily wrote when she was bored.

Lily switched books, since her next class was in the same room. It gave her a moment to figure out what to tell Doris. Finally, Lily decided to talk about the photoshoot instead. "I borrowed a trunk for a photoshoot. I had to ask the owners for approval." Lily relaxed her shoulders. "They told me the original owner was a man named Fred Cummens." She lifted one shoulder like it didn't matter. "He sounded interesting so I decided to write a story about Fred...just for fun." *I'm shocked the lie came out so smooth. Usually my explanations are a mess, and ramble all over the place.* Lily felt a small bead of sweat trickling down her forehead. *Was it enough to knock her bloodhound-best-friend off the spirit trail?*

Doris took a minute to re-read Lily's notes. Flipping from one page to the next, her expression remained blank. "Oh! That sounds cool." Doris pursed her lips, nodding slowly before she flashed a thumbs up sign. "Can I read Fred's story when you're done? So, is this one going to be fact or fiction?" She tossed the pages onto Lily's desk. "...like the others?"

Lily could feel another memory pulling her away, so she shrugged her shoulders, "Sure, why not?" Fred urged her to write more of his story, forcing Lily to flip to a fresh, clean page. She was surprised when Doris grabbed the pen out of her hand. "Give me that! I have to finish this story while the ideas are flowing." Lily glared at Doris.

"Before you disappear into your stories, can you answer me?" Doris threw the pen at Lily's chest. "Is this new one fiction or not? It's not a complicated question."

Smiling up at Doris, Lily tried not to be rude. "Totally fiction! Can you imagine all the research hours needed for a real story? It's just a fun way to fill boring school days." *Even though her hand ached from constant writing.*

Chapter 16

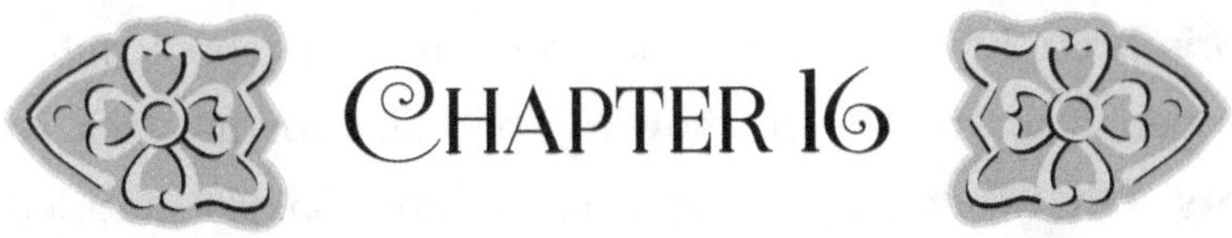

Doris suppressed the '*sigh*' that wanted to come out. "Sounds cool. Tell me when it's done so I can read it. Make it less depressing than the last one, please." With her chin propped on her folded hand, Doris watched Lily's pen fly across the page. Back and forth, ink scribbles flowed across the paper.

I can't keep this up much longer...please leave Doris. Was what Lily wanted to say, but instead she answered while gritting her teeth. "I'll try, but the story kinda...just comes to me...as I write. Can't make any promises." Lily looked between Doris and the paper, her hand still scribbling Fred's story as she spoke.

Doris turned to talk to another girl, leaving Lily to her writing. *Thank-goodness.* Lily exhaled the breath she had been holding since Doris sat down. It was extremely difficult to hold two separate conversations at the same time. Especially, when one was mental and the other was verbal. Her mind and mouth refused to operate separately.

Lily was glad she made the decision to filter the truth when her spirit journey began. She had been sick for a few days when Doris brought her homework over. Lily's notebook fell and happened to land open, showing the notes for her first spirit story. Lily needed to tell Doris something. So, she decided to say they were made up stories---fiction she wrote when she was bored. She even offered to let Doris read them after they were finished. Doris loved the idea, and pledged to be Lily's critique partner--reviewing every story as soon as it was done.

Doris was the only person to read every spirit story since Lily began writing them. The best part was, Doris didn't know the truth, so Lily didn't worry about hiding her notebooks. Which was a good thing because Lily discovered that no one cared about her notebooks if she left them out. The best place to hide a secret is out in the open. Once a story is finished, Doris reads then reviews it. If the ending is a happy one, she writes a gleaming, five-star review. If the ending is a sad one, then she adds a negative, one-star review, with a small note about how she would rewrite the ending.

"Why do you write such depressing stories? That last one, about the boy and the picture, made me cry." Doris paused, gripping Lily's hand with a gentle squeeze. Furrowing her brow, she softly smiled. "Are you ok? Do you need to talk about it?"

Lily was caught off guard for an instant. "Yeah! I'm ok. It's just a story I wrote."

"Ok. As long as it is just a story, and not you trying to hide how you feel."

Doris' response stunned Lily. Of course she thought about what anyone might think. Whether these were her feelings or not, in the stories. But she didn't expect Doris to be so attuned-- seeing through the story, so quickly.

"Hey, want to check out this new magazine that's being sold at that fancy store in town? Mom bought it for me and I brought it so you could check it out too." Lily felt impressed that she found such a perfect distraction for Doris. Thank-goodness for that magazine hanging out in her bag. Lily pulled out the now semi-crunched magazine out, handing it over to Doris.

"OOOh I love the cover. It's perfect for us! Vintage Teen Magazine. Checky title." Doris froze staring at the magazine cover. Realizing how smooth her best friend is. Lily not only avoided her questions but also threw her a distraction to keep her from noticing.

Lily didn't have time to respond before Doris slammed the Magazine on the desk. She pulled Lily in for a smothering hug. "Just know I'm here for you bestie! Any day, anytime." Picking the magazine up, Doris smirked.

The sincerity in Doris' voice was enough to bring a few tears. Lily's delayed answer was proof enough for Doris, she had hit the mark. Even though it wasn't true, Lily decided to let her best friend believe she was on the verge of a mental breakdown. Because the real answer was such a tangled web that Lily had no idea where to even start. *So in a way, Doris might be right. Maybe I am on the verge of a melt down.* Lily tried to hide her tears, but the harder she tried the faster the tears fell.

Doris forced Lily to scoot over. Using the magazine as a good distraction they explored it's pages as the tears stopped. Doris blinked hard, did she just reach her best friend. Her bestie who seems to be growing further apart each semester. Canceling their outings, movies and acting weird.

Before long they were both immersed in the magazine, pointing out outfits they would love to wear and hats they wanted to buy.

§

Lily wondered later, *Tears are childish, right? Why is that, exactly? Doesn't everybody cry?* Why are tears something we see as childish and not a normal human reaction? Lily decided from now on, she would cry and not be ashamed. Easier said then done. She would at least try to not be ashamed of a normal human thing. Besides, according to *Vintage Teen* magazine, crying is a healthy way to release stress and is completely normal.

"Why do you write such depressing stories?" Doris' comment brought Isaac's story to mind. To be fair, his story was very depressing. Even though Lily knew the feelings she experienced were from him, she did wonder if some of those actually were her own? Had she been suppressing them--even from herself? Going through that story opened her eyes to so many problems in life. Problems, that thanks to her sheltered, happy life, she had not experienced before.

At least some good came out of that very, sad story. Lily learned to appreciate her life and everything she had with a new zest. Her family, friends and the town she lived in, had become more precious to her. Not in a possessive way, but from a place of gratitude. Everything seemed to hold a new sense of wonder and beauty in Lily's sharpened outlook.

Is that why I'm cursed with this power? To learn life lessons like gratitude? I don't know for sure but it's one hard way to learn things.

Lily recalled helping her Mom make dinner, a few months before her Isaac spirit adventure. "Life teaches us lessons during every stage of life," Mom had said. "No matter how old or young we are, if we open our eyes and are willing to learn, we can become wise."

Lily didn't understand why she was sharing that piece of advice, but it was helpful and recently more relevant. *Mom has great intuition. It's like she can read my mind. It's weird and cool, all at the same time.*

Lily realized that her brain had taken a giant detour since class started. Looking up at the clock she saw the class was almost over. When she looked down at her notebook, Lily saw she had stopped writing without noticing it. Skimming through what she had written, she must have stopped shortly after the bell rang. *Was Fred listening in on her thoughts this entire time?*

That wasn't usual, unless Fred was connecting to her emotions at that moment. *Fred, did you go through a similar depression? I can't imagine going blind--never seeing daylight and color again.* Her chest tightened uncomfortably. The pain intensified for a split second as an answer from Fred. Lily sucked in a deep breath, slowly trying to mask the pain she was feeling. Another side effect to her closer connection with Fred--everything was magnified the more she understood his story.

Another class ended. During the 5 minute break Doris snuck behind Lily reading what she was writing. "So when will you be done with this story?" Doris reached over Lily's shoulders, trying to stop her from flipping the page that she was still reading.

Lily turned a mischievous grin toward Doris, then changed the topic with lighting speed. "So, Doris, how was the soccer game? Did a certain *someone* notice you?" Lily knew Derek was always the perfect distraction. Doris happily recounted every second of the entire game through the rest of their classes.

Mrs. Shels waited to pick up her kids in her usual spot at the school. Lily hurried toward the family van, then slowed to a walk when she spotted Patrick. He didn't notice Lily as he looked across the sea of backpack-laden classmates running toward escape. At least, Lily assumed he hadn't seen her. Patrick looked in her general direction, but didn't wave or anything else, like he used to. *Is he ignoring me? No, Patrick is such a hard worker, he's just too busy to be distracted by girls right now.* No sooner than that thought entered her head, a girl from the high school volleyball team ran up to Patrick and acted like they were best friends. Seeing their interaction and public display, Lily hoped and prayed that the girl was his cousin. Otherwise, Lily was going to be sick, right here in front of everyone. She darted into the back seat, hoping no one noticed. Heart pounding and red-faced, Lily pretended to be fully engrossed in the contents of her backpack. Thankfully, her brother's noisy entrance pulled the attention away from Lily.

Lily tried to melt into the car seat, hoping no one would notice her. But Max loudly shouted to anybody within four-square miles that 'Lily would never get a boyfriend with a frown like that'. Lily really tried to keep from blowing up at her brother, but her better angel was tired and she punched Max anyway.

Max's smile fell when Lily punched his shoulder. "Owwww, *Mom*! Lily's punching me again."

"Shut. Up. Max! You're lucky I'm *not* kicking your butt into next week!" Lily threatened, mimicking punching him again before buckling up.

Mrs. Shel's response as they headed home was, "Don't make me stop this van!'.

Both Lily and Max grumbled at each other while offering 'I'm sorry' to their Mom. After a quick nod, Mom asked how their day went. Each of them gave a vague answer before Theo asked, "What's for supper?"

Mrs. Shels practically sang the menu out loud as she drove them home. "Mashed potatoes...fried chicken...and apple cobble!"

The boys cheered while Lily wanted to cry. *Mashed potatoes!?? Ick!* Every time mashed potatoes were on the menu, she had to gag them down whether she wanted to or not. Mrs. Shels made sure she couldn't sneak them into a napkin, either. She had been praying for brownies, to make the potatoes worth tolerating, but with apples instead, she wasn't sure if she could choke them down this time. *There's a sad trade off...apples instead of chocolate fudge brownies. Was Mom trying to torture me with the most disgusting food combinations? I wonder if Mina still has chocolate stashed in her desk?*

Finally home, Lily tossed her book bag to the kitchen floor with a loud thud. "I feel like eating a plate of brownies, right now." She opened the microwave, hoping to see brownies. *No brownies. None in the fridge. No brownies anywhere.* Lily dragged her heavy book bag over to her chair to unload her notebooks.

Still muttering complaints under her breath, Lily remembered the last time her mom had caught her grumbling about dinner. She snapped her mouth shut to keep more whining from tumbling out. Last time, Mom made her sit through an entire lecture about 'how she should be grateful to get three meals a day' With a side of 'how some kids don't get half of what she does'. This regular lecture used to make Lily's eyes roll. Lily didn't see any starving kids around her school. The topic was in regular rotation, just like the mashed potatoes on the menu. Lily complained about clumpy potatoes, and her Mom would respond with 'The talk'--about starving kids all over the world. Lily used to feel guilty until she started asking, 'where are they?' She checked her school and around town, but Lily didn't see any starving kids. After a few months, she felt less guilty. Then Lily noticed her lunch was meager compared to others in her class. If she wasn't starving,...then was her Mom making it up to get her to eat the gross food? It wasn't like she could ship her gross potatoes to them. Which Lily was 100% in favor of doing!

Until her last spirit mission, the one with the depressed Isaac. *His story really opened my eyes. I used to ask Mom, 'where's your proof?' I would mumble, after she lectured me about being grateful, and I thought I was being smart since she had no proof. Boy was I wrong. Isaac set me straight, but that was a hard pill to swallow.*

During lunch shortly after I had met Isaac, I ended up in the girls bathroom crying. Before the tears rolled down my cheeks, I was about to happily eat lunch with my friends in the cafeteria. When I opened my lunch box, I thought about the stupid apple I had in my lunch today. How I wished I had extra chips instead. Then Isaac whispered in my head. He wanted my apple. He said, "It's been so long since I've enjoyed one. What I wouldn't give to taste apples again."

A simple pleasure really that we take for granted. But that's not what created the tears. It was his feeling of utter sadness that washed over me as I stared at that simple apple--feeling what he missed. Isaac just wanted to taste my simple green apple again. He didn't care about my chips, my sandwich with two types of meat, or the leftover dessert in the plastic container. He was drawn to the apple, it was more than enough for him.

That single moment was just one example of how crappy I felt writing his entire story. I felt overwhelmed, miserable and very moody. Lily felt his horrible childhood memories. The experience with Isaac made Lily see things differently. No one had noticed this kid at his school. He was a ghost long before he ever died. Lily wouldn't have noticed him either. Like most people, she would have assumed he was happy with his obscurity. *Just goes to show, no one knows who is struggling or even starving--for food or attention or help.* Lily offered a small prayer for Isaac-- so grateful that his spirit no longer suffered. *Sad, yes. Isaac's story was hard to deal with, but so far, I'm not falling into a hole of despair with Fred.*

Lily stacked her notebooks into a neat pile. Mrs. Shels gave her kids a choice: finish their homework, then go play; or play first, then homework after dinner. Max and Theo ran through the kitchen and out the backdoor to play. Lily could go outside if she wanted to, but with Fred nagging constantly, she needed to work on his story. Playing wouldn't be much fun with Fred tossing out random thoughts and memories every five seconds.

Lily finished her homework in record time. Maybe Fred helped her with a few math problems. He made it a little too easy to ask. Shortly after, Mom shouted 'Dinner's ready!'.

Lily had to compliment her Mom on the apple cobbler. It wasn't as good as brownies, but it did hit the sweet spot, after gagging down the gross potatoes. With dinner over and the kitchen cleaned up, Lily sat down to sort her notebooks as Mrs. Shels finished wiping down the last counter.

"I read...I mean I showed that Vintage Teen Magazine to Doris today. She really liked it like me. Even learned a few cute skirt styling tricks. Thanks for buying it, Mom."

"You're very welcome." Mrs. Shels rinsed out the dishcloth smiling before heading outside to check on the boys.

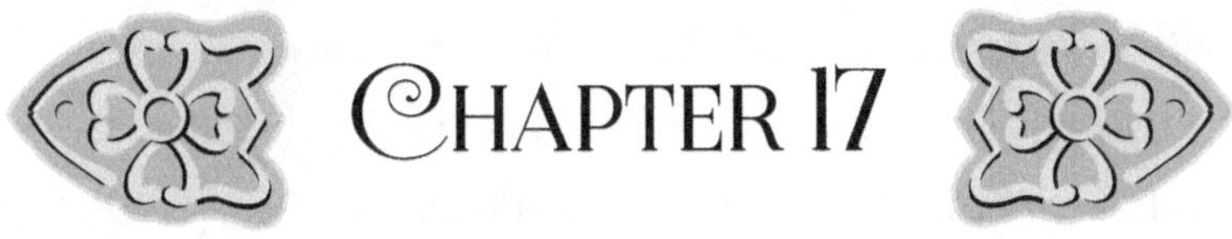

CHAPTER 17

Time to dive into the ancient world in Fred's memories. Scanning through her supplies, she pulled out her ear phones. De-tangling them, she plugged the jack into her cell phone. Right before she got comfy, Lily grabbed a water bottle, filling it up. Finally, she opened all her notebooks while listening to her favorite movie soundtracks. Lily tore out a few blank pages, to rewrite Fred's memories in chronological order.

Flipping pages, Lily began sorting through the memories from the beginning to present day. She left plenty of space for missing information. *Maybe I don't want to know what's missing.*

In later memories, Fred described his wife to the nurse at the nursing home where he lived. Lily's best guess was, the woman from his first few memories must have been Fred's wife. She matched Fred's description the best: black hair, with some grey peeking through, here and there; shorter in height, yet strong and beautiful. HIs wife was younger than Fred, but in his own words. *"Dorothy is the sweetest person I know. But don't be fooled, by those soft blue eyes. She'll match wits with anyone, and throw sarcasm back twice as fast. I love that woman."*

Lily wondered about Fred's wife. Dorothy didn't show up in any of the memories he shared with her. *Why? Did she die?* No, that can't be right. Fred would have confirmed that for sure. *Fred was either separated or divorced. Is that possible?* Lily wrote out the memories and placed them in a timeline. She discovered a huge gap in his memories. The gap started shortly after Fred moved into the nursing home. He had gone to the doctors office multiple times, before losing his eyesight. There was mounting tension between Fred and his entire family, including his wife before he left home. Fred refused to tell Lily exactly what happened. Even Lily guessing about it caused Fred to flare with so much anger that she stopped asking.

Major mood swings happening.

Lily stopped writing to take a short break. Feeling Fred's fierce energy lash out had taken its toll on her own energy. Her eyes felt heavy, like a knot forming in the middle of her forehead, with all the hard thinking. Rubbing the sore spot gently, Lily tried distracting herself and Fred with some new music--maybe something random and peppy? Trying hard to bust out some new dance moves, Lily bobbed and turned to the beat, but she felt as if bricks dangled from her arms and legs. Giving up, Lily collapsed onto a chair, a few angry tears escaped before splattering onto the papers.

After a second to compose herself, Lily confronted spirit stalker. *Fred...Even if I don't know you entirely, I can feel how you react when your wife is mentioned. You must have loved her deeply. So why won't you tell me what happened?*

A flood of emotions and memories slammed inside Lily. Her heart felt dead--empty, dark and full of...white noise? Lily saw a few stars before her head slammed onto the pile of notebooks, lifeless eyes staring across the kitchen table.

When Lily next looked up, Fred was sitting next to her. *Did I just die? Is this really the spirit world? This isn't what I expected. All this gloom, doom and nothingness. Where are the other spirits? Where are the angels? So then I can't be dead. The other spirits didn't say anything about a cloudy emptiness.* Lily reached over to tap Fred's shoulder, but her hand passed through him. *Of course, we are spirits.* Lily tried to project her thoughts into Fred's mind.

They left you--alone, in that home to die?

Fred's mind fractured, opening his wounded soul to reveal the abandoned, depressed and desperate man that he had become. No longer the strong, loving husband and father, he had turned inward, reveling in the very emotions he had been disgusted by. Angry, he lashed out at his loved ones. Fearfully, shutting himself away from everyone and everything that could help. Desperate, he was screaming for help in all the wrong ways. Unable to defend himself or his family from an attack, the despair dug deep into his soul and took over without him knowing it. No one saw the end coming. Fred fell into the deepest pit, mentally and physically. He felt overwhelmed and could see no hope for the end of his life's journey. Lily struggled against the slimy, shiny mass of shadows ensnaring her, sliding over her arms and throat. Every hopeless thought, every regret, every spark of animus infecting his soul slithering in from whatever dark corner they usually hid in.

A fiery sensation tore through Lily's throat, making it painful to swallow. She felt strangled from inside--her heart slowed dangerously, thud...thud, slamming against her ribs with every gasping breath. Instinctually, she frantically looked for an escape from Fred's nightmare. The nothingness was so dark when she reached out with her arms for someone to help, no one was there. She stumbled blindly forward searching for something, anything solid. She was so lost and disoriented, finally collapsing as she screamed for Fred.

Fred, Fred! She cried. *Are you here? Are we in Hell?*

Lily smacked her lips together tasting salt. Slowly opening her eyes, she blinked against the sudden brightness. Her throat felt raw from choking on her own tears. Jerking upright, she clutched her pen to fill in the blank spaces. She now knew why Fred blocked his family from his memories. Rubbing her eyes as she wrote, she tried to wipe away the tears.

Fred's immediate family sent him to the home to die.

They went so far as to forbid Dorothy from visiting Fred.

Shortly after being moved into the home, Fred's entire family severed all relationships with him.

Angry tears continued to fall. Lily couldn't believe it. Fred's emotional denial was starting to make sense. Who wouldn't turn into a heartless nasty person If going blind caused your own family to abandon you. Slamming her fists on the kitchen counter Lily held in the scream that wanted to burst out!

Lily's anger was abruptly disrupted by a new, unfamiliar voice inside her head. "Sir, sir. Please calm down. You're going to make yourself sick again if you don't relax." *It was a male nurse from the nursing home.* Lily quieted her thoughts allowing the voice to continue.

"Shut your mouth! I want to see my wife!" Fred's voice cracked, causing fresh tears to spill from Lily's eyes. "You have no idea what I-I-I...what I am fighting." He barely finished his sentence before his voice went soft, hoarse from yelling and trembling with emotion.

Oh Fred. "You're right, sir." The nurse spoke again, softening his tone . "I don't know what it's like to wear your shoes, but I can try." The mystery voice belonged to a much younger man.

Lily guessed he was at least thirty years old. His voice was firm, yet gentle.

"What did you say, boy?"

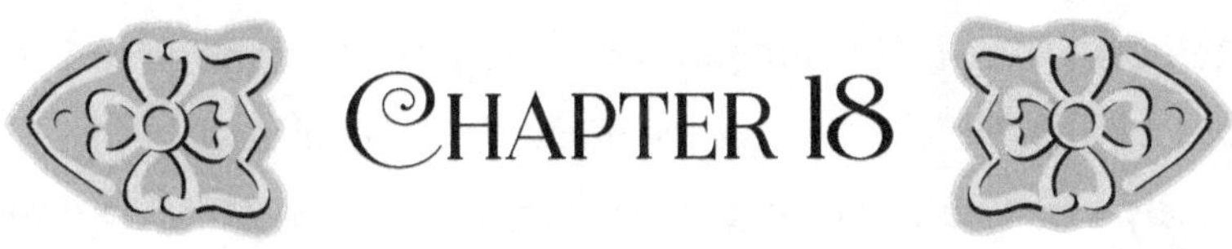 Chapter 18

" I said, I can try, sir. Do you want me to try?"

" You can't imagine the pain and loss I've endured…" Again Fred's voice cracked. This time he did not finish.

"I can't experience everything you have, that much is true. But, I can put on a blindfold and try to understand the struggle you fight everyday." The man stopped talking. Lily could hear something rustling in the background. It sounded soft, like a piece of cloth.

"Ok, Sir. I need you to say something, so I can find you."

Fred's dead silence was the only response, he refused to say anything.

Something plastic clattered to the floor, followed by an *Oops*.

"Boy, don't be stupid!" Fred's voice came out clearer than Lily had ever heard. "Stop pretending to be kind to me." He sounded concerned for a second.

"Sir-- May I call you Fred?" The nurse waited a moment, "Fred, I am *putting* myself in your shoes, as much as I can." He paused again, giving Fred a chance to respond. "My Mom used to tell us--*if you feel like judging someone, you better plan on switching shoes with them. 'Can't judge what you don't know yourself'.*"

Lily could almost feel the stranger's smile piercing Fred's miserable existence.

He continued, "Then, she would follow up with a swat to our head, finishing with. *'Judging is the Lord's business, so keep your nose out of it, period'.* The nurse laughed. Lily's first thought was, 'what a weird laugh'. It sounded like a braying donkey, friendly and inviting if you like farm animals, but a little disconcerting in her kitchen. She wondered if she had just formed a judgment herself. Chuckling, she pictured a mysterious spirit returning to swat her on the head some years in the future. *Is a spirit-smack as hard as a Mom-smack?* God works in mysterious ways, so who knows, maybe a God-smack is the worst of all. Lily didn't plan on finding out.

Fred and the male nurse faded into silence, leaving Lily alone in the kitchen, again. The mystery nurse had made a good point. The entire time she was trying to finish his story and she had not considered what it was like not to see. Lily hadn't tried putting herself in Fred's shoes. Closing her eyes, she stood up and tried finding her way around the kitchen. Barefoot was not the best idea as her pinky toe immediately met the chair leg.

Fudgesicles! Lily whimpered. *Ten points for the fricken chair!* Lily dropped to the floor trying her best to hold in the scream of agony. Rubbing her poor bruised toe, she wondered if she woke anyone up. *How did Fred do this?* She barely made it five feet. How did anyone walk around without seeing? The pain in her toe connected to one of Fred's memories. She couldn't see but she felt his frustration. Fred was feeling his way around the house, listening to the nagging voices expecting him to fall. The doctors kept telling him there was nothing they could do. He should prepare for a life of blindness. Lily's toe still ached, but as the memory went on, her feet, arms and other parts of her body began to throb. The constant stumbling, bumping and near misses added up--like small cuts and bruises popping up with every step. Lily knew Fred was sharing this memory so she would know what it had been like in the beginning.

Fred, I will never complain about anything ever again. I don't want you to suffer anymore. Let's finish this so you can move on.

A woman's voice interrupted Lily's train of thought. "Fred, you injured that same cut again. I told you not to try walking around the house by yourself. You need to listen to me, you stubborn old goat." Her tinkling laugh caught Lily off guard before she was suddenly transported into another memory.

Someone was with Fred, helping him. Lily's best guess was his wife. Their teasing and bickering was a good indication that they knew each other well. Plus she attended every doctor's visit with Fred. This must be his beloved Dorothy.

Dorothy spoke again. "Fred, please talk to me. I miss our long talks."

"Talk? About what, exactly?" Lily felt Fred's anger spike. "About the fact that I am blind? That I am useless? Or the fact that you have to take care of me like a small child? Is *that* what you want to talk about, Dorothy?! Why?!"--

Lily felt as if she was suddenly evicted from Fred's memories. She could still feel them moving to sit down, somewhere soft if the quiet *oof* was any indication. Fred's anger started to cool into a simmering frustration. She heard nothing else.

Lily returned to the present moment, opening her eyes to write in her notebook:

Fred's wife's name is Dorothy.

That's it? There has to be more than just one memory of Dorothy. Come on Fred. But, Fred was done sharing his memories. Lily scribbled a question mark next to Dorothy's name.

Since Fred was silent, Lily wrote and circled the biggest questions she had yet to solve.

Why did your soul attach to this stupid chest?

And, are there two different trunks? If there are two?

Walking around the kitchen island, Lily stretched her legs

after sitting for so long. Hoping to reconnect with Fred, she put on her jade ring, then pulled out her collection of crystals. *Dumb crystals. I wanted anti-anxiety crystals and I got crystals from the old testament…that do nothing for me. At least most of them look pretty.*

The real reason Lily wanted these crystals was to help her connect with the spirit stalkers, but she couldn't exactly tell her parents that. She had read, online somewhere, that some crystals help strengthen spiritual connections. Lily figured she would try anything at this point. Even if they didn't work, at least they looked pretty, and she could use them for decorations. *But for some reason Mom has a problem with that…she has a problem with everything now. Lily noticed, the older she got, the more her parents pushed her about being a good Catholic girl.*

Don't wear that, you shouldn't like this, that's not catholic enough. Blah blah blah.

Fred was suddenly back, interrupting Lily's rant. She felt a *whoosh* of anxiety flow through her as they reconnected. The hair on her arms stood up. Goosebumps popped up across her skin within seconds. It felt like a single spark catching on a dry bale of hay. Starting slow, but once lit, the flames quickly engulfed the entire thing inside a fiery inferno. Lily could hear Fred yelling beside her--screaming at someone she couldn't see. It wasn't until she felt a sharp stab to her heart, that Lily realized Fred was yelling at Dorothy. Fred's anger was growing more and more explosive with every new memory. This was what he had been trying to hide from Lily--the uncontrollable rage. He couldn't stop yelling. Lily knew Fred was so ensnared in his own anger and frustration that he had no idea what he was saying or doing.

Lily heard a loud crash, followed by a woman's shrill scream--then more voices shouting.

Abruptly, silence flooded Lily's mind. Fred had broken their connection again, ejecting Lily from his memories.

Poor Dorothy, attacked by the one person she loved so much. Lily wondered, what else happened? Did Fred throw something at Dorothy? Would he really do that to his beloved wife?

The last accusation Fred hurled at Dorothy stuck inside Lily's mind. She felt the slicing of her heart strings, a pain so intense she couldn't describe it. Part of her died hearing him scream at Dorothy like that.

Right before the loud crash, Fred's harsh words rang in the air. "Leave. Me. Alone. Everyone else did, why not join the party?" Lily knew Fred wanted everyone as far away from him as possible. He believed they would be better off-- safer without him.

Fred, you're going to lose Dorothy if you keep pushing her away. Why are you trying to hurt everyone that loves you?

Reining her emotions, trying to calm her nerves, Lily paced around the kitchen. She sat down, looking through her notes and decided this crappy day needed chocolate. She was able to fill in some missing memories--between Fred living with Dorothy until he moved into the nursing home. Lily was sorting through her thoughts as she mixed the brownies and stuck them in the oven. *Fred had messed up big time and was probably why he had been sent there--for everyone's safety.* Lily could understand why he separated from his wife physically until his anger was under control, *but why did they stay separated? Never seeing each other again?* The waft of the chocolaty goodness made her stomach growl.

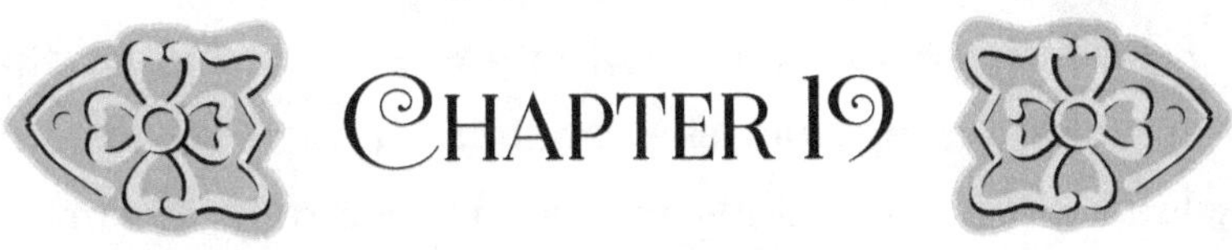

CHAPTER 19

Lily was still missing some memories after he moved into the home, but before his death. She worried that Fred had been left alone, to die with no one who cared near him. *Was that why his spirit couldn't move on?* She wondered while pulling the brownies from the oven. *Was Fred attached to the trunk or his regret?*

Lily packed up her notes, shoving a large brownie sandwich into her mouth. After half of a second brownie sandwich she was in a chocolate coma and barely awake enough to walk to her own room. Crashing face first on her bed, she let sleep overtake her, too tired to even pull the blanket over her body.

§

Over the next few days, Lily tried to coax Fred into reconnecting.

She talked to him as gently as she could, telling him she understood why he was so angry. Telling him that she knew he wouldn't hurt his family on purpose. That his outrage was another stage of his grief--not because he was a bad person.

*Fred. You didn't do anything...*Lily wanted to say 'he didn't do anything wrong', but she couldn't say that. Because after all, Fred did do something terrible. He not only screamed at his family but he also became violent. This was a sticky, tricky situation for Lily. *How am I supposed to help an unstable spirit? I'm not going to lie to him but again, it wasn't entirely his fault.*

Fred, I don't know how to help you. Sorry doesn't seem enough. Would you like to talk about it? I'll let you yell as much as you want. Still no answer, Fred was not cooperating.

Lily felt as if those last memories were a dividing point between her and Fred. She was fighting her feelings of anger and bitterness toward Fred--for what he did to Dorothy. It was a cruel thing to do, to his wife and his family. But then Lily could see the other side of the coin, and realize that Fred was not in a healthy state of mind. Fred was facing the inescapable demons only a blind person could truly understand. *Even, I couldn't pretend to be blind for a full minute. I can't imagine what it's like for Fred.*

Torn and feeling conflicted, Lily tapped softly on Mina's door. She needed her sister's advice again. It was Wednesday evening and thankfully Mina was home.

Lily plopped onto Mina's bed, pouring out the conflicting emotions she had about Fred. "I don't get it, Mina. He loved his wife, and she loved him. Why would he push her away like that?" Lily grabbed the closest pillow to exert some of her frustration.

"I don't blame Dorothy for leaving Fred in that nursing home. He was treating her like trash. No wonder she wanted him out of the house, I'd do that too if I were in her shoes." Lily flung the pillow across the room, barely missing the bookshelf. She ignored Mina's small jab. "But...at the same time...was it enough to separate them forever? After all, couldn't Dorothy see the effects of going blind on her husband? Maybe that's why she tried staying longer than the others." With one hand on her hip and the other flailing around, Lily paced, unable to sit still while her emotions flared.

"Did she leave him for good?" Mina asked. "Just because she's not in his recent memories doesn't mean she's out of his life. Maybe these memories are all from the same week." For a minute, silence took over the room Mina looked over Lily's notes, flipping the pages noisily, one at a time. "I'm no doctor or professional therapist, but I've been able to dive into some therapy with my massage therapy classes. Emotions can affect physical and mental stability. Fred lost his eyesight very quickly. To me, it sounds like a cancer of sorts. On top of that, from what you've described, he was alive around the 1940's." Mina peered over the edge of the notebook toward her sister.

"Yeah, I know. Emotions affect everything. We already went over this." Lily felt her aggravation swirling tighter and tighter. Mina repeated things Lily already knew. Plus it had been an entire week since she brought the trunk home. Lily was starting to get antsy, trying to solve Fred's story. All the memories from the last week seemed to blend together--yelling, anger, fear and loneliness. Strong emotions from Fred.

"Lily." Mina's voice was low and serious. " You have never dealt with depression like Fred's. You came close with that last spirit. But that was Isaac's depression, not yours. You didn't experience it when it started, before it grew into the sinking hole of despair." Turning in her chair, Mina crossed her arms to look directly at Lily. "My guess is that Fred is going through a very deep depression because of his blindness. When Fred was alive, therapy was seen as something shameful and likely ended your reputation in the community. Plus, it was not available to most people, as only the rich could afford to hide it. You can't understand depression exactly, because it is unique to each person. However, I can tell you that without the right help or therapy, a person is overcome by everything around them. Causing sufferers to cut out people without realizing it." Mina took a deep breath, giving Lily a moment to let what she said sink in. "He yells, but that's likely his emotions crying out for help. Fred is suffering, more than others know. And yet, they are the ones turning away from him. They only hear his words and see his actions. Assuming he has willingly turned into a hateful, bitter, old man. When in reality, he is emotionally distressed and needs love and hope." Mina was in full teacher mode, pacing with such purposeful steps Lily worried the carpet would have a permanent groove.

Lily was afraid to move for fear it would distract her sister. *Mina was definitely on a roll.*

"It's not his fault really--he's blind. Fred is fighting, thinking he can control something that he can't. If Fred had therapy, he likely would have caught the signs and been able to control his anger. Therapy, emotional support, and hope is essential, but Fred had none of those. I can't imagine how hard that would be for him." Mina picked the pillow up off the floor, squeezing it between her folded arms. "Don't hate Fred for something he can't control or fix without help. It's a shame really. People turn away from him instead of recognizing the warning signs or helping him with his trauma. But again, back in Fred's time, therapy was a new, experimental concept. People didn't know or understand depression like we do now. You understand where I'm coming from, right?" Mina knew she had probably overwhelmed her little sister with all the medical jargon. But, Lily needed to be aware of Fred's depression, even If it was a tough subject for someone her age. Mina sucked in a deep breath, exhaling slowly, as she waited for Lily to reply. *Did Lily get she was wading through an emotional swamp with Fred? Did she understand that what she was witnessing in Fred was the results of raw depression.*

Lily sat back on her sister's bed, trying to filter through the medical mumbo-jumbo. Thinking of Fred and pulling herself out of the mess to observe from an outsiders point of view. She didn't want to feel sorry for Fred since he acted like a bitter old man. But after Mina explained Fred's struggle, and how it affected him, Lily decided to give him a second chance. It all made sense now--his anger, fear and distress was Fred's way of expressing his pain without even knowing it. Lily decided to sympathize, even if he made plenty of mistakes. Fred needed Lily...to help him. *Someone* needed to care about him.

Mina watched Lily stare at the floor. "Does any of this make sense?" Lily shrugged her shoulders. "It's a lot to take in but I'm not upset with you. Therapy, depression and mental health are topics that I don't expect you to know about." Mina organized the pillows on her bed, keeping her hands busy. "And I wish you didn't have to know anything about them. It's a harsh reality that we live with this as a fast-paced, phone-absorbed world." Mina sat next to Lily. She looked entirely too pale for Mina's comfort.

"Yeah, I get it."

Lily's short and blunt answer had Mina even more worried. Mina had to bring up Isaac's painful depression in order to make her point. When she looked at Lily, the dark circles under her eyes seemed more hollow. Her exhaustion was obvious to anyone who cared to look. Mina gave Lily a playful nudge with her shoulder. "Tell you what--let's stay up late tonight and piece more of Fred's memories together. With my help, I'm sure we can get Fred and Dorothy's story figured out." As soon as she caught Lily's attention. Mina hopped onto her chair and wheeled toward some plastic bags in the corner. Grabbing the crinkling bags, Mina scooted her chair back to the desk and gestured for Lily to take a look inside.

Lily barely looked up, caught in a trance-like state.

Chapter 20

Mina added more enthusiasm to her voice. "Here we go! Let's enjoy our favorite snacks while we think." Tossing the bags at Lily, Mina watched as she rummaged through-- starting to look more like her sister again.

Lily pulled out two bags of chips, her favorite iced tea, and some chocolate-chip cookies. Feeling like her old self, Lily felt her mood rise, switching from haunted to happy. *Now this is the way to get things done. Good old sugar, helps boost the mood, mind and mission.* Lily looked at Mina, who exhaled. *Or maybe it's Mina. She's the one lifting the mood and my thoughts. Not the sugar. Is sharing thoughts and pain with someone you trust really that beneficial?* Lily took that thought and pinned it to her heart. *Mina is the reason I feel better.*

Mina remembered when she was a teen, watching Lily open

the chips and chow down, reminded her of her Mom. She used to do the same thing with Mina, every once in a blue moon, as a fun girls night. Nothing fancy--just snacks, a comfy bed and girl talk. They were part of Mina's favorite memories with her Mom. Mina's thoughts were interrupted when Lily asked if she could have the last bag of chips.

Mina snatched the remaining bag. "Those are mine! Get your grubby paws off them." Mina batted Lily's hands away from her chips. "Let's get down to business and finish up Fred's story--before we crash into a food coma."

The two sisters inhaled their snacks while arguing over Fredrick Cummens' memories late into the night.

"Also, I'm sure you are, but don't forget to pray for Fred and the other spirits you helped." Mina commented.

Lily looked at her sister, feeling tired and suddenly annoyed that this was being brought up by her now too. "Yeah, sure. I'll pray for the spirits that have already died. Heck of a lot of good that will do for them." Rolling her eyes, Lily wondered what on earth Mina was thinking. *Been talking to Mom and Dad too much again.*

"Ah, so you don't believe that then. Interesting."

"Believe what?" Lily asked, not so much out of curiosity, as much as reflex. "Well? Believe what?"

Mina smoothed out the pillow she had crunched while they chatted. "I'm just surprised you don't believe in the power of prayer. You're willing to believe in the power of some crystals that come from the ground, but not in the power of prayers that go directly to God. That's all." Looking up to see if Lily caught her point, Mina smiled. She remembered this very conversation she had with her Mom and soon after her best friend. Lily is just like her older sister.

"Look, I know you mean well but this whole 'be a good catholic girl' and all is getting really annoying." Lily emphasized her annoyance with her voice. "So, prayer is important, I get it. But these spirits are dead. Been dead for years. What's the point in praying for them now. Their judgment has been decided already."

Mina chuckled lightly. "Sorry, I just had a Deja Vu moment here. Except, I'm giving the snacks instead of getting them." Lily stared at Mina with a slight scowl. "Prayers work outside of time. It doesn't matter when you pray, because God takes that prayer and intention, and uses it when he see the best time for it. Your prayers for the spirits might have been already used years before you said them. But, because God knows all. He knows you're going to say prayers for them so He can act when it's best. Make sense?" Mina tapped on her phone. "I don't remember who's the fastest superhero, but take the fastest superhero and the Dr. guy who can manipulate time or is it teleportation? Whatever, take those too and…" Mina stopped, realizing her attempt to make some comparisons failed miserably. "Scratch that. Take all the superheroes and you still have nothing close to God and how He can do the impossible. We can't help Fred in the past. But our prayers right now can be what God used for his salvation now."

"I think you're over complicating it again. Basically God works outside of time and nothing compares to his power.

Right?" Lily took a deep breath. Clearly annoyed that this all made sense. "And because of that I should be praying for these spirits."

"Exactly! Thank you!" Mina relaxed further into her chair, feeling pride that her conversation made sense and her little sister listened. *See, I listen, sometimes.* She teased her guardian angel. Who she knows had made this same conversation happen for her as a teen many, many times.

§

The students rushed from hallway lockers to their 2nd period classrooms. Lily watched from her desk and wondered if she was ever that oblivious to real life? Fred was still silent, even after the late night snack fest with Mina. No matter how much Lily tried talking to him, Fred did not respond. Lily was ready to give up--exhausted and feeling lost. She had no idea how to reach Fred right now. She even resorted to praying for him, like Mina said too. *Please, dear God. Help Fred. Help me free him soon. Thank you.*

Her thoughts were interrupted by a loud burst of laughter from her classmates. The three girls, the popular clique, were sitting together, talking about someone or something. Knowing these girls, Lily figured they must be shaming someone. That clique was known for their cat fights and snarky, mean comments. In a word, Lily thought they were mannequins--pretty to look at, but completely hollow inside. Now that she was more in touch with her own feelings, their insecurities were obvious, and their reality check was going to be painful. *Is that why these girls are so toxic? Because they don't like themselves?* "Woah, I'm starting to turn into Mina. What a scary thought."

Another burst of laughter came from the group. "Hahaa! I wouldn't doubt it! It's like they never heard of blending or contouring." Lily looked away once the three girls noticed her staring.

Moving on, Lily noticed random, new things about her class--different groups within the same classroom--the popular ones to the introverts to the troublemakers. Paying attention to how they acted, when they reacted, and why, she couldn't help but wonder. *Are they like this because they're struggling? Would they be different if they had help? Le sighhhhhh...another problem for another day. Let's try to focus on Fred for now. But, maybe just in case, I'll add them to my prayer intentions.*

The bell rang signaling the end of classes for the day. Lily checked her unreadable notes from her History class but they made absolutely no sense. They looked like ancient hieroglyphics because she couldn't concentrate on anything except Fred. His story was nowhere near done--a frustrating situation that was picking away at Lily's mental stability.

Mina made sure to point it out to her the other day. "Hey, be careful with that eye rolling thing. You can do that with me because I know about Fred, but you can't get away with that around Mom or Dad... just don't even try. You don't want to know." The last comment from Mina made Lily wonder. Was Mina a bad teenager or something? Or do all teens go through the eye rolling stage?

Lily could feel the clock ticking for so many things--Fred

story, graduating high school, hiding her spirit connection from her family, Lily's neglected social media, Mina's mental health check-ins, resurrecting her love life with Patrick, appeasing Doris with a fake photoshoot. And of course last but not least not losing it all by having a major mental meltdown, even just so Mina can't say "I told you so".

Just to make things even more interesting and bizarre, Fred was not communicating. It had been almost a week since Lily had borrowed the trunk, and she was running out of time. As the list grew longer, Lily's ever expanding anxiety bubble was approaching its limit!

Max and Theo were grating on her last nerve all the way home. Finally able to escape the van, Lily stomped to her room immediately, like a fire-breathing dragon. Alone at last she screamed her fury into a thick, fluffy pillow. It's like her little brothers could sense when she was at her weakest moment. They kicked her seat, spoke as loudly as they could and made obnoxious noises the entire trip home! She clenched her teeth, chewing on the words she wanted to spew at her brothers, except Mom was listening. *Life was so unfair! It's always the case, Mom will yell at me for their misbehavior. They could get away with anything I bet.*

After a good long scream, Lily felt ready to tackle the trunk. "Ok, Fred, my man. Let's take a closer look at this trunk of yours. Feel free to pop in with any helpful information or maybe another memory or two." She stared at the trunk hoping a magical sign would appear. Lily was open to any possibility. When nothing happened she collapsed to the floor with a dramatic plea. "Please

God, Fred, anyone up there. Let me find something helpful!" She begged Fred while sending up a prayer to God for help.

Lily sat between the trunk's lid and bottom piece, ready to examine every inch. Using her fist she knocked on each side. *Sounded solid enough. This reminds me of that book, 'The Black Townhouse'. When they were looking for the missing gun and found it in the secret compartment inside the desk. I wonder if this trunk has a secret compartment? This is exactly how they found the compartment, too!*

The trunk was layered in a thin embossed metal covering the wood on the outside. The interior at one time was wallpapered, but now had practically dissolved--little scraps of thin paper barely clinging in some corners. Lily carefully ran her hands along the inside of the trunk, trying not to destroy even more of the delicate wallpaper. In the lid there was a deterianting, velvet lining covering the small storage containers built into the trunk.

The wood exposed, not covered by the metal layer, looked old and solid. No wonder these trunks were heavy. Obviously they were made to last during harsh sea voyages, jarring cross-country travel, plus endless years of use.

Sliding the two pieces next to one another, Lily tried to imagine how she would fit her belongings inside the heavy trunk. She noticed, on the inside of the bottom, a long thin wooden ledge jutted out. Her internet search showed images of old trunks with little boxes and rectangle-like storage containers. These rails were often used to support these added boxes. The boxes were removable and gave the traveler more organizing options.

Pulling out her sketchbook, Lily copied each detail of the trunk.

Metal layer covering the entire wood trunk.

Metal hinges on all the corners and wood strips running across the lid and bottom piece.

The detailing on the metal was beautiful.

Every piece of metal had something elegant embossed on it.

She noticed the flowers right away. Simple design really. Flowers with swirls surrounding each bloom in a repeating pattern. Lily couldn't decide if the pattern would be considered retro or vintage design. Since the trunk was vintage, the elegant floral design probably was also vintage.

After her sketches were finished, Lily moved on, looking for any signature indicating the company that made the trunk. Or, if she was lucky, maybe she would find Fred's name embossed inside, claiming it as his property. Lifting the bottom trunk, she flipped it over, but no signature or embossed name was evident. Flipping it back over, she inspected the inside of the bottom piece--keeping her touch light and avoiding rubbing too hard to preserve the remaining wallpaper. Unfortunately, a small corner of the delicate paper flaked off anyway, landing in one corner where there was already a small collection of fragments. But still, no trace of a signature or embossed name.

When Lily leaned over, a pain in her stomach and loud growl reminded her that she needed to eat. *Time to take a break. Hopefully, a yummy dinner is ready.*

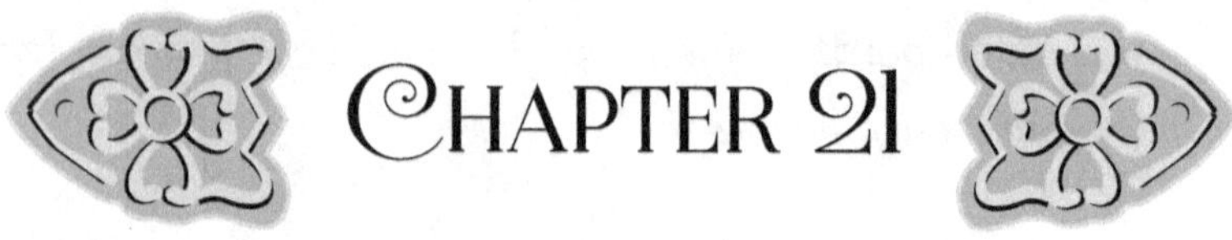

CHAPTER 21

After dinner, Lily asked to borrow her Mom's laptop. Mrs. Shels didn't hesitate, giving Lily permission. "Sure Sweetie, just put it back in my room when you're done please."

Setting up her research center in the kitchen, Lily checked for any information about these specific trunks. She entered questions in the browser window.

How do you tell how old a vintage trunk is?

After scrolling for fifteen minutes, Lily found the lids' shape was a Saratoga style. Typically built during the 1800's. It's obvious Dome top was categorized as either a Humpback or Camel trunk.

What type of vintage trunks are there?

Most of her searches confirmed that the trunk was either Humpback or Camel.

How do you find out where a vintage trunk was made?

This search led her down a path with lengthy articles, but no real answers.

Lily found similar looking trunks, but nothing exactly like Fred's. She read plenty of articles about companies that used to produce that style of trunks--steamer trunks, wooden v.s. metal inlaid trunks, round-top trunks, and flat-top trunks. Lily even tried asking:

Do any vintage trunks have secret compartments?

But even that search didn't give her anything useful. She had hoped that touching the trunk would cause Fred to reappear, stirring up some emotional reaction. Regrettably, just like her searches on the internet, Lily's results were dismal with Fred as well.

After returning the laptop to its proper place, Lily scrutinized the trunk again. Knocking twice on the bottom, then all over both pieces, the only odd sound was in the lid. The rap didn't sound as shallow. She tapped across the rounded top, turning the lid over to feel along the torn velvet lining. The domed lid had a built-in flat partition for extra storage, but that also left about five inches of empty space in the curve of the lid. Feeling around and gently tapping, searching for any gap that could hide a secret compartment. Pulling away a corner of the loosened velvet lining, she wedged one finger underneath until she felt only wood. Nothing was budging, it was another dead end. Lily resisted the urge to rip the velvet lining away, since she couldn't damage it because she was only borrowing it, after all. *I could say that Theo or Max ripped it. Let them pay for the damage. Call it payback for annoying me. They totally deserve it.*

Even after hours, fiddling with the trunk, Fred was still missing in action. No matter what Lily tried, he made no effort to reconnect. Her attempts to joke, cajole, and annoy him had zero effect. Another day without memories or progress and Lily was starting to feel a little desperate. *Come on, Fred! I'm starting to feel like I'm going nuts, again. I don't have enough to finish your story. Plus I don't know what will happen to either of us if we run out of time.*

Lily was lying as still as a statue on her bed, her mind straying like driftwood along a soft babbling creek. *Whatever is going on in your little bubble world, Fred, please reconnect soon. I can't do this alone!*

§

Lily felt like this week of school would never end. Thursday, 4:30 pm was almost here--one more day to go. Fred's silence was like a rickety wall, building aggravation and frustration inside Lily. The cacophony of students grated Lily's nerves, causing her irritation to grow by the minute.

Deep in concentration, Lily put a lid on her emotions, trying to not lose her cool in front of her entire class. *Keep it together, Lily. It's only because you're extra tired. Blame Fred for that one, not your classmates. Breath.* Unfortunately, Lily didn't notice her best friend, Doris, sneaking up behind her.

"So…" Doris was cut off, stepping back when Lily jolted upright from her desk. The sudden move caused her desk to teeter on two legs, dangerously close to falling forward. Her thick Algebra book slammed to the floor, along with her bag of pens and pencils. The noise covering her low muttered cursing. Everyone was staring. Lily stood frozen in shock with a frazzled look on her face. Doris, just as surprised, stared back.

Doris carefully walked around Lily's desk, helping her pick up the mess. "Are you alright? Sorry, I didn't mean to startle you like that. I'm really sorry."

Lily silently collected her pencils and pens, while mentally calming her shattered nerves. That kind of shock was enough to turn Lily's black hair completely white. If only Doris could make some kind of noise rather than scaring the life out of her.

After a quick clean up, Doris and Lily sat across from each other. Lily's arms folded stiffly across her chest, her fingernail tapping while she waited for Doris to pounce. Doris tipped her head, studying her clearly distrubed friend, trying to figure out where to start the conversation.

"Sooo...how close are you to finishing Mr. Fred's story?" Doris asked Lily in her gentlest voice.

Lily released the breath that she had been holding, with a quick sigh. "I'm stuck at the moment. But I'll be done soon." Lily realized her stiff answer was the only greeting she gave Doris. She looked hurt. "I'm sorry for snapping, I didn't get any sleep this week and...I've been feeling really crummy." Lily smiled, trying to guess her best friend's response.

Doris pasted a smile on, but Lily saw right through it. She had really hurt Doris's feelings. "Hey." Lily reached for Doris' hand. "...let's change topics so you can update me on your love life. We haven't talked about Derek for a few days." She leaned across the table to encourage Doris even more, with her undivided attention.

"Really? We just talked about Derek a few days ago. But...if you insist!" Her genuine smile beamed brighter as they chatted.

While Doris talked about cheering during her brother's soccer practice, Lily couldn't help but wonder about their friendship. *Doris is my fun, dorky friend. I want to tell her about the spirits, but I can't. For now, She will just have to read my stories.*

Lily felt alone again--conflicted about so many things it was tearing her apart. *Could she explain everything about the spirits to Doris? With Mina's help, she would be more likely to believe it. But... what if she doesn't believe me? Are we still best friends? What if she freaks out and tells everyone?* **They'd all think I was insane!** *What if she thinks I'm possessed or dealing with the devil type thing?? Then, the white-jackets would show up for sure after I get exorcized.* Lily could see it coming. With every scenario, she ended up at some toonville in a straight jacket, shunned from her Catholic society. *But Doris is my best friend--she wouldn't do that. I know she wouldn't. However, that's not a chance I can take, right now. I couldn't take my best friend thinking I'm insane and never talking to me again.*

Having a secret so big that Lily couldn't trust anyone with it was lonely and scary. This must be how Sabrina, from that teenage witch show, felt. Although having a talking cat would make a great partner in crime. Lily decided Mina was as close to a sarcastic, scheming cat that she would ever get. They are both huge pains, although Mina doesn't suffer fools easily and works hard for everything. Plus, she's just a really nice person when you get to know her. And she keeps me stocked with snacks! *Best sidekick ever!*

After school Lily was surprised to see a message from Mina.

Mina to Lily: *Trunk pieces waiting at the antique store. Mom knows and will take you. C U L8R, @work.*

Followed by a smiley-wink face. Lily tucked her phone into her pocket, then rushed to find the family van.

Mrs. Shels stood beside the open doors, ushering the boys inside. "Hurry up Lily! Mina said someone left something for you at that antique store. Once the monkey brothers get in the van, we'll head there first." Mrs. Shels walked over to the driver's side and yelled "You have 30 seconds before you're left behind. I'm not kidding!"

Lily was confused by a couple things. *What pieces were missing from the trunk? What took them so long? Why give them to her now? What's the point?* She was distracted by those questions while her brothers piled in the car as slowly as humanly possible. *I've seen slugs move faster than that.* Once inside the car, the Shels family headed to the antique store.

Max noticed they were not taking the usual route home and asked, "Where are we going?".

"Don't you listen to anything I say?" Mrs. Shels gave an exasperated sigh. "We are stopping at the antique store for Lily. She will go inside alone. You will leave your seatbelts on."

Soon enough they pulled into the parking lot and Lily hopped out to run into the shop. She could still hear her mom yelling at the boys to put their seat belts on. Both of them were ignoring Mrs. Shels, trying to make a run for the store before she could catch them. But Mrs. Shels clicked the child-lock button in anticipation, Max and Theo were nothing, if not predictable.

ANTIQUE STORE
OPEN

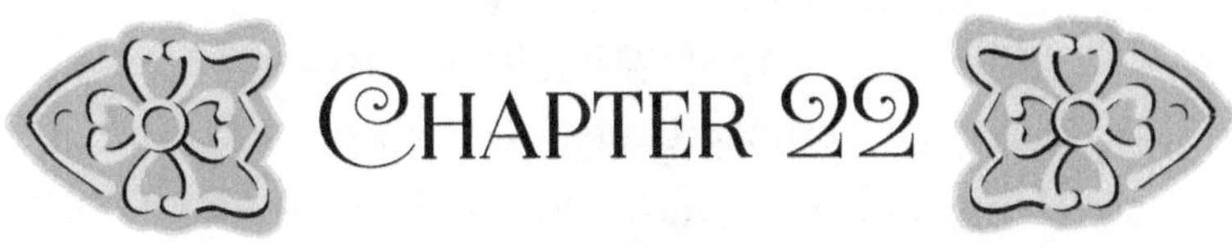

CHAPTER 22

Lily didn't bother looking around, walking right to the front desk. "Hello, Zoe. Mina said you..."

Zoe cut her off with a raised hand. "Yeah, give me a minute." She left the desk, returning after a few minutes, holding two odd shaped boxes. "The Brookes came by and asked me to give you these. Mrs. Brookes said they belong in the trunk?" Zoe piled the boxes onto Lily's outstretched arms, "Oh,...there's a letter too." She added an envelope to the top of the heap, before waving her to the door. "Here you go." Zoe opened the door just enough for Lily to squeeze by, wobbling her way to the van.

Her brothers pouted while she gently placed the wooden boxes on the van floor, grabbing the envelope on top before climbing in and fastening her seatbelt. "We are good to go, Mom."

"What are these?" Theo asked, reaching from the back seat to pull one of the boxes onto his lap.

Before Lily could snatch it back, Theo opened the top and peered inside. His disappointed facial expression was comical to watch. Obviously he was expecting to find treasure.

"They gave you empty boxes? *Old* empty boxes! You got scammed. How much do they charge for antique air?" Theo started to toss the box into the back of the van with all the other useless stuff that no one wants to carry into the house.

"Don't do that Theo! Give me that. It's not mine, I borrowed it--be careful!" Lily lunged for the box and almost had it safely in her hands, but Theo jerked it just out of reach. "Mom!" She whined, imploring Mrs. Shels to intervene on her behalf.

"Boys!" Her "mom voice" was deadly, and her brothers knew better than to push their luck. They might be safe now, inside the van, while driving home, but once they arrived home, they were on Mom's turf. Chores were a big thing in their house--getting into trouble meant extra chores. Really pushing Mom's buttons led to a world of hurt.

Once home Lily rushed the boxes and the letter to her room. Her plan was to read the letter then figure out how the boxes fit into the trunk. That was the plan.

When she entered the bedroom, Lily could immediately see where the boxes belonged. The letter dropped to the floor, unnoticed and forgotten, as she hurried to the trunk. "They must fit here." Lily carefully aligned the two wooden drawers with the trunk, sliding them between the side ledges. Standing back, Lily studied the two new pieces. " Hmmm, adding those makes

It looks like there is even less room for everything." Shrugging, Lily could not see how anyone could fit their entire wardrobe into one trunk.

Something else was missing. There was still a gap big enough for one more drawer. Or maybe...something else. Lily felt like she was grasping at straws, but she had to figure this out for Fred's sake. She needed to borrow her Mom's computer again. But until she finished her homework she didn't dare ask. By then, Max and Theo would be playing games on it, and once in their hands, Lily had no chance of stealing it away. *Maybe Mina will let her use her when she gets home.*

Lily pondered her options. One, She could sneak in and grab her Mom's computer now. Use it and return it before dinner without anyone finding out. Or two, she could beg her Mom right now and reserve its use tonight, no matter what. After all, her research was more important than playing video games. Lily was happy to stress the difference to her Mom.

In Lily's mind she had already worked out the conversation with her Mom, including Mrs. Shels telling her 'What a great daughter she was'. She marched herself downstairs to the kitchen, rehearsing her perfect speech the entire way.

"Hey...Mom. I really need to use the computer tonight. So, after I'm done with my homework, can I use it--even if the boys want it?" As soon as the words came out of her mouth, Theo and Max strutted into the kitchen.

"No way!" Their shout rang through the kitchen overpowering the music Mom had been listening to. "If we are done first, we get the computer first! That's the house rule!" All three of them turned to Mrs. Shels, waiting for her judgment.

"No way. Hold on, that's incredibly unfair." Lily turned to her Mom, pleading. "Mom, you know the boys have way less homework than I do. There's no way I can get done before them." The argument would have escalated further if not for three loud snaps from their Mom's fingers.

"Whoever finishes their homework first can use the computer first,..." Both boys began cheering, with grins of triumph. "...however." Mrs. Shels continued. "...if someone needs it for more than video games, then that has priority." Mrs. Shels held up a finger to stop any further argument. "Lily, when you need the computer, the boys will give it to you...without delay. *Won't you boys?*" Mrs. Shels' big smile meant the boys only had one option, 'Yes Mom.'

The boys knew they had lost the battle, but not the war. Revenge promised once Mom's back was turned.

"You are good boys. Now go set the table please." Mrs. Shels shooed them away with one hand. Grumbling, both Theo and Max left the room with the plates and silverware for the dinner table.

"Thanks Mom!" Lily saved her joy and jump of triumph until she reached her room. Leaving the kitchen with a small grin, she couldn't help egg-on her scowling brothers when she passed the dining room. *HEHHEHEHEEHE Take that!,* danced through her mind.

An hour later, dinner ended with both brothers finishing in record time. Lily couldn't help but notice how fast they moved when their precious computer time was on the clock. But who cared anyway, she decided. They did their chores faster than usual, so that's at least a silver-lining for everyone.

Chores done, Lily moved on to her own homework. Which thankfully, was even shorter than the day before. The sudden decrease in assignments had both Lily and Doris worried. It seemed every time they had days with less homework, the teachers bombarded them with tests, quizzes, plus mountains of homework, the next day. The teachers did it on purpose--they liked pumping the students' hopes up with less homework, before dropping a tornado on top of them. Doris says it reminded her of the wicked witch when the house dropped. Lily imagined the teachers and principal in a dark room with a single bulb, plotting. "Let's see how many tests and quizzes we can possibly squeeze into one day? If you don't have a handy test, give them extra homework--make it double!" The teachers cackled. "Yes! Yes! Make them suffer." The scenario played inside Lily's head, picturing the teachers evil plans. *There's something suspicious about three days with little to no homework. A nuclear bomb must be coming. I know it.*

Speaking of suspicious behavior, Lily's mind wandered to

her brothers. *I wonder how much homework they skipped to get done so fast?* Usually it takes them hours to finish, so the timing was very suspicious. Lily had half a mind to check their book bags... but on second thought...she decided to just let it go. *Some things are best left alone. If they didn't finish their homework, Mom will find out eventually.*

"Done!" Lily slammed her Math book shut with a loud *thump*. She had sped through her assignments as fast as she could. To her happy surprise, Fred finally showed up during Math, a particularly tough problem she couldn't solve and he helped her with it. *Evidently, Fred was good at Math. Maybe he should be my new tutor, but then how would I explain that to Mom or my teacher? Welcome back Fred! Now let's get your story solved, ok!*

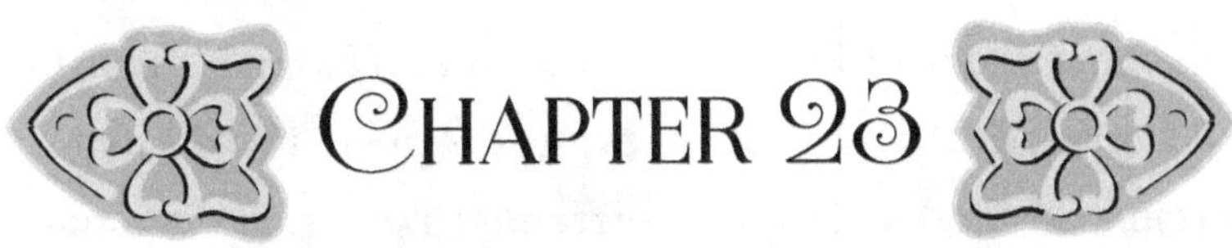

CHAPTER 23

As soon as Lily zipped her book bag, a new memory flashed inside her head. The memory had no visuals, like normal, so she could only hear what was going on. Something had changed in Fred. Lily knew he was present, she could feel him there, but he wasn't shouting like before.. In fact, he wasn't speaking at all. Lily heard two new voices--a man, and a younger woman--not Dorothy, someone else.

"Dad. We can't take care of you, right now. Mom...umm. Mom isn't doing well."

Lily felt Fred's fear and anxiety explode into a hot ball of anger. He didn't speak, but he was thinking--his thoughts moving at a million miles per hour.

The man's voice sounded closer. Lily felt his hand gripping Fred's shoulder. "We didn't want to tell you, because you didn't need to be stressed out more. The family decided to move you to a care home. A really nice one, where a special staff can take care of you. Help you manage your...blindness." The room flooded with a heavy tension. Lily felt like she could cut through it. She was shocked Fred remained quiet. His internal struggle died a quick death--any will to argue dropped away. Lily hadn't experienced Fred's complete surrender before, and wondered. *Was this the moment he finally accepted defeat? That his fate, to die alone, now merged into depression, had killed any hope he had left. Is he going to die soon?*

"Dad? Dad, what do you think?" The woman's voice was insistent. Lily realized this had to be Fred's son and daughter.

Fred didn't respond.

The next comment was an angrily muttered, "Fine, be that way." then a set of footsteps moving away.

Fred's memory ended.

Lily could have sworn, right before Fred ended the memory, she could hear him sobbing.

Lily's heart ached, feeling the pain and frustration his children dealt with, because of both parents' situations. Besides Fred's blindness, now their Mother was sick as well. They didn't say what ailed her, but it sounded just as hopeless. *No wonder so much anger and resentment was passed down through the generations. They were all so devastated with their own emotional trauma, they couldn't see anyone else's struggle.*

Fred, don't give up on everyone yet. Lily begged. *You can't do this to yourself! You don't <u>want</u> to go to the stupid nursing home, so say something! Now!* Frustrating as Fred was, Lily knew her words could do nothing to change things. The past was the past. Only God can move outside of time--so Lily prayed again. Offering up what she could for Fred's soul made her wonder. *Were her prayers in that moment, the reason Lily was drawn to Fred's trapped spirit, in the first place? Maybe she was his last hope.* Perhaps her simple plea had led her to Fred. To free and remind him that hope is eternal and never lost. Sometimes the unknown prayer saves a future we can't imagine.

Opening her spirit story notebook, Lily added more notes:

Fred has given up. He is not talking or fighting.

Dorothy is sick. We don't know with what yet, but it sounds extremely serious.

His son and daughter are sending Fred to live in a nursing home.

The entire Cummens family is miserable, angry, and falling apart.

Lily entered the parlor--a new word she learned from Fred--where her brothers were playing games on Mom's computer. "Ok guys, it's time." She held out her hand, hoping they would give her the computer without a big fuss.

Max and Theo looked up from the computer screen, obviously annoyed. Pretending she didn't exist meant--no way. Max even shook his head, determined to keep playing for as long as possible.

Lily folded her arms together. "You know what mom said--so fork it over or else." Lily hooked a thumb over her shoulder to mom's sitting room as a reminder.

Max stuck his tongue out, taking his good-old-time to turn

the game off, before offering the laptop. "You better not use it all night! We had it first, fair and square. So you've got 2 hours--don't waste our game time!"

Lily couldn't stop her eyes from rolling. "I don't make promises I can't keep." She closed the laptop and strolled to her room taking as much time as possible. As their older sister, it was Lily's duty to teach them that whoever held the keys, owned the castle. In other words "Good-luck getting the laptop away from her anytime soon."

After setting up her work station on the bed, Lily realized she still had not read the letter that came with the trunk containers, from Mrs. Brookes.

"Where's that letter?" Lily muttered to the empty room. Lifting the corner of the trunk base, then the boxes, she found the envelope under her bed. "There you are! Let's see what Mrs. Brookes has to say?" She slid her finger under the flap, tearing it from one end to the other in one quick rip.

Unfolding the pristine, single sheet of paper inside, Lily read the letter.

"Dear young lady,

Forgive me, I do not remember your name. I wanted to give you these two wooden hat boxes that go inside the trunk. I'm not sure If I'm too late, but I hope you can use the new pieces in your photoshoot. There used to be more containers and small compartments that fit inside the trunk but through the years they were either lost or broken.

I also wanted to give you some history about the trunk in question. The trunk belonged to my late grandmother, Dorothy Cummens, who I am named after. It was passed down to my Mother when she died. It is very old, so I will understand if some pieces break while you are using it.

My parents took care of my grandmother while she battled with dementia, so after she passed away, the trunk was put into an attic, where it stayed until I inherited it--after my Mother's death. My daughter and son-in-law decided to donate it, against my will. I appreciated your unplanned revelation, when you asked to borrow it. If it weren't for you, I still wouldn't know the trunk had been missing. It's nice to know someone still cares about history and antiques.

If you want, after the photoshoot, you can keep the trunk, or donate it. The antique store can take care of it whatever you decide.

Thank you, Dear.

Sincerely, Dorothy Marie Brookes

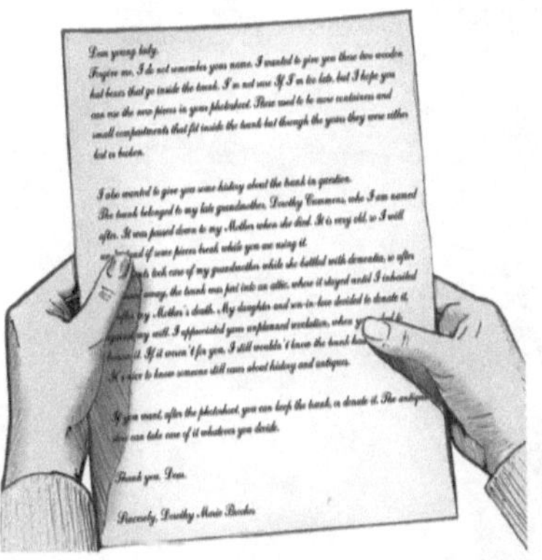

"Ahhhhh, what a cute letter!" Lily squealed as she finished reading it. Mrs. Brookes sounded just like a sweet old lady. Just as Lily imagined she would be-sharing the history behind the trunk, telling Lily about the Cummens and Brookes family. *Wait a second, speaking of family, why wasn't there any mention of Fred?*

Lily quickly scanned the contents of the letter. Not one mention of Fred, Frederick, or even a grandfather. *Does Fred's family still resent him?* The Brookes barely acknowledged his existence, even after all these years. The trunk *belonged* to Mrs. Cummens, not Fred. *Is Fred attached to the trunk because his marriage ended on a bad note with Dorothy, or was his family's resentment the thing that needed to be fixed?*

CHAPTER 24

While Lily refolded the letter, another memory pulled her attention away from the questions. *Fred, I've already seen this one.* This memory was Fred being yelled at by his son, for treating Dorothy so terribly.

The young man's voice boomed with a fierce anger. He spoke above where Fred sat. "Mom was crushed by your yelling and cruel words. I never thought you of all people would treat a woman, one who you love, like this. You pounded into my head that you treat the women like queens, especially the ones you love. With respect! I've never been so ashamed of anyone, let alone my own Dad. I can't look at you anymore. I don't know who you are, certainly not *my father*!" His loud footsteps, as he paced and stomped from one side to the other, reminded Fred how far he had fallen from the man David knew.

Fred just sat there, silent, while David's words lashed at his soul. Even though Lily experienced this memory before, she was still shocked by Fred's punishing silence--from yelling and screaming to this detached acceptance. Lily felt her stomach drop, like riding on a roller coaster. She had expected the worst fight between Father and Son, instead nothing happened. Now her tension needed an outlet. In some ways, Lily felt Fred giving up was worse than when he fought back. Fred decided he was done fighting, it was better to accept his fate instead of holding out for hope. He gave into despair, burrowing deeper into a tunnel of black anguish.

Lily's patience reached its breaking point as she paced back and forth. "Fred, this memory doesn't help me. I need something more, something that tells me why you're connected to this stupid, old trunk. I can't finish your story until I can fix whatever is keeping you attached." She waited, trying to relax, sitting next to the trunk. *Thud, thud,* Lily lightly bumped her fist on the trunk. "Something is missing, something big. Fred's story doesn't make sense. Why he is attached to the trunk has to be the key!" Gritting her teeth, Lily tried to figure out what the answer could be.

"AHA!" A thought occurred to Lily--another way to get her questions answered. *The letter.* Lily realized she dropped it when she was pacing. Picking up Mrs. Cummens' letter, she quickly formulated a plan. *Let's ask his granddaughter, she might be able to tell me something about his wife and this trunk.*

Pulling out paper and pen, Lily wrote her very first real letter.

Dear Mrs. Brookes,

Thank you so much for sending those extra boxes belonging to the trunk. It really is a valuable piece of your family history. I think it's perfect for my photoshoot. If you want, I can send you some of the pictures after we are done.

Speaking of the trunk, can you tell me anything else about it and/or the family members that owned it?

Lily paused in her letter writing, realizing that this entire time she was using the photoshoot as an excuse to borrow the trunk. But, she had no idea when, where or what this photoshoot would involve. In fact she never planned on having one.

"Oh man," Lily pressed her palm against her forehead, feeling the tense pressure build. "I've been so busy with Fred's story that I really haven't planned anything."

Lily grabbed another sheet to plan a simple photoshoot. *Maybe Mina will help me again. I can have the trunk as the centerpiece , then drape myself over it or pose next to it. Outfits...I need outfits. Make-up, lights, maybe an assistant. Since the trunk was old aka vintage, her entire outfit should be vintage too. The choices were endless. Lily let her mind go absolutely wild with possibilities. It's been awhile since I've dressed up to match a specific theme.*

Opening her limited closet, she pulled out anything that would perfect her vintage look. "I could do a retro dress, with a cute hat, Oh these shoes will fit perfectly too!" Tossing all of her scarves and belts on top of the pile of clothes, she dug to the bottom of her closet. Lily knew the perfect outfit was in here somewhere. She even pulled out a pair of old white lace gloves she wore once for a Halloween party. Turning around with the last item in her closet, Lily was shocked by the volcano of clothes sliding off the side of her bed. Not one inch of carpet could be seen under all the shoes, belts, hangers and miscellaneous clothes that had fallen to the floor.

"Oh no...I could really use that assistant right now. Mom is going to kill me."

"What's going on here?" Max asked carefully from the doorway. "Woah Theo, come look at this! Lily's closet threw up all over her room."

"Get out of my room Max!! It still looks better than your room ever will!" Lily chucked the rice-filled stuffed puppy at Max.

Choosing the outfit is the best part of a photoshoot. The outfit Lily picked out was one of her favorites and most expensive. She had saved for months, doing extra chores and taking on babysitting just to buy this particular outfit. Her creative juices flowed when she imagined how well the outfit and the trunk would look together. She had no idea at the time she bought the dress that it was considered vintage. She just liked the color.

Lily continued the conversation with herself, her planning skills fired up and ready to take on any challenge. "Next is location, hmmm the park. There's a really nice garden with a ton of flowering bushes. The green background would contrast with the boring brown and grey trunk."

Perfect. Her photoshoot--completely planned in 15 whole minutes. "I have to remember to ask Mina for help though. LOL. She's kinda important to the plan" Lily grabbed a sticky note, writing a quick reminder to ask Mina, later.

Lily noticed the crumpled pages, it was her letter to Mrs. Brookes. Pulling the papers hidden under the layer of scarves, she flattened the bent corners.Ironing the full page with her hand. Grabbing the red pen off her desk, Lily crossed out the last line, adding:

I hope I'm not being too inquisitive, but I have some questions about your grandmother and grandfather. If you could be available to talk, I would be more than happy to…

Lily stopped writing. "I can't ask her like that--right out, about her grandparents. She doesn't know that I know about Fred. If I ask her about his blindness or about her grandmother's dementia, she'll think I'm trying to blackmail her, and wonder how I got that information. ButI can't tell her--so that's out." *Think Lily, think!* Scribbling questions on another piece of paper, she tried forming the perfect ones to ask Mrs. Brookes.

What can I say to get Mrs. Brookes to trust me and tell me about her grandparents?

If I don't find out soon, I won't be able to disconnect Fred from the trunk. Who knows how much longer I have before he completely loses *it. Plus, If I can't disconnect him from the trunk, does that mean <u>we</u> are connected forever?? Will something else worse happen?* Lily didn't want to think about that possibility.

If I do ask her, will she freak out? Either way, I'm screwed. Balancing the needs for both of them, really sucks. I'm not even part of the equation, I'm just the greasy filling in this weird family saga!

Turning back to her unfinished letter, Lily considered the wording of the question. *No, that doesn't make sense.* Scribbling through one attempt after another. *Nope, that doesn't work either.* Her paper descended into a scribbled mess before she started over on a fresh piece of paper. The letter consumed Lily, making her forget about the laptop that the boys were waiting on..

After four more tries, Lily finally found the best way to phrase her request.

Dear Mrs. Brookes,

Thank you so much for giving me the missing boxes to the trunk. I will use all of them in my photoshoot. If you want, I can send you a few shots after the finished project.

Your offer to keep the trunk is very kind, but I don't think I will be able to honor it. There is not enough space in my bedroom at the moment. Since I'm not keeping it, do you want the trunk returned? Since it belonged to your grandparents, maybe one of your children or grandkids would want the trunk as a keepsake?

If you want it back, my sister and I will bring it as soon as possible. I did wonder if you would be willing to share more about the trunk's owners? I would love to hear more about it. It is a very cool piece of history. I wonder if my family has any old pieces like yours.

Thank you again!
Sincerely
Lily Shels
Finally! I'm done.

CHAPTER 25

Lily grabbed the letter, selecting a white envelope to shove it into. Clumsy, she stuck a cute kitty sticker on the flap, then ran downstairs to catch her Mom. Mrs. Shel's was standing by the front door and Lily thanked her lucky stars she had reached her Mom before she left.

"Mom! Wait a second, can I come with you tonight?" Lily folded her hands in prayer, hoping her pleading and smile would sway her Mom.

Mrs. Shels stopped to give her daughter a side-eyed glance, before grabbing the van keys. "You want to come with me?...to my painting class?" Finally noticing the white envelope Lily was clutching she raised one eyebrow.

"Well kind of. I want to put my letter to Mrs. Brookes in her mailbox tonight." Lily held up the sealed envelope. "Since your painting class is in her town, I was hoping we could swing by her house." Lily beamed her mom with her best, cutest smile. *Please work.* Lily prayed for Divine intervention.

Mrs. Shels took one look at Lily's puppy-dog eyes, before giving in. "Where do they live? Better yet, give me the letter and I will drop off." Mrs. Shels waited for Lily to hand over the letter.

Lily quickly gave her Mom the street and house number to the Brookes home. "AW thank-you Mom!!!"

Once the letter was safely in Mrs. Shels grasp, the situation became very clear to Lily. *Mom doesn't want anyone going to her painting classes.* Which is the only reason she would volunteer to run an errand for Lily.

Lily knew her Mom wasn't the biggest fan of arts and crafts, nor was she very good at them. When her Mom brought the paintings home, Dad immediately bribed us to "accidentally" destroy them. He said, "There wasn't enough bleach in the world to erase everyone's nightmares". *Sarcasm runs deep in the Shel family.* But, any reason to get out of the house was good for her Mom, right now. Lily could sympathize. *Yep, If I had to deal with the terror twins everyday I would lose my mind! I would want one night for myself to recover too.*

On the way to her room, Lily heard Max and Theo yelling at each other in the parlor. *Lee Sighhhh...brothers.* She shook her head as she walked up the stairs.

§

Mrs. Shels held the letter for a moment after Lily walked upstairs.

Should she check what's inside? Mrs. Shels couldn't decide which was worse, Lily writing to strangers, or strangers contacting her daughter? As the mom, sometimes Mrs. Shels got a gut feeling that warned her something--the situation, the people--something wasn't right. Not necessarily wrong, just off.

Mrs. Shels took a deep breath, putting the letter in her purse. *I'll ask Lily about it later. Shoot! Gotta run.* She dropped the purse strap on her shoulder, snatched the keys, then checked on her boys one last time before heading out. "I'll be back in two hours. Behave yourselves, and call me if you need anything. Lily is in charge, *so behave!*" Usually Mr. Shels or one of the older siblings would watch the younger ones, but not today. Mrs. Shels knew Lily at 15 could be trusted to watch the boys. But still you never know when crazy things will happen. She just felt better with adults in charge of them. But it was time to trust Lily, she was old enough, thankfully mature and responsible for her age. Saying a quick prayer for their safety, Mrs. Shels drove away.

Lily ran back downstairs to lock the door behind her mom, then double checked on the boys before heading into her room to do her research. The boys stayed in the parlor watching a movie. *Perfect. They'll be occupied and hopefully won't cause any trouble for at least 3 hours.*

Lily stared into the computer screen. "What was I supposed to be looking for?" She skimmed through her notes about Fred, hoping to find something to jog her memory. "Ah yeah, the secret compartments in the trunk. There we go." Lily searched:

Barrel trunks and their inside containers, images.

Immediately several pictures flashed across the screen. Lily tried to sort through them to find what was missing from Fred's trunk.

Didn't Mrs. Cummens mention two wood containers for hats? Double checking the letter, Lily was surprised to see that Mrs. Brookes description wasn't accurate. They weren't specifically for hats from Lily's research, they were actually for anything that fit.

"Wow, there are so many styles with different lid shapes. Each trunk had a very special container layout." Lily noticed most of the barrel trunks had a permanent container in the lid on one side and the option to add two removable containers to the base.

Again, Lily wondered how women packed all of their belongings into one or two of these trunks. Her gaze zipped back and forth between her closet, the trunk and the tall dresser. Even if she used all of her Mom's vacuum bags, and only packed up dresses, it still wouldn't fit inside the trunk or be enough clothes for a week. *How did women in the 1900's pack all of their clothes inside these teeny tiny trunks? That's not only a good question, it would defy physics.*

"Surely they had more than one or two outfits?? Having just two outfits to wear everyday for years would be awful and boring! Not to mention gross. Did they even have washers and dryers? How did they clean their clothes everyday? Ewwww!" Lily stuck her nose inside the trunk. Smells like dirty socks and old moldy basements. Lily couldn't imagine what that would be like. *Only two outfits, those poor women.*

After Lily got over the shock, she spent the evening in deep thought. She reviewed all the notes and memories about Fred with a fine toothed comb. *Details. She needed more Details. Details would crack this case! Fred, when are you going to stop pouting and talk to me? Remember you helped solve that math problem. Just look at this mystery like a math problem…wait, I am horrible at math. We're doomed.*

If Lily was being honest with herself, Fred's case had become boring. Not less stressful, just boring. No matter which side she came from the story, nothing connected Fred to that trunk. *This big wooded monstrosity is the biggest pain in the butt.* "Maybe I'm asking the wrong person?" *Bingo!* Lily's mind raced as she added Fred's wife, Dorothy, to the equation. "Dorothy Cummens. What are you trying to tell me? Or are you hiding something from me?"

§

"I'm home!" Mrs. Shels walked into the parlor, checking on Max and Theo. "Hey boys."

No response. The boys' bodies in a hypnotic state, stared at the bright tv screen.

"Oh ok, if that's how it's going to be. I'll just enjoy this ice cream by myself...in the kitchen." She walked out of the parlor toward the kitchen. The boys suddenly snapped out of their trance, tripping over each other to get to the ice cream.

A few seconds later, Theo and Max shoved their way into the kitchen. "Mom, you got ice cream? What kind of ice cream did you get?"

"Shh Lily might hear you and want some. That's less for us!" Max mock-whispered.

Mrs. Shels stopped in the middle of pulling out the mint ice cream, to glare at her two incorrigible sons, tossing the noisy plastic store bag onto the counter. "We are not eating this entire carton. Just for that I should give you less--now go get Lily."

"YAAAAYYYYYY!! Mint Ice-Cream!" Their cheers were so exuberant that the boys' voices carried upstairs to Lily's room. Within a few minutes she was downstairs grabbing a bowl from the cupboard.

"See I told you she would hear you. She's got ears like an eagle." Max shoved Theo.

Theo shoved back. "Stupid, eagles don't have ears."

"Don't call your brother stupid." Mrs. Shels said as she scooped the ice cream.

"Even if it's true?" Lily muttered under her breath, grabbing a spoon to dig in. Mrs. Shels death stare activated. Lily expected to combust in 3.5 seconds. "Thank you MOM!! Best Mom ever!" Sweet-talking her Mom, Lily shoved the frosty treat in her mouth, stopping her mouth from getting her into more trouble. This break was just what Lily needed.

Mrs. Shels set the ice cream filled bowls on the counter then directed everyone into the dining room. She followed them and sat at the head of the table. "Now that you all have some ice-cream, can I get 30 minutes of your time to play Uno®?"

How could anyone refuse to play a game with their mom, when she brought home ice cream at 9pm on a weeknight? In the Shels household this was a rare treat. Late night ice cream and a game with her family. Lily looked around the table as the cards were shuffled and the ice cream slowly disappeared.

Lily picked up her cards. *Great, nothing good.* She let her mind wander, waiting for her turn. *Did Fred ever play cards with his family?* Lily sighed.

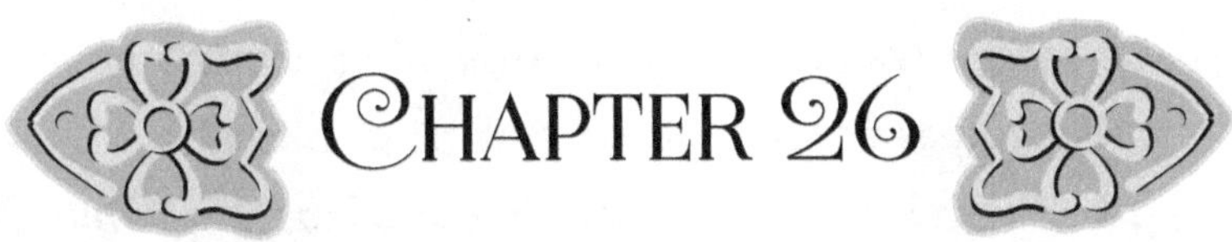

Chapter 26

"Lily, did you say something? I'm kicking your butt." Mrs. Shels slapped down the worst card. "DRAW FOUR, COLOR CHANGE!" Her Mom was already down to her last two cards. "Let's change the color too........RED!" She was waiting for a groan or some sort of reaction from Lily. But she was disappointed by Lily's silence. "Lily?"

Lily looked around the table with a confused expression, adding a blue skip card to the pile.

"You can't do that! You have to pick up four and the color is red, not blue!" Max pointed out her mistake.

Confused, Lily looked at the top card on the discard pile. "What? When did the color change?"

"It happened while you were daydreaming." Theo laughed. The boys got a kick out of their sisters' bewildered look.

"Looks like you're not going to win this time after all!" The sound of giggling wrapped around the dinner table. Lily laughed along with her family. *That's what you get for spacing out during Uno®.* That was the beginning of her quick slide into loserville.

"Maybe she was too busy daydreaming about a booooy!" Max whispered as he shot Lily an evil grin. "It is a boy! Look at her blush!" Both boys started pointing and laughing while Lily distracted herself with cool ice cream.

Mrs. Shels threw the winning card onto the pile. The game was over.

"But I only had two more!!!" Lily threw her hands up in frustration.

"Noooooo…" The boys, feeling the same, tried adding their cards to the deck to show how they could have won, if only they had two more turns.

"Oh no you don't. I won and you guys lost. Ha Muahahahahahahahahaha!" Mrs. Shels enjoyed the victory with all the humility of a mom whose kids often flaunt their wins. She bowed several times as though she was standing before a large crowd of cheering fans.

"Mom, you can chill now." Lily added dryly. Mom pretended she couldn't hear Lily over the crowd. "We let you win this time, that's all. Theo insisted on it." Elbowing her brother, they winked in solidarity.

After a short victory dance where she ignored her children, Mrs. Shel helped them clean up. The table was cleared, the game put away and cleaned dishes returned to the cupboard.

"Thanks for playing tonight, kids." Mrs. Shels gave each of

them a hug good night. She had to sneak in kisses with the boys when she could, since they had reached the age where it was embarrassing.

"Mooom." Her youngest son whined as she gave him a quick kiss on the cheek.

"Good night Mom! Love you!" Lily wasn't shy with kisses and hugs. She would tell you, to this day, hugs and kisses are necessary for human and animal happiness. So happily, she offered them to her Mom, before heading up to her room.

"Don't forget your night prayers!" Mrs. Shels yelled upstairs as her childrens wandered off to bed.

§

Lily woke up late for school, but as she rushed, changing clothes and grabbing her lunch, she still almost missed the van. Her only thought was it's Friday at last!!! The entire school caught her Friday Freedom Fever. The fever hit hard leaving students less responsive to school life or requirements. Creating flustered teachers school-wide, spending their day trying to get students to pay attention.

Sitting quietly in her chair, Lily's mind was preoccupied with Fredrick and how to unstick her current spirit quest. She was disappointed, especially after expecting she would move forward with Dorothy's part of the story. Stuck. That was her story for the past 2 weeks.

Doris crashed into another one of Lily's daydreams. "Besides the photoshoot, what else are you doing this weekend?" She noticed the same notebook as before was out, and Lily was still working on the same line as Monday. Doris studied Lily's blank expression. "You know, sometimes I wonder if you're daydreaming about a boy or pretending to write those stories." She grabbed Lily's open notebook. "It's Friday, and you still haven't written anything new?" Doris shook her head, her utter disappointment clear. Her arms over her chest, she slowly shook her head side to side. "As your critique partner, I must say I am unimpressed."

Lily smirked at her friend's attempt to display her acting skills. "Yeah I'm still stuck." *Still stuck...with Fred and all his emotions."* The words floated up, adding to the black cloud of anxieties in Lily's mind. "I wish I had a boy to dream of."

"Yeah, that was pretty darn harsh. Patrick should have taken your number just to be polite." Doris shook her head wishing her friend better luck in her love life.

The two best friends sat in silence for a minute.

§

Doris recognized Lily was still in a bad mood. It's weird, she could almost pinpoint the very day Lily's mood took a nosedive. Stranger yet, the stories Lily wrote seemed to coincide with her mood swings. At first, Doris ignored the coincidence thinking she was making connections where they didn't exist. She even asked her Mom if she should bring it up or just ignore it. Her Mom's response was:

"Ignore it unless it keeps happening, teenagers go through lots of

emotional changes. You might end up experiencing something similar. And those stories might be Lily's way to work through them."

Her Mom made a good point. After the last semester, Doris was keeping a watchful eye on Lily--her mood and actions especially when she is writing a new story. The second Lily started her current story about Fred, everything changed. Lily stopped texting Doris. She never wanted to hang out or was snapping at everything and everyone. *Maybe I'll ask Mina if she knows what's going on? I don't think this is just teenage mood swings. And it can't be Patrick, he's only ever spoken to her once.*

§

The room teacher tried gaining the class's attention. "Today's class will...Quiet down back there. Yes, I'm talking to you three." The teacher stopped writing on the chalkboard to reprimand the whispering students in the last row.

"Ok, back to the lesson." The teacher droned on about something for the rest of the period. Forty-Five minutes never felt so long--dragging on forever. Lily tried her best to take notes, but something was distracting her. *Did she forget to add something to her notes about Fred and Dorothy?* The weirdest feeling surrounded her, as if she were being engulfed by a black cloud she kept hearing a question repeated--one she didn't have an answer for. *"Why is Fred's connection to the trunk?"* *"Dorothy"* Dorothy was the only link she could imagine. Lily looked at her notebook, surprised to see the letters D-O-R-O-T-H-Y written out in red ink in her math notebook, surrounding it with question marks. *Did I write that? Or has Fred taken over?* Her eyes locked with Doris, she worried she might have unscoincensely alerted her best friend. *What do I do if she asks me about this again? Should I tell her the truth or make something up?*

Instead of deciding on what she would do Lily scribbled on a scrap paper *"Boring…RIGHT?*

And held it up for Doris to see.

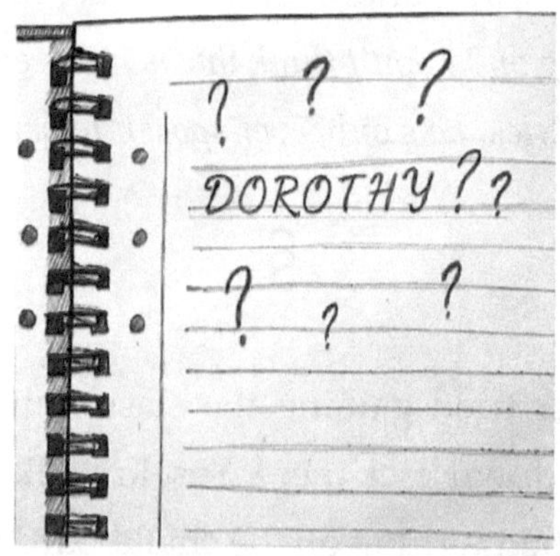

Doris held up a response *"Blahhh…"* With some creepy looking face next to it. Both girls giggled quietly keeping an eye out for their teacher.

Lily mentally organized her weekend plans while the teacher droned on.

Saturday morning: photoshoot with Doris

Saturday evening: hopefully have some clue on solving Fred's connection with the trunk.

Sunday morning: Mass

Sunday afternoon: Ask Mina to take her to the computer store and print out the pictures from the photoshoot.

Doris and Lily had synchronized the time on their phones, a

few days ago. Planning to meet at Lily's house at 9am, Saturday morning. Some of Lily's original plans did not work the way she wanted. Mina ended up working Saturday, leaving the transportation part in the lurch with no car or driver. Lily knew she should ask her Mom, but Lily knew her last minute plan would frustrate her Mom. Mrs. Shels liked sticking to a schedule. And Saturdays her schedule was always full. Lily could feel her brain start to curl up and die. *How would she get that trunk down to the park?*

When the final bell rang a high pitched tone, Lily beamed, it was the best sound she heard all day. Students ran like the hounds from hell where on their heels the minute they were released from the classes. Doris strolled beside Lily. They both decided to walk today in order to finalize their photoshoot plans.

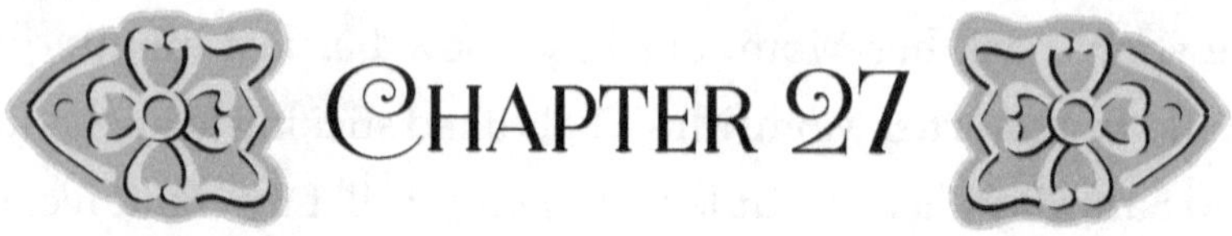

CHAPTER 27

Lily started down the sidewalk filling Doris in on a few ideas. "I think the park is usually pretty empty in the morning time so we should have privacy to do our photoshoot. Plus, It's cooler first thing in the morning. The summer heat peaks in the afternoon."

"I'll come by earlier to help pack up the car." Doris added, tightening her book bag straps as they walked towards their neighborhood.

"Yeah, about that. Mina is working tomorrow--" An intense wave of emotions hit Lily, knocking the breath out of her. She tried concentrating on the sidewalk as she fought off Fred's sudden anger and frustration. *Where is this coming from and why now Fred!*

" Oh man, really? Can your Mom take us?" Doris noticed

something had changed. Something was wrong with Lily, she had slowed down, staring at the sidewalk. "Lily? Your Mom does know about this, right?" Doris knew Lily and her Mom had a good relationship so why wouldn't she tell her Mom about the photoshoot? Except when she looked back at Lily her face was blank. "Did something happen between you and your Mom?" Doris paused waiting for an answer. "Lily? Lily? Hello?"

Lily bit her bottom lip, keeping her eyes glued to the sidewalk. Thanks to Fred, occupying her thoughts, and trying to take over her emotions so often, she said the only thing she could. "I figured we would carry the trunk to the park. It's not that far away from our house."

Doris stopped dead in her tracks, grabbing Lily's shoulder. "What?" She was getting really sick of being ignored. "Are you nuts? We would need to make at least four trips to carry everything for the photoshoot. Why won't you just ask your mom?" Doris's patience was spent. Feeling the anger rise, she got in Lily's face. "Lily! What is your problem? You ask me to do this photoshoot, then ignore me when I ask simple questions. What is going on?"

Lily looked at anything but Doris. She had already thought of this solution. It's not like her mom would get angry or say no, maybe a little annoyed but she would help them. *Why am I hesitating like this?* Usually Lily had a plan A, B, and C ready to go. But with Fred's intrusions constantly battling her emotions, Lily was too exhausted to even care about the photoshoot at this point. *Why did I start this stupid lie. It's more work than it's worth.*

Doris, her hand still on Lily's shoulder, tried redirecting the conversation. "Don't Max and Theo have soccer games around ten tomorrow morning?"

Lily replied absently, adding kindling to Doris's growing anger. "Yes, but Mom will be taking them and I don't want to bother asking her to drive us too."

"You are overthinking this, Lily. Your mom is super nice. I bet she would say yes if you just asked her." Doris' grip on Lily's shoulder relaxed. Offering her best smile, Doris continued. "Is something wrong? Usually you have at least three back-up plans when it comes to these kinds of things."

Lily's head flooded with questions, barely hearing anything Doris said. *Am I really overthinking this? Will Mom say yes? Am I losing my mind?* With every passing second, Fred was invading her thoughts. *Is someone talking to me? Fred, please stop trying to influence my emotions.*

I don't want to be angry anymore.

Lily wondered, was that her thought or was Fred's thoughts twisted in there too? When the next thought popped up, Lily knew they were from Fred. *I hate feeling this anger, I hate being alone. I hate feeling empty...I hate...myself.*

Lily clamped one hand over her mouth and the other over her stomach, trying to stop from spewing her miserable lunch across the sidewalk. A familiar tingle and throbbing in her jawline, her only warning. She sucked air through her nose as she choked back the bitter bile. *Oh my gosh not this again!*

Lily suddenly stopped, bent over, taking deep breaths. Doris was done with Lily's over-dramatic nonsense. "HELLO! Lily? Are you even listening to me?" Doris stopped walking, her hands fisted at her hips.

Lily could barely push the words out, praying she didn't puke on her best friend. "No, we can just walk to the park." Inside, she was battling hard against Fred's sudden attack and the ensuing nausea. This wasn't good and she knew it. Lily could barely keep her thoughts straight. Usually if she stayed quiet and focused on nothing in particular, she could contain the spirit's emotions. But today, it was not working. She needed to get home immediately, before she said or did something worse, like the last time--when Isaac took over.

Doris grabbed Lily firmly by the arm. "You're acting weird again. What's going on?" Doris could see Lily's eyes were glassy, and she was barely responding. "Lily, you're scaring me!" Doris quickly pulled Lily toward a grassy hill and pushed her to sit under the shaded trees.

After getting Lily to calm down, Doris exhaled realizing her earlier frustration had now been replaced with fear. This was a repeat of last semester when Lily turned into a zombie. The week she almost...Doris stopped her mind from finishing that thought.

I know better, this time I'll step in and stop her before things get out of hand. Lily will just have to get used to me sticking around like a bad tattoo.

It's never easy having difficult conversations with your best friend, especially when it ends in tears. Taking a moment to calm her nerves, Doris started out shakily. "I've been watching you, Lily. Watching you change--when you started these stories--after that weird depression thing last semester. You scared the crud out of me, and I don't want to experience that again." Taking a deep breath, Doris smoothed her wrinkled skirt. "Lily, you're acting weird--again. I can't watch you do it a second time. But, I can't help you either, if you won't tell me what's going on."

Lily couldn't look at Doris. Even if she tried, her mind was completely at Fred's mercy. His shattered soul was quickly exhausting all hope. Lily felt like her body was tangled inside a spider's web--escape was hopeless. Fred had depleted her power, immobilizing any movement or response.

"Something is going on Lily. Something to do with those stories. Or maybe it's just me? You were normal before you started writing them. Then you started acting weird. Sometimes you scare me. I didn't say anything before, because I was hoping things would go back to normal. Like they did after you finished Isaac's story..." Doris sucked in enough air to push the rest of it out as fast as possible. Just in case Lily decided to interrupt. "...but they haven't. I talked to Mina about when you tried--'' Doris stopped talking. She couldn't say the words. Just thinking about them was making her hyperventilate. But Doris forced the words out anyway. "We thought you were going to hurt yourself. Mina told me you would explain when you were ready, except that never happened." Doris's voice broke, tears filled her eyes until they overflowed, streaming down her cheeks. Dripping onto her school uniform. "Why can't you talk to me?" All the anger evaporated leaving Doris lost and feeling betrayed. She let her body sink to the ground next to Lily. She didn't have much fight left. Being friends with Lily was exhausting. And it didn't used to be this way.

Lily sat frozen unable to move or answer until Fred allowed it. Tears spilled down her cheeks, as she battled all the different emotions bombarding her--Fred's problems, Doris' hurt feelings, and her own regret. She couldn't do anything about her own regret, that was on her. Doris' hurt feelings, Lily would like to reassure her but Fred was the bigger problem she had to deal with first.

Lily gained just enough control of herself. Bolting up she yelled at the invisible Fred. "Fred, if you don't get your boney spirit butt out of my head, I'll make sure you spend another hundred years trapped in this crumby, old trunk!"

Doris seeing her best friend act like she was losing her mind was speechless for a few minutes. *Was this the real Lily? Is she insane?* Doris coughed a few times, clearing her throat. "Mina told me your behavior is connected to these stories. Is Fred an imaginary friend you like to talk to?" Doris wiped the tears with a tissue. "Here." She offered Lily the tissue. She had planned on talking to Lily about it but she didn't expect to be this emotional. And Lily, who she expected to overreact, was silent like a mannequin. Whatever was going on, as her dad would say, "Find out today". Doris was fed up. She was determined Lily would listen to what she had to say.

"I was going to wait but you're strange, freaky behavior is too much! Just like you talking to yourself. You need to tell me what is going on. I'm your best friend, you can trust me and I will try to understand. But even I have limits and you are pushing it." Doris's body shook with frustration. She was angry and hurt--her best friend ignored her even when she was trying to help.

Lily heard Doris talking but it sounded far away--distant and muffled. Her entire body felt heavy, like it was weighed down with cement blocks. Lily couldn't lift her head, her arms or her legs. Her arms were pinned to her body. She felt like a marble statue. She wanted to answer Doris, but Fred made it impossible.

Doris bolted to her feet. "Fine! Be that way! I'm not going to take this anymore. You either tell me or I'm leaving. I mean it Lily! No more playing around." Doris waited a moment, her anger building with every silent second that passed. "Alright. If that's how you are going to treat your best friend, then you're on your own. No more help. No more listening. Nothing. Until you explain what's going on." Doris's voice cracked as she turned to dash away. Doris ran home and didn't stop until the bedroom door slammed behind her.

CHAPTER 28

Doris fell face first onto her bed, screaming all her frustration into her pillow. *Lily wouldn't even look at me! Like she didn't care that I was there. Like I was invisible. I tried to be there for her and she didn't even care enough to say anything. What a jerk! I hate her!* Doris hugged her pillow while the violent emotions raged. Trying to muffle her frustrated tears.

Doris didn't hate Lily, far from it. She cared deeply about Lily. She wanted her to be safe and share what was happening in her life. Why was that so hard? Isn't that what best friends do?--be there for each other, tell secrets you can't share with anyone else. Shouldn't you trust your best friend like no other. *If Lily can't trust me, are we even best friends? Is Lily keeping secrets that are that bad?* Doris' mind rushed thinking of horrible possibilities. *No! Stop it! I'm sure it's nothing like that.*

A loud knock rattled her door before Danny, her brother, walked in. "Hey Dorky! Dad wants us to come down now to eat dinner before we go to the game." Danny dropped the soccer ball he was holding onto the floor chasing it out of the room. Ignoring Doris' obvious red face and tears.

Doris yelled, reaching for a tissue. "Shut up! I'm not coming down."

Danny shrugged leaving the room. "Girls don't make any sense." He commented as he ran down the hallway.

§

Doris closed the door and sat crying for a few minutes before a second softer knock sounded, followed by her Dad's deeper voice.

"Doris, open this door right now." Her dad's voice was loud and clear.

Wiping her face Doris climbed off the bed, donning a baseball cap before opening the door.

Mr. Casdy stepped into his daughter's room looking around. "Ok, Doris. First, you yell at Danny. Then you refuse to come down for supper. Ya wanna tell me what's up?" Mr. Casdy moved further into the room and caught a glimpse of Doris' face. Immediately, anger rose inside of him. "Are you...*crying*? Doris, did someone hurt you? If something happened, you can tell me."

Doris could tell her Dad was getting anxious. He was known for being protective in general, but Doris knew that he would do anything to keep his family safe. "No, Dad. Nothing, I mean, no one hurt me. I'm sorry. It's just...just." She couldn't finish her sentence without shedding more tears. Mr. Casdy, seeing his little girl cry, couldn't help but wrap her in his thick arms for a warm, strong hug.

Mr Casdy could feel the warm flush creep across his bearded face. Feeling awful for making his daughter cry even more. "Hey. Hey, Daisy-chain, calm down. I didn't mean to make you cry." Rolling his eyes, he couldn't believe he let his wife sweet talk him into checking on Doris. This was exactly why he didn't like handling girly things like this. Emotional girls need their moms for comfort. When he tried getting out of this very situation, Mrs.Casdy replied, "You're her father, and I always take care of these problems. Go up there and see what is bothering your only daughter. Who knows, you might learn something about your children."

There was no way around it. His wife gave him *'the look'* then pointed to the stairs. *Maybe after messing this up, she'll think twice before sending me up to deal with crying kids.*

Doris sniffed loudly, tossing her used tissue onto the floor. "It's not your fault, Dad...I had a horrible fight with Lily, after school today." Doris burst into a torrent of tears while wrapped in her Dad's safe arms.

While Doris cried, soaking his tee shirt, Mr. Casdy thought about what he was supposed to say to his distraught daughter. *Great, this is why your Mom should be here. What do I do now?* He sat down on the small sparkly pink bed wondering what to do next.

If this was Danny, I'd just punch him in the shoulder and tell him to toughen up. Maybe that will work. "Ok now, stop your tears and tell me why you're so upset this time? I thought you and your best friend argued all the time." Mr. Casdy just realized how little he knew about his own daughter's life. Working all day, then busy with Danny most weekends, he didn't really notice who Doris' friends were.

Mr. Casdy just remembered what his wife said about hormones and letting girls cry when they need it. His wife's words rang in his ears. "It's better if you let them get all the crying out. It's healthier than telling them to keep it in" *Maybe he was getting the hang of it. This isn't so bad.* "Umm...wait--cry if you want. Let it all out. You'll feel better and stronger."

Mr. Casdy peeled Doris off his shirt, handing her half a box of tissues. Stealing the other half to wipe the mess from his shirt. *Ewww, maybe it would be easier to change my shirt. But Daisy would say 'It's not worse than the sweaty-mess you bring in from the soccer fields'.*

"I'll wait 'til you're done, Doris. Do you need more tissues?" Mr. Casdy checked his watch, Danny's soccer game was only an hour away. He prayed Doris wouldn't have an extended meltdown. *He didn't have time for this--maybe he could speed things along with a few questions.* He could almost hear his wife's voice, lecturing him for rushing their daughter through an emotional moment. Andrew decided against that plan.

"Dad, Lily won't tell me what's wrong. Something is going on with her. But she won't say a word to me about it. And today... after school..." She took a tissue from her dad's hand, dabbing her tears. "...today, I asked her to tell me....and she **just ignored me!**" Doris blew her nose. "I felt so stupid--standing there--I just ran away. *After* I said I won't speak to her unless she tells me *everything.*" She tried to catch her breath between explanations. "I didn't really mean it. I just couldn't take it anymore! She made me so angry just sitting there. Doing nothing. Like I was the one being weird or **overreacting.**" Doris depleted all of her energy relaying her woes to her Dad. Feeling like a wet noodle, she deflated into her pillow-strewn bed. Her dad nodded, trying his best to listen. "I don't want to lose our friendship, Dad. But I think I just ruined everything...**she won't talk to me!**" Mr.

Casdy grabbed another tissue from the box to offer Doris. "What do you think, Dad? Was I **really** overreacting?"

Mr. Casdy opened his mouth to answer, but he hesitated a second too long.

"I don't think I was." Doris slid off the bed, starting to pace around her room as she continued. "She can't keep secrets from me. *I'm* her best friend--since first grade! *And,* I tell her **everything**!" Each step around the room became louder than the last.

Mr. Casdy tried to remain sitting quietly on her bed, waiting for Doris to finish her story, but finally cut in when she paused to take a breath. "You know what I would do? I would march over to Lily's house and demand answers. You need to confront your problems head on. Then at least you will know if your friendship survived instead of moping around until Monday. Plus, that makes you the stronger best friend since you are willing to confront problems and solve them."

Doris put her hat on then threw away all the used tissues. "You're right Dad! I need to confront Lily. Head on! Just like sports, we have to play offense, not defense."

Feeling the adrenaline surge, Mr. Casdy fist-pumped into the air above his head. "That's my girl! Get over there and confront your best friend!"

Doris grabbed her jacket, running toward the front door. Mr. Casdy proudly cheered his daughter on, following her out the door and onto the porch. After watching Doris leave, Mr. Casdy strutted into the kitchen, where Daisy, his wife, was setting dinner on the table.

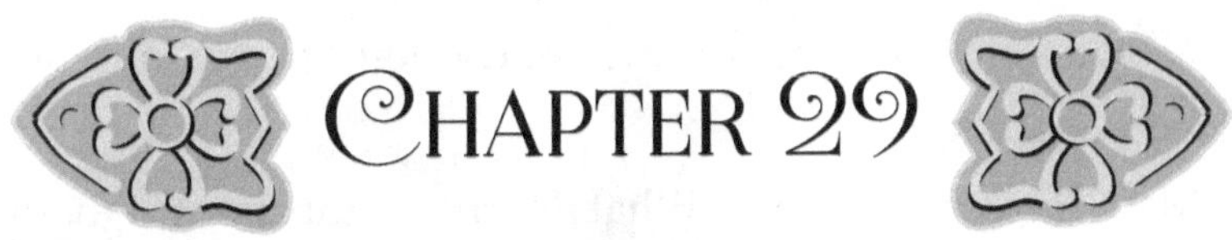

CHAPTER 29

Mrs. Casdy noticed his satisfied grin and confident walk. "So, how did it go?" She couldn't help but chuckle at his peacock-like manner. "I take it *the talk* went well? What was Doris' problem?"

Mr. Casdy sat down ready to give details on his 'father of the year' moment.

Mrs.Casdy handed her husband a plate of chicken-fried rice when he started talking. "She yelled at her friend, and was scared that their friendship was over. So I told her to go over there and confront their problem head on. Play offense not defense." He was beaming--happy with his successful dad moment, dealing with his emotional daughter.

His wife smiled, which made him nervous. "You did a great job, Honey!"

Being acknowledged by his wife for this, was well deserved. Mr. Casdy felt his triumph should earn him 'father of the year' title for sure. Many years ago, when Doris was in kindergarten, she brought him a small plastic trophy that said, "Father of the Year." He still had that trophy, somewhere. It was one of his prized possessions.

Mrs. Casdy continued. "What did they fight about? I thought I heard the front door close, did Doris go somewhere?"

Mr. Casdy nodded. "Doris said she had something to tell her friend. Loran...Lisa...L something. She refused to tell Doris something important. I think it was something to do with acting weird." He shrugged, continuing to eat his dinner.

Mrs. Casdy bit her lower lip, thinking about Doris' fight with Lily. "Lily, dear. Doris' friend's name is Lily. Doris and Lily fought over something important? And you told her to confront Lily right now?" Looking down at him with an arched eye-brow, Mr. Casdy could tell he did something very wrong.

"Honey, did you ask what they fought over? Because maybe, her friend, Lily is going through personal problems that can't be fixed with one conversation. You know, some people need more time to open up about sensitive issues. Lily might need that extra time. It could be something personal, or family problems, or girl problems. Tons of things could be happening with Lily-- or Doris."

Mr. Casdy stopped eating, waiting for his wife to finish her lecture. He knew the victory would be short lived. *No one ever appreciates when a man tries.* He slowly chewed his food and considered whether to tell his wife what he really wanted to say.

"See, this is why I didn't want to take on girl problems. I don't get girl talk, and Doris doesn't feel comfortable talking about all that with me either. That's why you should have gone instead." He followed that crushing thought instead, with a strong nod to his wife. *Maybe this screw up will change her mind about me dealing with girl problems.*

Mrs. Casdy suppressed her laughter while considering how best to encourage Andrew. *His heart was in the right place, execution wise sports analogies aren't great for all girls.* "Oh well, I hope the girls can work it out. After all, they are teenagers. Everything seems to be a life altering problem to them." Mrs. Casdy caught her husband off guard with a kiss. "You did good honey. Thanks for handling this one."

Mr. Casdy forgot his prepared argument, the kiss shocking the annoyance from his mind. Eating happily, he figured his wife would think twice before asking him again.

Mrs. Casdy put her plate in the sink, and headed for the kitchen door. "From now on, I think you're capable of handling all the girls' problems. You have to earn that 'Dad of the Year' trophy somehow. And as you love to point out, this is the perfect vehicle to earn it." Chuckling, she walked out, leaving Mr. Casdy choking on his dinner. She took that as a good sign-- he was nervous but ready.

§

As Doris moved closer to Lily's house, her nerves felt like ants were racing across her skin. *Confront your problems head on.* She repeated to herself with every step. She only lived a few blocks away, which through the years had been an amazing benefit-- until now. In a few short minutes, Doris stood before Lily's front door, wishing she had walked even slower.

Pray.

The thought popped into Doris' mind like a neon sign. She figured saying a prayer that Lily opens up to her tonight was a good idea. *Please let us still be best friends. Please, God.*

Doris swallowed hard as she knocked on the Shels' door. A few seconds later it opened when Mrs. Shels appeared.

"Hey Mrs. Shels, Is Lily home?" Doris shook as the anxiety surrounded her. Up until that moment she had been afraid that Lily would answer the door. But now, new worries popped into her head when she saw Mrs. Shels. *What if Lily already told her mom? Would she side with Lily and yell at me?* Doris hadn't considered any of that...until now.

Mrs. Shels smiled, even though her eyes held concern. "Hi, Doris. Yes, Lily is in her room." She stepped back, leaving room for Doris to enter. "Doris, did something happen? Lily locked herself in her room and it sounded like she was crying."

Doris froze. *Lily hadn't said anything to her mom.* "Yeah...we kind of had a fight after school. I yelled then she ran away--so..." Doris didn't know how to finish that sentence. Actually there was no good way to finish what she had to say. Tears blurred her vision.

Mrs. Shels noticed Doris' abrupt ending. "Ahh, ok. Well I'm glad you're here to fix it then. Girls should work through their problems. You and Lily are too close to let a fight come between best friends. I hope you work this out. Let me know if you need anything. ok?" She gently squeezed Doris' shoulder. Her encouraging look helped Doris relax. *See, Lily, I knew your mom would understand.*

Mrs. Shels led Doris to Lily's room. Knowing Doris needed some support, she knocked gently on the door. "Lily, someone is here to see you." Mrs. Shels turned the door handle and shoved Doris into the room quickly. Walking away Mrs. Shels dusted her hands, considering it a job well done.

Doris was shocked by Lily's state. Her face was bright red, tears streaked her mascara--she looked miserable. The room was one, huge disaster. Clothes strewn everywhere, paper scattered across the floor. It looked as if a small tornado had blown through. After Doris was shoved into the room, Lily glowered then stomped back to her bed

Doris took a courageous step forward. She could only manage to mumble, "Hey Lily."

Lily looked up, giving Doris a shocking view of her red, puffy eyes. But Lily wasn't looking at Doris.

CHAPTER 30

F red's panicked emotions were scrambling Lily's thoughts. She felt every painful, heart-crushing moment that Fred endured after he lost his family.

Drowning in Fred's misery, Lily was about to give in when a single knock sounded. The loud noise made Doris flinch at the unexpected interruption.

Mina poked her head through the slightly opened door. "Hey Lily--" Seeing the disaster in Lily's room, Doris looked ready to flee, and Lily was crying, Mina pushed the door open. Walking into the war zone, she locked the door behind her. "Alright Lily, this is the same crap again!" Mina waved her arm at the chaos in the room. Turning to Doris, she asked "Hey Doris, are you alright?"

Doris managed a reassuring nod and a weak smile.

Mina studied the girls carefully. Lily was a wreck and had

been crying, Doris looked shell-shocked, keeping her distance from Lily. *Something must have happened.*

Mina draped her arm around Doris' shoulder, guiding her to the chair across from Lily. "Doris, I'm guessing from your response, that Lily hasn't told you everything, right?"

After sitting down, Doris lifted her head, holding back her tears. "No, she hasn't told me anything. That's...what we fought about after school." Doris' gaze fell to her lap, the tears gathering again.

"Ok. Lily. It's way past time to include Doris. You need to explain everything to your best friend. I warned you about waiting too long. But first...let's clean up this post-hurricane disaster."

Mina waited, but Lily didn't respond. She stood still, frozen, her eyes closed, her hands folded at her waist.

Mina stood next to her sister, realizing Lily couldn't answer right now. "Lily. Are you there? Is Fred showing you something?" Mina touched Lily's hand. No response. Yep, she must be trapped, dealing with some of Fred's issues, right now. *Thanks, Lily. Or maybe I should thank Fred?* Mina didn't realize she had been slowly shaking her head until she heard a panicked cry from Doris.

Doris tried muffling her shock as she watched Mina touch a corpse-like Lily, then start shaking her head. *Did my best friend just Die right in front of me??* Doris couldn't believe what she was seeing. *Did I just kill Lily?* A horrendous sob escaped Doris. *Oh my gosh I am going to prison!*

"Oh, no no no. Doris, it's ok. Lily's just sleeping...or something like that." Mina couldn't help but laugh at the weird situation she was now in. Her sister comatose, dealing with a spirit, and her best friend, freaking out because she doesn't know what's going on. And Mina, the lucky sister--had to explain the complicated story to Doris, without Lily's help.

Mina looked to the ceiling as if praying to God. *Please...help me find the right words.* "OK. Doris." Mina clapped her hands together, furrowing her forehead and twisting her lips, before attempting to lighten the mood. "I know this seems weird, but Lily is ok. I'll try to explain what I know--just keep an open mind."

"Why? What's going on? What's wrong with Lily? Why are you acting like everything is normal?" Doris could barely push the questions past her trembling lips. *Something is seriously wrong here.* Doris had half a mind to run out of the room screaming.

"Doris," Mina waved, gaining her attention. "Hey, don't worry. This happens every once in a

while. Think of it like an internal struggle between good and evil, Lily and the spirit." Mina stopped, her explanation was obviously not helpful when a horrified look crossed Doris' face. Rubbing her own face roughly, Mina took a deep cleansing breath. "Lily will snap out of this...eventually. She's safe, she's just inside her head."

Mina tried composing her thoughts. She needed to explain the Fred thing to Doris, plus keep an eye on Lily. Just in case Lily tries to harm herself. *What a mess. How did I get stuck in the middle of all this?* "Ok, so Lily's text said that you had a fight after school, but then it got weird. That's why I rushed home, to check on her.." Mina rubbed the back of her neck and tried to laugh. "Ah, where do I begin?" She picked up Lily's math notebook on the desk, holding it upright for Doris to see. "This right here, is where we will find all the troublemakers. These stories...that Lily writes...are more than just stories. A couple years ago, Lily found out she had some weird, spiritual power…" Mina raised her hands like a stop sign. As if to say, 'Don't ask me, it's Lily's story, I'm just telling it', kind of shrug. "..it allows her to feel or sense trapped spirits that are attached to an earthly object. For example this guy..." Mina pointed toward the wooden trunk pieces, the only items not buried in the mess. Taking a second, Mina was relieved to see Doris without the horrified expression, focused on her every word. "This trunk has a spirit stuck to it, and when Lily touched it, the spirit attached to her as well. Not possession, exactly, more like pestering her until she figures out why they haven't moved on. Are you following me so far?" Mina forced a stiff smile onto her lips to reassure Doris.

Doris nodded with a frown as her gaze darted between Mina and Lily.

Mina was glad to see Doris was keeping her emotions in check. At least for now. It was hard enough to explain Lily's weird situation, even worse when tears were involved. "Ok. The trunk's spirit is called Fred. He's a blind, old man who died sad and alone. For some reason he's attached to this piece of junk." Mina kicked the trunk. "That's what Lily and I have figured out so far. Right now, Lily is either fighting Fred or he is sharing something important."

Suddenly Lily gasped, before opening her eyes. Mina and Doris jumped at the abrupt change. Doris screamed, her heart pounding out of her chest.

Lily looked around, her eyes wild. Noticing Doris and Mina staring at her, she asked. "What happened? Mina? Doris?" Lily ran over to her friend, hugging Doris as tight as she could. "I'm so so sorry!!! I didn't mean to ignore you or hurt your feelings! I'm so sorry! It wasn't your fault, I didn't know how to tell you. Can you forgive me?" The girls hugged until they ran out of tears.

Mina started cleaning up, around the bed, to give the girls some space.

Doris sniffed loudly. "Of course I forgive you! I'm sorry, too. I didn't mean what I said. I was so worried. So many freaky things happening, I didn't know what to think."

Lily grabbed a tissue, wiping her face. "I know, it's time I told you about the weird spirit stuff."

Before Lily could continue, Mina interrupted, holding up a folded letter.

"Hey Lily, Sorry to interrupt, but did you finish Fred's story yet?" Waving the letter, Mina raised one eyebrow. It looked like Mrs. Brookes shared a few new things about the trunk with Lily. Mina hoped they were near the end of this spirit's story because she was tired and needed a long break.

"Wait, we need to explain everything to Doris first." Lily began the long explanation when Doris cut in.

"I know, I know--you randomly find spirits that are trapped in objects, like this trunk, and end up having to free the spirit by writing their story. Or something like that, am I right?" Doris looked to Mina for confirmation, not noticing Lily's shocked expression. "While you were vacationing over by the bed and I was freaking out--Mina explained the important parts to me." Turning to Mina Doris said, "Thanks, Mina."

"Oh my stars and garters, Thank you so much Mina! You are the best sister anyone could ask for...but how did you know to come home?" Lily wondered what happened while she was fighting Fred."Doris, are you sure you're ok with my spirit power? I mean, you don't think I'm a bad Catholic or anything do you?"

Total silence enveloped the room. Doris and Mina stood with their mouths hanging open.

Lily said "What? Do you?"

Mina sputtered, "Oh my stars and what?!? What does that even mean?"

Doris started laughing as Lily explained. "It's just something Fred says. Stars and garters. It has something to do with bracing for a storm and socks. I don't fully understand, but it just popped out."

Mina shrugged and pulled out her phone. "Shortly after I got to work, I got this weird message from you, Lily. The text read: *"I hate being alone, afraid...will I ever be free?"* I knew you were in trouble so I rushed home. When I got here, Doris was watching you frozen like a statue, so I had to do something to calm her down. You're welcome, by the way and you owe me Big time!" Mina grinned when Lily hugged her as if her very life depended on it.

"No, Lily, I don't think you're possessed or a bad Catholic. Maybe this is a weird cool power God gave you for some reason! I think it's kinda cool. Well, except the fact that you get freaky and weird sometimes. Maybe that's something we can help you control."

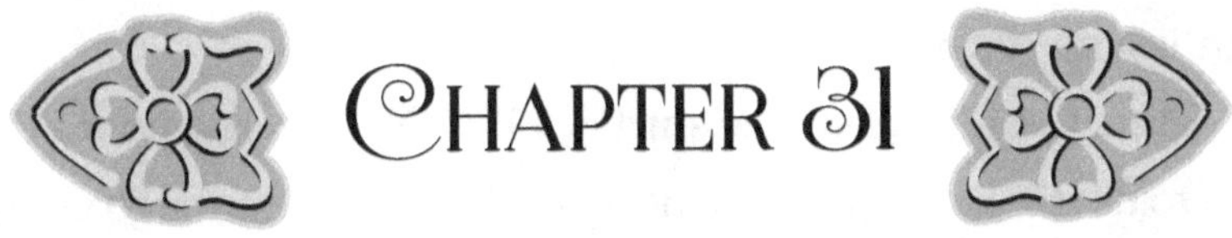

CHAPTER 31

Lily released Mina. "Thank you. Thank you! Thank you! I'm so close to being done with Fred! The letter is from Mrs. Brookes, Fred's granddaughter. She told me about him and why their family refused to forgive him. She said that her Mom told her that her great grandfather ruined his marriage, after he went blind. He was basically sent to a nursing home because no one wanted to take care of him. Mrs. Brookes never met Fred, but was told before he went blind, he had been a very good man. Her great-grandmother tried reminding her kids until she died that Fred was a good man. Unfortunately, she had dementia, so no one listened to her. I think that was the missing piece. Something else happened between Fred and Dorothy that no one knows about. Or maybe Fred's family has to forgive him before he can move on. Something like that." Lily was prowling around the room, feeling excited. In her gut, she could feel she was on the right track. Fred's story was coming together at last.

Doris reached out her hand. "Are you ok jumping around like that?" Doris hesitated "You were in a trance for a long time, fighting spirits, right?"

Mina tossed a clean tee shirt at Lily. "You scared poor Doris half to death. Even made me nervous. If you have enough energy to hop around, you could at least pick up this mess."

Lily grabbed the tee shirt and folded it, laying it neatly on her bed. "I'm feeling much better now. Fred's sadness hit a new low for me. He's completely crushed and lost." Lily shuddered, the emotional battle she fought with Fred wasn't quite over. At least until he was free, she would be dealing with his shattered feelings. "I'm sorry for making you both worry so much. And Doris, I am sorry I kept so much from you. The spirits, the stories, Fred." Lily grabbed Doris's hand. "I wanted to tell you months ago,years ago, but I didn't know what to say. Mina told me to just tell you, but I...I was scared you wouldn't believe me."

Doris replied. "I'd like to think I would have believed you. We are best friends. Next time, just promise me, you'll tell me what's going on. Then I'll try my best to believe you."

Lily shook Doris' hand. "Ok, deal. I wish I could say this was my last spirit case, unfortunately I can't. But I will promise you, I'll tell you about them, no matter what."

Doris stuck out her little finger. "Pinky promise?"

Lily linked pinkies with Doris'. "Pinky promise." In the past their 'pinky promises' were never broken--the ultimate promise. Making one meant they were serious.

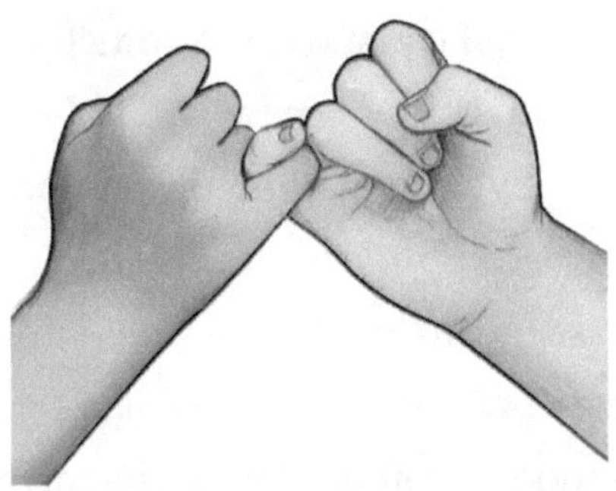

Mina proudly clapped both of the girls on the back. "I'm glad you two are friends again! Now let's get back to work!" Faster than a ninja, Mina dumped clothes on both girls. Doris and Lily shrieked, batting the clothes away from their heads.

Mina stood with her hands on her hips surveying the room. "Lily, I know this spirit stuff is complicated, but what in the friggin 'heck were you doing in here? It's a wreck!"

Lily stopped, taking a hard look around her room."Well, half of the mess is from trying to find outfits and props for tomorrow's photoshoot. And the other half is me trying to work through Fred's tirade. I tried imagining what it would be like to be blind. Then I shut my eyes for a few seconds and immediately ran into something. Then something strange happened. I actually became blind, for a few minutes--*like literally blind!*" Lily waved one hand in front of her eyes, trying to retrace her steps. "See I closed my eyes, then opened them when I touched the bookcase over here. But after that I couldn't see anything! Everything was black. Or not exactly black, but I couldn't see anything. Then I really started to panic, which is why that box was tipped over. While I was freaking out, I had to feel my way back to my bed--

where I started crying. Praying I didn't permanently go blind." Lily's face looked like she just bit into something bitter. "I spent half of my school life, laying here wishing I never met Fred, or any of these spirits. Every one of Fred's emotions: fear, sadness, anger, anxiety, frustration, loneliness...they all finally made sense. It felt like Isaac, during his last days--utter despair."

All the laughter and joy was sucked out of the room, by Lily's revelation. The mood had shifted with the mention of Isaac.

Mina and Doris exchanged concerned looks. Each clearly thought that Lily was heading toward another episode, the conversation had taken a nosedive.

Usually Lily broke the tension but Doris felt like it was her turn. "Well thank-goodness you're not blind. Imagine the fun Mina and I would have mixing up your outfits. And lying about them being cute."

Mina snorted, high-fiving Doris.

Lily couldn't help but smile while she compared Fred to Isaac. They seemed to have the darkest emotions of all her spirits. Lily stretched out on her bed. "I was so scared, I thought I had finally lost my mind. Right before that, I prayed for a sign--an answer to Fred's story. Then I thought, *what would it be like to be blind?* Which I often wondered. Then I literally was blind. I felt like my life had flashed before me. Then my memories were mixing with Fred's. I was so scared, I prayed to Jesus, Mary and Joseph. Begging for my eyesight to come back. I begged and pleaded until I felt a strange calmness overcome me. As if someone said *'You'll be alright.'"*

The tension in Lily's body evaporated "I opened my eyes

and guess what? *I could see!! It was like God was listening just for me!!"*

Simultaneously, Doris and Mina exchanged looks. *Be careful what you wish for, I guess.* They both seemed to think.

"Everything came back, bright and clear. I wanted to jump up and down with happiness, but Fred's emotions invaded, with so much hostility. I spent the next few minutes containing his intense anger." Waving her hand at Doris. "That's when you knocked and came in." Lily paused, worry wrinkling her forehead. "I don't remember much after that, until my connection to Fred was interrupted."

The three of them fell silent. Each lost in their own thoughts about what Lily had revealed.

Doris broke the silence first, with a few questions. "So, this is the same Fred that you've been writing about? He's trapped in a trunk and is blind? How horrible and sad...no wonder his pain was so intense."

Lily pursed her lips before smiling. The fact that she could finally talk to her best friend, about all the stories without having to make up something as a cover story, was a relief. At last she felt less alone and isolated. With Mina and Doris by her side, the spirit stories would get easier to handle, hopefully.

Seeing Doris' serious expression, Mina stopped cleaning. "What's the matter, Doris?"

Doris was afraid to ask but she had to know the truth. She whispered as softly as possible. "Lily, last semester...was all that crazy, scary stuff caused by a spirit?" Doris looked directly into Lily's eyes. Now that she knew about Lily's gift, she needed to know if Lily had been influenced by a spirit. During that semester, Doris spent so many days and hours worried about her best friend. She was certain Lily's weird behavior had something to do with those stories. Her intuition was right on the money. The only missing element was the spirit stuff. Doris lapsed into silence thinking about Lily's stories.

Looking down quickly, Lily replied. "Yes, all of that was because of another spirit. Remember the last story you read? Before Fred? The one about the boy named Isaac?" Lily paused, her body breaking out in goosebumps. No matter how much time passed. Isaac's story always gave her the heebie-jeebies.

Doris sat on the bed, feeling nauseated. "Isaac is real? As in, alive and breathing like you and me, before he *died*. When I first read his story, it was just a sad story. But now, that poor boy! He went through so much--suffering." Doris wished she could hold back her emotional response to Isaac's demise. "I'm sorry. I guess I just realized the pain he went through was real. *It's a true story?* It's weird that your feelings can change by knowing it's true. I cried a lot when I read his story, but I thought you made that up. Now that it's not, I'm almost ashamed that I felt comforted by that fact." Doris realized, true or not, stories were full of life lessons to guide us. The story felt so real, because it was real. After reading it, Doris started to notice things about people around her. How they acted and treated others. Especially bullies. *I wish we could stop all bullies.* Doris scowled, glowering at Lily. "We have to stop the bullies, or we'll end up with a bunch of Isaacs."

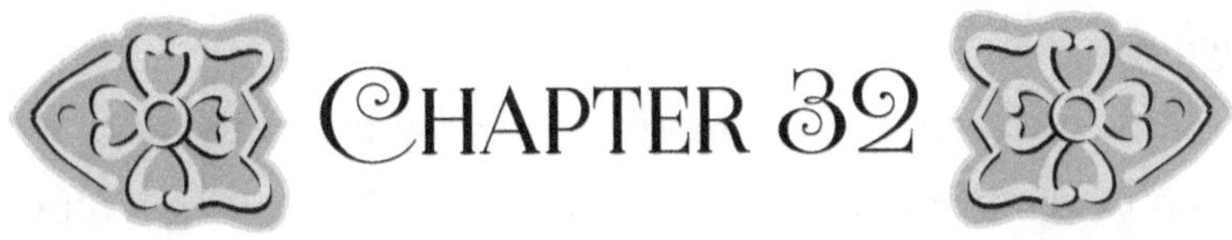

Chapter 32

Lily felt the same way. They had been bullied enough in school to understand. It's not something that can be avoided. *Could something be done to help prevent it?* "You're right! We have to do something, anything. Maybe the teachers will let us give a speech about bullying, and how to cope with self doubt?"

Doris punched Lily with lightning accuracy. "Yeah! Or how to stop being a bully. Maybe we could get the class bully to be our bad example." The two girls giggled. They knew it was wrong, but thinking about the class bully finally getting her just desserts was a wonderful dream, no matter what happened.

Lily joined Doris on the bed. Both girls completely abandoned any attempts to clean the room. "I wish! But the teachers, priests and nuns will say. *'Revenge is mine, saith the Lord'*." Lily repeated the well known scripture in her best 'teacher voice', raising one finger to wag at the offender. Laughter erupted, chasing the last of the dark mood away. After a good laugh, a new calm settled in the room. After all the tension from the serious conversations, the three seemed to be thinking the same thing. *We needed a good laugh.*

Mina paused her cleaning, realizing that Lily and Doris weren't even pretending to help her. "Hey! You two get off your bums and get back to work!"

The girls looked at one another with surprised expressions. *Who us?* Turning to Mina, they added mischievous grins before shaking their heads. *We refuse to comply.*

Mina dropped the armload of scarves she had collected from the floor. *Fine, live like pigs!*

Shaking her head, she gave up on Lily's room looking like anything other than a barnyard. "Fine. Clean it yourselves. I tried, but I'm not playing nice anymore!" Mina crossed her arms and stomped one foot, emitting a loud huff. Mina was being as dramatic as possible, mocking Lily.

Doris sighed, falling back onto the bed ignoring Mina. "Lily, how did you end up solving Isaac's story anyway? I thought there was something missing?"

Lily grabbed the closest pillow, hugging it to her chest. "Mina helped me solve Isaac's story. There was a piece missing and I tried getting it from Isaac's family. But my letter was never answered. I guess Isaac knew I was digging, so he helped me. Afterwards he was able to leave in peace...because Mina figured it out. I don't know what happened exactly, but he left after Mina contacted his counselor. So it's all good. But I don't really know, I sort of made up the last part of his story."

Mina stomped over to the chair, collapsing in a big huff. "Fine, if you're going to ignore me, I guess we can talk about that. Isaac's story was a rough trip through Hell. One I don't ever want to repeat!"

Lily looked around the room, sighing. She stood and began picking up the mess again. Following her lead, Doris joined in. Within a few minutes, the room was almost back to normal. Tidy and peaceful.

Mina flipped through Lily's notebook with Fred's story. "Lily, how's Fred doing anyway? From your notes, it looks like he is really struggling--*WAIT! Did Fred just die??*" Mina's mouth dropped open when she read the last paragraph. "Fred revealed his death to you?" Mina pointed to today's date. "If he already told you, then why did you have that weird episode? Shouldn't he be released, or free. Whatever you call it?"

Doris grabbed the notebook out of Mina's hands, reading the page as Mina waited for Lily to respond.

Lily shrugged, then scratched the back of her neck. "That's the thing. Fred revealed his death this morning. Usually when a spirit shares how they died--or their final moments, I can usually connect their death to the earthly object. But...when Fred shared his...nothing happened. I couldn't make a connection between Fred's trunk and his death. His entire story is a huge mess and now I feel more lost than ever. *I didn't think that was possible.*" Lily could feel her energy collapsing under the stressful confusion, again.

Doris looked up with a scowl. "Lily, maybe you need to

explain this to me." She shook the notebook toward Lily. "Better yet explain his whole story to me. I'm trying to make sense of this, but…I am definitely lost."

Lily held out her hand for the notebook. "Sorry about my scribbles, I was so annoyed that I left some details out." Looking at her notes through squinted eyes, Lily had a hard time deciphering the chicken scratch. "Let's see. Basically Fred took me literally to his last few minutes. I couldn't see, but could hear what was going on. The Priest was performing Last Rites, because the Father asked him to receive Extreme Unction. Once done, I heard a female voice, a nurse or doctor, speaking to the Priest. Their conversation was easy to hear and the person apologized, saying, 'no one from Fred's family would arrive in time'."

"Poor Fred," Doris muttered. "…he really was left to die alone."

"You'd think so huh? Or that Fred would be at rock bottom--he's on death's doorstep, alone and unloved…" Tossing the notebook onto the desk, Lily started pacing, lightly massaging her temples. "…but here's the thing. He's not. I've never sensed so much peace or happiness in any spirit right before their death. Fred was happy! Completely composed--even his family not making it, didn't upset him. He was entirely calm, as if looking forward to the end." Lily flopped onto the bed, gauging Mina and Doris' reaction.

Both frowned, lost in deep contemplation.

Mina fiddled with a pencil, flipping it between her fingers while she twirled in the chair. Stopping her circular motion, she searched through the papers and letters tossed across the desk. "Lily, did you ever hear back from Mrs. Brookes? You wrote her another letter or something, didn't you?"

Lily had resumed pacing, but stopped in her tracks at Mina's question. Turning toward Mina, her frown morphed into a wide grin. "Mina, you're a genius!!" Lily rushed to the desk. Giving Mina a kiss on the cheek, Lily began tossing papers. "The letters! Where are they?"

Mina pushed away from the desk, leaving room for a frantic Lily to search.

After 60 seconds rifling through her disorganized desk, Lily triumphantly held up a letter. "Aha! Here it is. I totally forgot all about this. It came just today, but I was so preoccupied with Fred, and our fight, that I forgot to read it." Ripping the envelope, Doris and Mina moved closer as Lily read the contents aloud.

Dear Lily,

I'm glad you like the trunk. You are welcome to keep it or donate it. I'm happy to hear you got the extra pieces in time for the photoshoot.

If you don't want to keep the trunk, maybe someone else will use it for something. If you return it, my son will simply get rid of it again. He doesn't understand history or family heirlooms. I suppose it's time for me to let it go. It just collects dust in my attic, so maybe someone else can cherish it.

Sometimes it's hard to let go of the past. As I said before, this trunk belonged to my late grandmother. It was passed down to my mother after her death and my Mom rarely talked about her parents when I was growing up. As an adult, I asked her why and she told us about her parents--how her father ended up going blind around his 50's, and died a miserable lonely man. It destroyed their marriage. Dorothy, his wife, my Grandmother, moved in with my parents. During those first few months, Grandma went missing for an entire day--scaring everyone to death. Especially since we had just learned she had dementia. Shortly after that, my Grandfather died. After the funeral, I was left alone with my grandmother for a few minutes. She told me something I remember as clearly as if she were telling me right now.

She said:

"Dorothy, your Grandpa loves you and he is a good man. I saw him before he died. Did you know that? If you check my trunk, you will find our hidden letters. I loved your grandpa and will miss him terribly. Find the letters and show your Mom. Maybe she'll believe me then."

I did ask my Mom if I could look inside the trunk. She said yes and I was surprised to find it was empty. My Mom said that

Grandma told her the same story, after she moved in. *"It's the dementia. But I'm glad it made her happy at least."*

So my dear, the short of it is, I kept my grandmother's trunk, hoping that one day her letters would be found. My Mom said 'it's all in her head', but the way my Grandmother looked and spoke, I know she was completely sane in that moment. But because I was just a child, maybe I wished it to be true.

I hope my story helps answer some of your questions. It's nice to know young people still care about the lives of those who can't tell their story anymore.

Thank-you for your letters. I look forward to seeing those photoshoot pictures.

Sincerely, Dorothy Marie Brookes

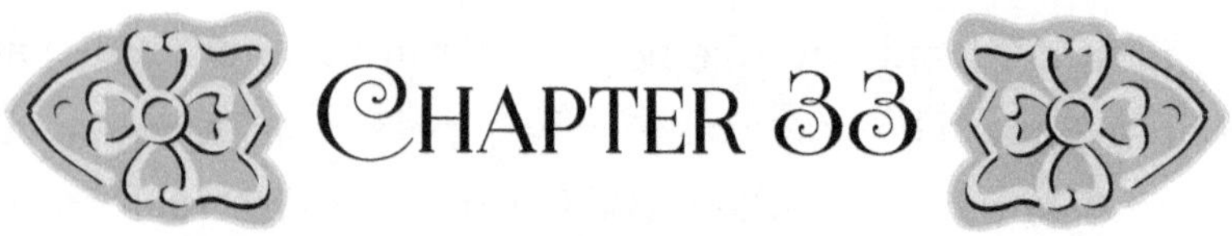

CHAPTER 33

Lily's hands trembled. She could feel Fred reacting to the letter. It felt like a warm fuzzy hug blooming inside her body. As if Fred was saying, this is the missing key. *Find Dorothy's letters.*

"That doesn't help at all, does it?" Mina chucked the plastic water bottle across the room. "The trunk is empty. If Mrs. Brookes doesn't have the letters, then where on earth are we going to find them?" She asked, ignoring her missed target or the bottle rolling across the floor.

Doris retrieved the bottle, tossing it into the trash can, before adding. "Maybe there's a secret compartment? You know, like in the book, 'The Black Townhouse'."

Both of Mina's eyebrows shot up. "You read that book, too? Was that a class assignment or something?"

Doris nodded. "Yep, our entire class already read it. Now we have to either make a speech about it, or hand in a book report. I think I'll do the speech--on hidden compartments. It's been a while since I had to create a poster board for fun. What are you doing for the assignment, Lily?"

Lily didn't answer, she moved to the trunk, her mind focused elsewhere. *Fred. If those letters are the key to releasing you, please tell me where they are? Please, Fred. I can sense your frustration. You know where, don't you, but you can't tell me?* Lily touched the trunk lid, Fred's emotions cartwheeled though her mind--one of the few times Lily knew Fred was happy. She touched another part of the trunk, eliciting the same response. She touched the left side, the top, then the bottom--Fred was sending her the same happy emotions.

Mina interrupted Lily's train of thought."Lily? Are you talking to Fred again?"

Lily snapped, "Shhh!" She frantically waved for Mina to leave her alone. "Yes I am, but you're interrupting makes it hard to focus." *Too late, Fred was gone. Le sighhh.* "Noooo!" Lily stomped her foot. "I was so close!"

Lily looked peeved. "Sorry Lily," Doris reasoned, "we just never know when you zone out, if it's good or bad. Is everything ok?" Lily nodded. "Did you check for any secret compartments yet?"

Lily took a deep breath, reminding herself that they were only looking out for her. She's lucky to have such a great sister and best friend. "Yes I checked, unfortunately I found zip, zilch, nada. I checked everywhere I could think of. I even researched this specific barrel trunk to see if there were any hidden compartments built into them. No such luck." Lily kicked the trash can over. "Those letters have to be somewhere...or maybe they're with the original trunk lid? That's the only reason we can't find it."

"Original? As in there's another trunk somewhere? Oh my gosh, we'll never find them now!" Doris rested her head on her hands. "Why would Dorothy hide the letters in the first place? That's what's bothering me, as if separating them from each other wasn't enough. Did her family keep Fred and Dorothy from even communicating with each other?" Doris thought about that. About how painful that would be for a couple married so long. *How tragic.* She clenched her hands into fists to keep herself from crying.

"It makes sense to me," Mina said, moving to where Lily stood beside the trunk and avoiding Doris' death-glare.

Doris' jaw snapped shut. "Mina! You did not just say that!"

Mina held up a hand, "I meant, just think about how scary the situation was for her family." She sat next to Doris. "The Dad goes blind, and turns into a mean depressed ogre, who no one wants to be around. Then moving the Mom away because he's violent and she has dementia. Next she goes missing and tells them she's been writing to her husband--I'd lose my mind. Her daughter probably thought keeping her Mom away from Fred was best for her safety and health." Mina shrugged before resuming her position next to the trunk. "From the daughter's perspective, discouraging communication between them makes sense."

Doris wanted to argue with Mina, but she had read Fred's

story. He was violent and it was probably best to keep Dorothy away from him. "It's still cold-hearted to not let them even write to one another."

Mina continued while she inspected the outside of the trunk. "It seems that way. But after what Fred said to his family, and how miserable he made everyone, the environment would be very stressful. It scared them to see their Dad become a stranger. He changed from a caring, sweet man to a horribly, miserable person they didn't understand. At that point, the family had to do whatever was best for everyone's safety."

Doris and Lily grimaced as they made eye contact. Mina was on a roll, embedded with the physiological mess surrounding Fred's family. Both of the girls knew they were in for a long Fruedian profile.

"Another thing, if Fred had seen a good therapist, he could've handled his blindness better. The transition would take years of therapy to cope. It's an extremely, emotionally-fragile time in his life. Fred went through so many changes, mostly by himself. Dorothy tried to help, but without professional assistance, even she couldn't handle his drastic changes. I can only imagine how awful those last few weeks must have been."

Lily scoffed, "Fred lived through it, he's not a case in one of your books. You don't know--you can't feel what I *know*."

Mina "You're right Lily, Fred lived it, I didn't. But, you only *know* his side of things, his feelings and his thoughts. You *don't know* the family's or Dorothy's side." Mina tipped the trunk on it's side feeling around. "It's heartbreaking to imagine that Dorothy only dreamed she sent letters to Fred. That would be awful, especially for Fred."

Doris asked. "But what if Dorothy did send them? They have to be somewhere."

Mina waved Doris closer. "They could be right here. Let's take a good look at this trunk, to make sure we haven't missed anything."

The three girls meticulously examined every inch--inside and out.

Doris sat on the floor, tapping carefully against the trunk lid. "Maybe we should ask Mrs. Brookes if they have more of Dorothy's stuff in their attic. She might have misplaced them or couldn't remember where she put them." Doris pointed toward the Shels' attic. "You know, no one ever looks through attic junk."

Lily felt defeated after another fruitless search. "I guess I could ask her. But I'm too tired to send a letter tonight. Let's just get through tomorrow's photoshoot, then I'll send our questions with the pictures. See you tomorrow Doris?" Lily's long day had finally caught up with her. Her eyes felt heavier by the second.

"Yep! I will be here at 8 am sharp. We'll pack up everything and get it done. You still need to ask your Mom for a ride though, so don't forget." Doris could tell Lily was exhausted. If she waited more than 5 more seconds to leave Doris might pass out too. "It's been a long, exhausting day so I'll head home." Standing to stretch quickly, Doris hugged Lily then headed out the door. She stops halfway through the door. "Best friends?" She asked, winking at Lily.

"Yes, best-best friends!" Lily yawned back. Mina followed quietly behind Doris, leaving Lily to sleep.

Alone at last, Lily thought while she drifted toward sleep. *I can't believe I forgot about family movie night. Good night, Fred.*

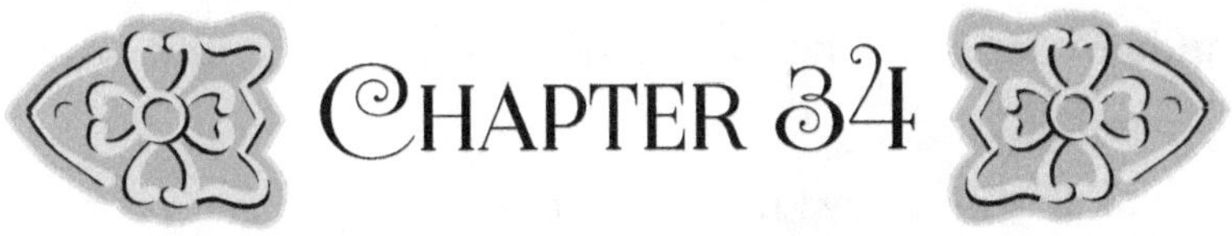

CHAPTER 34

Fred sat in darkness. He could hear movement, the squeaking of hard-sole shoes on the tile floor, someone's clothing, as it brushes against their body. He felt isolated, even surrounded by people. Fred recognized the smell of his new home, disinfectant and desperation. His son, David, brought him to visit this nursing home once, before forcing him away from his family.

A male voice asked, "Mr. Cummens?"

Fred instinctively looked toward the voice, but the stranger was hidden in the darkness. *Will I ever accept, this is my life now?* Until a few weeks ago Fred could pretend he wasn't going blind. Only a few weeks, and it already felt like forever.

The same voice spoke again, "Mr. Cummens, my name is Mat. I will be your nurse while you're here." Matt grabbed Fred's hand, shaking it firmly. "Sir, if you need anything, push this button," Matt moved Fred's hand over the large button, "...or just call out to me."

That was Fred's first memory of Matt. He remembered the hand shake, the first one he had in a while. Matt's voice had sounded young, strong, like how Fred used to sound when he began in banking.

Over the next few hours, Matt stopped by his room only once. He had found Fred stumbling around, looking for the bathroom, instead of asking for help. Matt simply moved him to the bathroom, then had Fred feel around to familiarize himself where everything was. Matt didn't comment or rush before leaving him in privacy.

Matt told him once, that moment was all he needed to know everything about his new patient. That Fred would refuse to call for help, and that he was a stubborn man.

Matt returned to the bathroom and helped Fred back to his chair. "Mr Cummens. Should I call you that or would you prefer Fred?" Fred refused to cooperate or answer the young nurse. "I like using first names, so Fred it is." Matt recognized a difficult patient, so he decided remaining calm and respectful was his best approach.

Weeks later, when Fred still refused to call for help, creating multiple messes in his room, Matt kept his cool with him. Matt checked in on Fred almost every hour from then on. The night shift staff kept a journal, updating Matt when he arrived how Fred did during the night.

Fred overheard the night shift nurse ask Matt, "Why did you accept this job? You witnessed his temper tantrum when they brought him in. Mr. Cummens is the worst patient we've had in years."

Matt's reply shocked Fred. "Thanks Jan." Matt tucked the journal under his arm. "I took this job because--what I saw was a man battling with his condition, who should be taken care of with as much compassion and love as possible. Plus, a good challenge teaches me more."

The other nurse chuckled, "Matt, you're one mixed up kid."

Matt chuckled too, "Yeah, well why did *you* take him on as a patient, if you think *I'm* crazy?"

"Because no one else would take this shift and I can't stand seeing someone in pain, no matter what. Goodnight Matt. Don't forget to add something nice in that journal today."

Fred heard the door latch click as the night nurse left.

That morning Matt pulled out a plastic table and placed a piece of paper and pen on it. "Fred, let's try writing today--a letter." He wrapped Fred's fingers around the pen then moved it over the paper.

Fred yanked his hand away abruptly. "No."

Matt tried pulling Fred's hands back to the paper. "Fred, at least try. I know a way you can learn to read with your hands." Matt had tried to explain how Fred would read letters with his fingers, instead of using his eyes. But Fred jerked his hand back, hitting Matt when he ripped the paper, flinging it across the room.

Matt tried to calm Fred down, gently touching his hand and speaking in a firm calm voice. "Fred, hold still while I grab a paper towel. You cut your hand." As soon as Matt was gone, Fred jumped out of his chair, not seeing the small droplets of blood splattering on the floor behind him.

Fred counted the twelve steps to his bed, but the echoing footsteps were confusing him. *Where was he?* He could feel something wet running down his hand. Fred stumbled, just catching himself when he slipped on the wet floor. The near fall, caused Fred to panic. He threw his arms about wildly, smacking anything within his reach. *Is anyone there? Please, help me, I'm lost and alone.*

"Woah there, Mr Cummens. I'm right here. I just had to grab a paper towel. Here's your chair, just sit down for a minute." Matt guided Fred to the chair. "There we go. Let's take care of this war wound." Matt dabbed a cold towel against Fred's palm.

Matt continued to wipe up the blood. "You cut yourself pretty good, this time." Fred's heart was racing as Matt gently applied pressure to the cut. After making a quick call to a nurse Matt moved Fred into his room for a bandage and disinfectant.

Fred felt a sharp sting, and pulled his hand away. Matt pried his hand open.

"Fred. I have to clean your cut. Don't fight me. Just one more minute and I will be done."

Once finished, Fred examined his bandaged hand with his fingers. He couldn't see it and trying to imagine it was difficult. *Did he remember what white looked like?* Fred tried picturing what a white cloth would look like--the texture, the color, and the overall appearance. With every passing second, Fred's heartbeat sped up, his body began to shake as panic overtook his control. *I don't remember white!*

Fred whispered. "I can't see...*anything.*" As he sat in the chair, gripping his bandaged hand, Matt's familiar hard sole footsteps moved closer.

"What's wrong, Fred?" Matt waited for a response. Surprised when Fred replied.

"What does white look like, I can't remember?" Fred choked on the words, his raw emotions pouring out. "My eyes, I can't see anything. Not even in my head. *What is white?* How can I forget something so easy, so quickly? What does the color white look like?" His hands trembled as he ripped the bandage off.

Footsteps warned Fred to Matt's approach. "Fred. *Fredrick!* FREDRICK DONNIE CUMMENS!"

Fred's mouth hung open. *His full name?*

Matt didn't sound angry, he sounded worried. The bandage dangled from his throbbing hand.

While Matt rebandaged his hand, talking about random things, Fred's anxiety dissipated. He felt safe back in his room. Fred knew he was making the nurses job harder when he acted that way. He couldn't help his reaction. Once the panic began--feeling alone and abandoned--Fred lost control. His body shook uncontrollably, his mind and heart raced like a harem of spooked, wild horses. The frustrating situation always morphed into rage, causing Fred to overreact and irritate those around him. When the trembling began again, his thoughts crashed like waves against the shore. Relentless, without interruption.

"I know they forced you to live here, Fred. But, your stay with us doesn't have to be awful or a tortured experience." When Matt noticed that Fred was sliding into panic again, he grabbed his hand. "Fred, calm down. It's alright." When he felt Fred's body relax he continued. "Sir, I'm going to tell you something--but you have to keep it a secret." Matt rummaged through something on the floor.

Fred turned his head toward the sound. He guessed it to be a cloth bag or pillow case.

"Fred, your wife wanted me to read you a letter. It came in the mail this morning. Do you want to hear it?"

Fred's hand trembled as he reached into the empty space in front of him, until Matt placed the familiarly scented envelope into his hand. Tears trickled down Fred's unshaven cheeks. He squeezed the letter against his heart. After a short pause, clumsily wiping his face and sniffling, he choked out. "Whaaaat, what did she say? What does Dorothy say...to me?"

" I'll just read it to you." Matt patted his hand, extracting the letter from Fred's grip.

Fred let Matt take the letter, then place the empty envelope in his hands. Fred held onto the delicate envelope. *He could still remember the day he bought the stationary set for his lovely wife-- white with purple Lilacs. He did know what white looked like.* Mat read the letter aloud.

My dear Freddy,

I fear the worst has happened, our family has been torn apart. It's my fault, I should take the blame. My dear, I want to take back all the hurtful things I said to you. We were both exhausted and so frustrated with how fast things were changing. We can't control that anymore, and must put out Faith in God. He knows what is best for us. Even when I have so many doubts and concerns.

I am truly sorry, my dear Freddy, for everything. I love you so very much.

Remember God gives us nothing we can't handle.

If you are weary, turn to God.

You are always in my thoughts and prayers. You are the very air I breathe.

Yours truly, now and forever,

your loving wife, Dodo

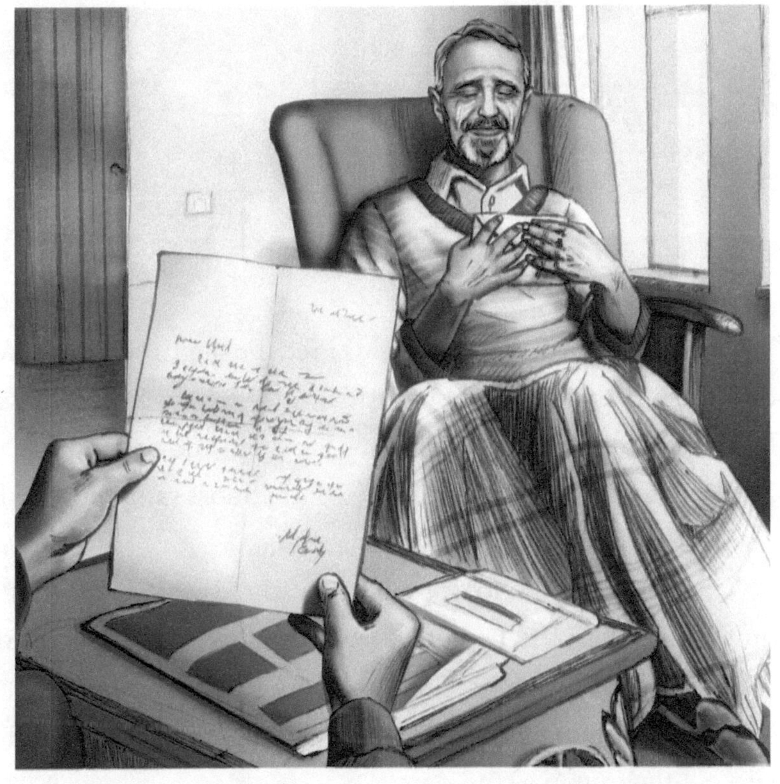

Fred felt a soft handkerchief tucked into his hand.

"Dorothy. Dorothy, my dear Dorothy." Fred sobbed, crushing the envelope in his fist. *She still loves me.* He didn't notice the soft footsteps as Matt left the room.

Chapter 35

Once he felt composed again, Fred pushed the button for the nurses station. It buzzed faintly when he held it down. Seconds later, he heard the familiar footsteps moving closer.

"What can I do for you, Fred?" Matt almost sang the words, he sounded so happy.

"Can you take me to the window?" Fred waited for Matt's arm to guide him the 10 steps to the window seat. He couldn't see the sun, but he could feel it. He couldn't remember what it looked like, but one thing he could remember was its warmth--like a gentle hug on a cold day.

He remembered the first time Matt found him by the window. "Wow, take a look at that gorgeous sky today." The instant the words fell from Matt's lips, he apologized for being inconsiderate. "I am so sorry, Fred. I forgot...I didn't think..."

The apology died away, leaving an awkward silence in its wake.

Today, Fred leaned into the sunshine. He felt the warm rays touch his face and arms. "Matt, is the sun and sky beautiful today?"

"Yes it is, Fred. Would you like me to describe it for you?" Matt opened the window, letting in the warm breeze. Fred nodded in approval, smiling for the first time since he arrived.

Matt described the bright sun, the blue sky and fluffy cotton-ball clouds. As he talked, he placed objects in Fred's hands, allowing him to feel the images he was describing.

"Thank-you. Will you still teach me how to write now? I want to respond to Dorothy's letter." Fred swiped the tears with his sleeve.

"Of course I will, Fred! Here you go." Matt grabbed a pencil.

Fred felt something long and skinny rolling across his palm. Gripping the foriegn object, Fred growled, "I can't write like this, Dorothy won't be able to read it!"

"Sorry, are you right- or left-handed? I knew you would ask, so I've been carrying this stuff in my pockets, until you were ready."

Fred raised his right hand. "They only allowed us to be right-handed, son." Gripping the pencil, he felt the wood press into his skin.

Mat guided Fred's hand's to the paper he had placed on the table. "Feel the paper under your fingers. Can you feel the tiny bumps, they create a straight line. To help keep your writing from going all over the page." Matt waited for Fred to explore the paper. When he didn't, Matt intervened. "Here give me your other hand. Feel the lines with this hand, and write with your dominant hand." Mat helped Fred write his first sentence. Fred pushed Matt's hands away wanting to write on his own. "Well, as I guess, you are one determined, stubborn man." Each time Matt tried to help, Fred swatted Matt's hand away.

Over the next few weeks, Matt filled Fred's days with reading and writing lessons. He taught Fred about the braille books that they used for their lessons.

§

Two weeks later, Fred overheard Jan and Matt as they switched shifts.

"Hey Mat, are you finally leaving for the night?" Jan asked, as she knocked on the door to Fred's room, ready to take over for the night.

Matt replied. "I will, in a few minutes. I have something I need to do first." Fred had finished another letter to Dorothy, that Matt said he would mail out as soon as possible. Matt sealed the envelope and tucked it into his pocket before heading out the door.

Dorothy's letters were coming weekly. Matt and Fred both noticed her letters had become shorter, and less coherent. Almost as if Dorothy forgot what she was writing about. In the last two, she wrote that she was not allowed to visit Fred, because she was sick— even though she assured him she was fine. Dorothy didn't understand their children's reasoning for keeping them apart. But, since she couldn't drive herself, her only option was to write to Fred.

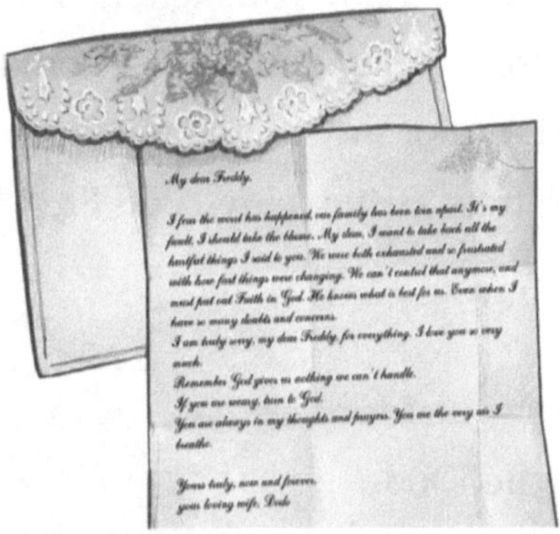

The more Fred read, the more he worried. *Was Dorothy alright? Was she really sick and just trying to put on a brave face for him?* After the apology in her first letter, Dorothy signed the rest, *I love you Freddy,* and *I miss your laugh,* in her swirly handwriting. Even though Fred's concern for his wife's health grew with each letter, he still looked forward to each one.

On Monday mornings, Matt would arrive with Fred's breakfast tray. As Fred enjoyed his breakfast, Matt would read Dorothy's latest letter. Each time one of her letters were opened, Dorothy's perfume would fill the room. Fred inhaled the familiar scent, able to relax as though his wife was near.

Matt commented that his sister also scented her letters. But he liked Dorothy's perfume better.

My dear Freddy,

I received distressing news this weekend. Louise wants me to go to the Coast for a month or two--to visit her in-laws. I asked to stay here, but she insisted I go. So my dear Freddy, I will be gone for a few weeks. But, I will continue to write every week, my love. I have felt slightly under the weather lately. Even so, I want to stay close to you so you won't feel alone, even if they refuse to let me visit. Your letters are the only secrets I am allowed to keep from my family. You could always draw the mischievous spirit out of me. I hope you are smiling more, like I am when your letters arrive. I love you Freddy, and miss your laugh.

God bless.

Yours truly, now and forever

Your loving wife, Dodo

Fred stopped eating when Matt finished the letter.

"Dorothy is going away? My Dorothy is leaving me?" Fred's voice broke. The joy evaporated from his face, replaced with a mixture of hurt and betrayal. His eyebrows furrowed, as he clenched and unclenched the spoon in his hand. "I'm losing my Dorothy all over again." Fred cried, slamming his fists against the breakfast tray. The half-eaten bowl of oatmeal crashed to the floor. Ripping the blanket away from his legs, Fred slid to the edge, standing up quickly.

"Fred, no, don't, the oatmeal!" Matt tried catching Fred before he fell and missed.

Fred felt the warm oatmeal squish under his foot too late to avoid disaster. He slipped as Matt tried to grab his arm. Fred's momentum pulled them both down in a heap. Followed by a sickening snap and a horrific yell that echoed down the hall. Intense pain engulfed his entire body.

"Nurse! Nurse, call a doctor, immediately!" Matt yelled.

Fred writhed in pain, Matt holding him down as best he could. *Something had broken, but what?* Fred had never felt pain that intense.

§

After a trip to the emergency room, Fred returned to the home.

"Well Fred, the good news is you only fractured your left wrist. The bad news is, I'll be writing your letters for you for a while. Not too bad as a compromise." Matt's short laugh died quickly.

After Fred's wrist was wrapped in a splint, he fell further into melancholy. The last letter from Dorothy had frightened Fred immensely. *I will never see Dorothy again.* Fred's stomach lurched when he realized he would never see his Dorothy again--even if she was here right now. He could touch, smell and hear her, but never see her beautiful face again. *Dorothy, my darling. Can we meet before you leave? I'll ask Matt to add that to my letter.* Fred couldn't believe he was losing his wife.

"Fred, What do you want to write about today?" It had been two days since Dorothy's last letter and Fred hadn't spoken since. Matt asked the same questions every day, trying to get Fred to answer him. Fred had overheard Matt talking about his meeting with the Supervisor. Matt didn't notice Fred listening the night before. Matt had waited until the shift change to talk to Jan about it.

"How did your meeting go, Matt?" Jan asked, barely loud enough for Fred to hear.

Matt answered, "It didn't go so well. They refused to let me take Fred to see Dorothy, because they have complicated medical issues. Their children think they are both a danger to themselves and others, keeping them away from each other seems best."

Matt sighed. "I don't know Jan, I've nagged the Supervisor to death, trying to convince him to let me take him. Just 30 minutes together could make the difference for them both."

"I'm sorry to hear that, Matt. Maybe you should accept it. The Supervisor can't overrule the legal guardians. It's just not going to happen." Jan replied.

" *Too much of a danger to themselves and each other!* That's what they said, but he's been so much better since he started getting her letters.But they don't know that, because **they don't want to know.**" Fred could hear Matt wadding paper. "Separating a married couple for the rest of their lives because the kids don't like their dad, is not a good enough reason. Dorothy loves Fred. Have you read any of their letters to each other? They need each other, are the reason they both keep fighting--why would you keep them apart."

"Matt, I'm sorry but their kids made their decision, and we cannot change that. It's just not possible." Fred heard footsteps fading down the hall. Matt had left.

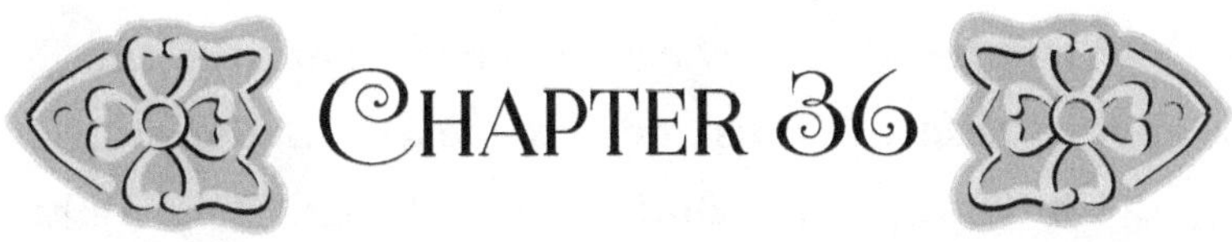

CHAPTER 36

Saturday morning at the Shels house was chaotic. The family van was packed for Lily's photoshoot, plus Max and Theo's morning soccer games.

"Did you grab the last bag, Doris?" Lily yelled as she descended the stairs. Doris confirmed they had everything, and the girls headed out to the van.

"You have everything, right?" Mrs. Shels asked. Lily and Doris followed the boys into the van.

"Yep, we are ready. Let's go!" Lily felt better after a good night's sleep. Fred was still with her, he even seemed happy today. She hoped that was a good omen, and she would finish his story soon. *The answer is near, I can feel it!*

A short time later, Mrs. Shels parked the van next to the garden. The girls quickly unpacked before waving goodbye to Mrs. Shels. Lily led the way to the area of the park she had selected for the photoshoot. When she described it to Doris, they agreed the brown tones of the trunk would look awesome surrounded by green plants and bushes.

Doris emptied the many bags and boxes onto a bench. "Man, this spot is perfect!" Doris and Lily looked up, the sun shined brightly through passing fluffy, white clouds. They could not have asked for better weather. There was a slight, cool breeze passing through, giving the girls a break from the heat.

Lily pulled the wagon that held the trunk closer to the bushes. "Let's set up the trunk here. Drape the blanket over one side." Carefully, the girls assembled the trunk, trying not to scrape the pieces together. Lily pushed on the lid, making sure it was steady. "Ok, looks like everything is ready." Kneeling beside the trunk, Lily whispered. "Fred, I hope we can complete your story today. So help me out a little here, ok?"

Doris moved away from the trunk. "It looks great Lily!" She had the large camera, ready to start snapping pictures. She held the camera up, moving back again, trying to capture the entire scene. The trunk, the brown and gold blanket with tassels, draped halfway across the trunk, and Lily in her yellow, retro dress with a green detailed sweater. Lily's hat was slightly crooked, allowing her face to peek out from underneath the hat's brim.

Lily perched on the edge of the trunk, posing until Doris gave her the cue to change positions. Lily moved to the middle of the trunk, this time holding her hat, and allowing her beautiful black curls to catch the sunlight.

"That's it! Ok, now look down with your eyes, and keep your face forward." *Click click click!* The camera snapped another picture. "I'm so glad your Mom let us borrow the professional camera, Lily. These look like great, quality pictures."

After a few more pictures, Lily switched with Dors. "Ok, Doris, move to the left, yeah look up toward the sky and hold your hat blocking the sun, then lean back. *Be careful, don't lean too far.*" Doris wore her favorite, white, summer dress paired with a straw hat. Pink flowers embroidered the edge of the dress. *What do you think, Fred? Ever imagine something like this? Two gorgeous girls hanging out with your old trunk.* Lily felt a sudden jolt bounce through her body. *Guess not.*

Forty-five minutes later the girls were ready to wrap up their photoshoot and go home.

Doris scrolled through their pictures. "Wow! We're already over a thousand pictures, Lily."

"Just a few more with me. I want to try that same pose on the trunk, again. But this time, let's do something a little different." Lily moved to the middle of the trunk, holding her hat like Doris, she posed.

Doris directed Lily. "Alright! Now face the other direction and do the same pose." *Click click click click.* "PERFECT!" A gust of wind caught Lily's hat, yanking it out of her hand. Doris captured the moment with a quick snap.

"That one will be our best one of them all." Doris ran to show Lily the image, retrieving her hat along the way.

Both girls laughed at Lily's surprised expression, then decided to take a short break. After the emotional day on Friday,

Lily and Doris were glad all their secrets were out and they could get back to their normal friendship. They always had fun together on these photoshoots.

Lily checked her phone while they relaxed on the ground. "Mom says, the boys game is over in about 15 minutes, so we can chill until they arrive."

They were warned waiting was a possibility, so Lily prepared for the extra downtime. Reaching into her purse, Lily retrieved two king-sized candy bars. "Which one do you want? Peanut butter and chocolate or Peanuts with caramel?" Grinning, she waved them in front of Doris' face.

Doris clapped, replying in a sing-song voice. "*Candy bars! King-Sized Candy bars! Give me the peanut butter and chocolate, please!*"

Of course, Lily knew Doris wanted that one. She had bought it specifically for her. After the emotional rollercoaster the other day, Lily thought candy bars would be a good peace offering. Lily handed the peanut butter one to Doris.

Lily moved over to the trunk, striking a pose while she held the candy bar. Smiling while she displayed it, like she was filming a commercial. Lily was so caught up in pretending, she leaned too far back on the trunk. One moment she was acting then she heard an ominous crunching sound. The next instant, Lily was falling backward, her dress flying over her head revealing her large white petticoat.

CANDY

Doris could only laugh--hysterically. She walked over, still trying to catch her breath.

"Are you ok, Lily?" Doris tried to hold in her laughter, but failed. Falling to the ground beside Lily, the two girls cackled until their sides ached.

Doris fanned her face, trying to catch her breath. "That fall was epic! All I saw was a blur of white petticoat, a flying candy bar, then you in a heap."

"Please tell me you did not take a picture of that? I'm ok, physically, nothing is broken. I'm not sure if my dignity will ever recover." Rolling over to her side she got on her knees. "You don't think anyone else saw that, do you?" Lily looked around, horrified. "Oh my Gosh! What if a video gets posted? I'll never be able to show my face at the St. Catherine High school again!"

Doris wrapped her arm around Lily's shoulder. "Don't be so dramatic! It wasn't that bad."

"Easy for you to say. It wasn't your undies flashing in a park full of children." Lily dropped her face into her hand, moaning. "Will you defend me when the stroller-moms attack? We might get a few modesty lectures today."

"No way, you're on your own if that happens. Those ladies hold real power and can lecture for hours!" Doris backed away, waving her hands in front of her. "I really don't think that would ever happen, though. I'm sure they have all had their dress flying moments too. Any dress or skirt wearing girl has. It goes with the territory, especially in a windy state like ours. You're overreacting, like normal. Let's go check the trunk."

Lily groaned when she saw the small dent in the trunk lid.

"That's not too bad, maybe we can just push it back out? Dang it. I was hoping to avoid any damage. Me and my big butt."

Doris joined her, flipping open the lid to assess the damage.

Lily grimaced seeing a large crack running across the inside lid. "Shoot. I broke it and tore the lining. See right here, where the satin is pulled away from the corner?" Lily felt along the edge where the lining had separated from the curving lid. Feeling between the lining and the wood, her fingers caught on something else. "What's that? It feels like paper. How did paper get stuck in there?" Lily tugged on the paper to see what it was. "It's an envelope." Lily and Doris gasped at the same time. "A secret letter!"

Doris helped cautiously pull the lining so Lily could extract the envelope. When the opening was big enough, Lily carefully pulled out a thick stack of envelopes. *Letters? Addressed to Fred?* Lily reverently held a pile of letters addressed to Fredrick Cummens, c/o Valley Hills Care Home. Tears streamed down Lily's cheeks.

"Are those what I think they are, Lily?"

"Yes! They're Dorothy's letters, and they were here the entire time. All of Fred's and Dorothy's love letters were right here! I'm so happy, these letters are why Fred's spirit is attached to Dorothy's trunk!" Lily lightly hugged the letters to her chest, not caring if anyone saw her bawling her eyes out.

Doris gave Lily a moment, knowing this was a big moment for Fred and Lily. "Does that mean you can finish Fred's story?"

Sniffing loudly, Lily delicately counted the letters. "One, two, three...*ten*. There are ten letters. Just look at them!" She gingerly fanned the envelopes onto the blanket.

Doris looked at the fragile letters, slowly picking up one before asking again. "So, is Fred free now? You found the missing piece, does he just move on when that happens?"

Lily picked up the letter with the oldest date. "No, Fred's still here. I think once I read these letters, or return them to Mrs. Brookes, then Fred will be released from Dorothy's trunk. At least that's how it's always worked before."

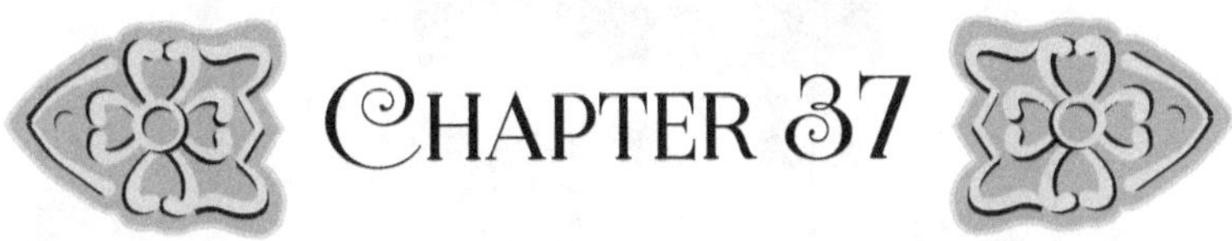

CHAPTER 37

Doris noticed a few of the envelopes showed worn and frayed edges. "Be careful, look how old they are. Oh my gosh, smell this one! It's scented with perfume." She sniffed one letter. "They smell like lilacs. How romantic! She spritzed his letters with her perfume." Doris sighed, imagining how dreamy, adding perfume to letters for the love of your life.

The girls sat on the blanket, reading one letter after another. Carefully opening the tattered envelope, then pulling out the faded letter inside to read it.

"This is like our own personal romance movie." Doris said.

"I don't know, at first I was excited. But with Fred reading over my shoulder, it feels like we are intruding into a private conversation." Lily grabbed Doris' arm, squeezing lightly. "Doris! Look at this one. A third person is mentioned here. His name is Matthew." Lily read on:

Dear Mrs. Cummens.

My name is Matthew, I am your husband's caretaker at the Valley Hills Care Home. *Fred has been a little under the weather since your last correspondence. He fell, breaking his left wrist. Since then, Fred stopped talking, and we are concerned that his depression is hindering his recovery.*

I have tried to arrange a visit for you to see your husband, before your trip. If you can meet us for an hour, I can pick you up from your home and allow you and Fred to talk in private. This arrangement must be kept absolutely secret.

Sincerely, Matt Geno

Doris broke the silence that followed. "I have a bad feeling about this...*what if they get caught?*" Folding the letter into the envelope, careful not to mangle the corners.

Lily looked through the remaining envelopes, scanning for

Dorothy's response. "I think this is the next one. It's from Fred's wife to Matthew." Lily read aloud.

Hello Matthew,

Your secret plan is safe with me. I must see my Freddy before I leave. I only have a few days until then, so we must act quickly.

Thankfully, I've become more clever in my old age. I can easily sneak out for an hour or two, while the children are out. The nurse that comes to check on me, leaves for a two-hour break at 1pm. I am supposed to be napping, but I will be waiting outside by 1:05pm tomorrow. I will wait for you at the corner near the bus stop. We need a code name. When you pick me up, call me Dodo.

Thank you for your assistance, Matthew. I cannot express my gratitude for helping us. I know you are risking more than just your job.

God bless you, Matthew

Sincerely, Dorothy Cummens

"Where's the next letter!" Doris impatiently flipped through the letters, ready to hear the rest.

Lily found the next one in order. "Ok, ok, here we go." Opening the letter, she cleared her throat before reading. "This one is from Dorothy to Matthew."

"Dear Matthew,"

"Wait!" Doris scattered the envelopes, rechecking the dates. "Where's the response from Matt? Did he pick her up? Did Fred and Dorothy get to see each other one last time?" Grabbing Lily's sleeve, pleading. *"Please tell me there is a happy ending!"*

"Would you just chill! You say I'm dramatic. This is the next letter, from Dorothy. So shhh!" Lily resumed reading:

Dear Matthew,

Thank you for granting my final wish--to see my Freddy one last time. I received word of his death, shortly after we arrived on the coast. Due to my health declining, I will not be able to return for the funeral.

I cannot express the depth of my sincere gratitude for helping us meet one last time. My heart can now rest easy, knowing my Freddy and I spent that final hour together before he left this world. I shall miss him dearly, and my heart aches that I will miss the service. I thank the good Lord, that you came into our lives when we needed you. You are truly a blessing.

God bless you.

Thank you again,

Sincerely, Dorothy Cummens

"They did it! Fred and Dorothy met one last time. I'm so happy!" Doris wiggled with excitement, squealing so loud Lily covered her ears. Her enthusiasm died immediately at Lily's frown. "Lily? What's wrong? They made it--they died *happy*. Why do you look so upset?" Doris moved closer, waiting for her to respond.

"You don't understand. Fred just realized he is actually *dead*. For some reason he thought, even though he is a spirit, he wasn't *actually* dead." Lily rubbed her forehead. "I don't know how to explain it, but he's just now mourning his death, or something. After I read that last letter, he remembered and finally understood that he was dead...and that Dorothy died, too. The letter, from Dorothy, finally convinced him. Now I get a weird, morbid feeling from Fred." Lily stopped talking, feeling the pain inside her chest expand. Fred's emotions swirled, a heavy weight filled with overwhelming anxiety. Realizing for the first time that he died over 50 years ago." Lily shuddered. "That's frustrating, but repressed anger has clouded Fred's good memories."

Doris sighed dramatically. "Yeah, I don't get that. Why would Fred mourn his own death? Why not focus on the last happy memory with Dorothy before he died? That's what I would tell Fred to concentrate on--their everlasting love."

Lily couldn't help but scoff. She knew Doris wouldn't understand, but she tried explaining anyway. "It's not that easy. Fred is a 50-plus-year-old spirit. He's been trapped by this bundle of letters and he didn't know why? This last letter from Dorothy made him realize he is dead. But now what? Both of us thought this would be the answer, yet *he's still here*. Now, I have to figure out what's still keeping him here!" Fred's emotions tumbled around Lily's head. Frustration arcing between them. *The letters were supposed to end his spirit time, but Fred hasn't moved on. Why?* Lily blinked back tears of irritation, frustration, and exhaustion.

"Hey." Doris nudged Lily with her elbow."There's one more letter. It's addressed to the *Cummens Family* from the old folks home. Maybe it's Matt." Doris looked up at a loud *honk*.

Lily looked up, too. "Shoot, we can't read it right now, Mom just pulled up." Lily gently tucked the bundle of letters inside Dori's large purse. "Be careful with your purse, don't crush the letters inside."

"Ok, I won't. Let's get packed up." Doris slid the strap over her shoulder, then folded the blanket. Theo and Max ran over, helping the girls pack up. Once everything was back in the van, Lily and Doris buckled their seatbelts.

"How did your photoshoot go, girls?" Mrs. Shels asked them on the drive home.

"It was AMAZING!" Lily giggled as she winked at Doris.

Doris laughed nervously. Lily's acting was flawless. Lily was depressed and sad just a few minutes ago, but now she was laughing as if nothing happened. "Yeah, Mrs. Shels, Lily *fell off the trunk*, it was epic!" Doris remembered the fall and couldn't hold in her hysterical laughter.

"Did you catch that epic fall, Doris?" Mrs. Shels looked at the girls through the rearview mirror. "I would pay money to see that."

Doris regretfully sighed. "No, it's only in my memories."

"Well darn, I could have shared that on all the Christmas cards." Mrs. Shels winked at Doris, chuckling.

Lily's laughter died, before she spoke up. "Mom! Don't you dare. I delete every picture before I let you do that." Lily folded her arms over her chest with a pout. "Speaking of pictures, I wanted to ask Dad if he could take the pictures to be printed, on his way to work Monday. Unless...you are going shopping tomorrow?" Lily thought about it and decided she had one more idea to solve Fred's problem. She was going to give everything--the trunk, the letters, and the pictures--back to the Brookes. Maybe then Fred would be free to move on. Mom interrupted her thoughts.

"Sorry Lily, You will have to wait until Monday." Mrs. Shels replied. "And you know I don't do any shopping on Sunday."

Lily didn't care if she had to wait a day or two. Her newest plan was the last chance to help Fred, and if it didn't work out, then a few extra days wouldn't matter. *Hang in there, Fred. I have a plan. Maybe your wife isn't the only one you need to mend fences with? Your entire family was involved in that time of your life. I'm not sure if they're holding you here, but I will fix this for you, Fred. Hang on a little longer.* Lily rubbed her temples hard. *Dear God, please help this to be the answer I've been waiting…that Fred's been waiting for. Please!*

Fred's answer was filled with frustration. *I should be with Dorothy already!*

Now that Fred was aware of his death, he drifted between anger, frustration, and depression. A moan slipped from Lily. The situation should have been solved hours ago, but once again Lily was stuck between Fred's rising anger and a permanent solution.

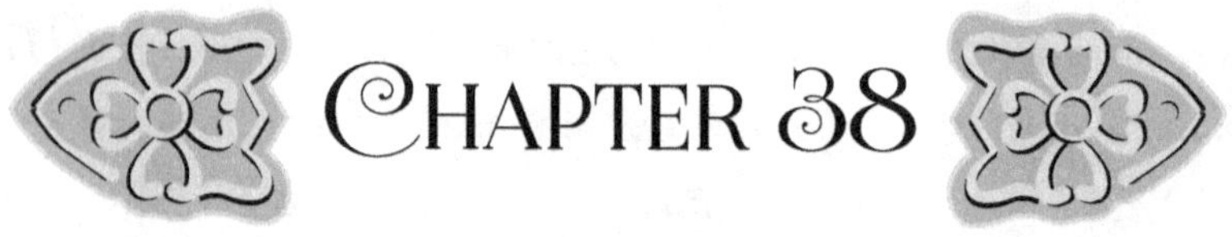# Chapter 38

Once the van pulled into the Shels' driveway, the kids unpacked quickly. Theo and Max rushed off to play video games, while Lily and Doris disappeared into Lily's bedroom. The girls waited impatiently for Mina to get home, so they could show her the letters. They spent the time plotting how they would tell Mina about everything they learned.

§

Mina was halfway through the front door when she stopped abruptly. Doris and Lily stood with their arms outstretched, blocking any other path except the stairs. "Ummm. Can I help you?" Mina grimaced, glancing at both girls while closing the door.

Lily grabbed Mina's bookbag from her shoulder. "It's about time. We need to talk." Doris swiftly looped her arm through Mina's, pushing her up the stairs.

"Woah, wait a minute." Mina tried to pull free from Doris. "I'd like to grab some food and recharge with some mindless tv, before the spirit-talk, please." The girls shared an intense glance at her request. Mina reconsidered and gave in, this was more serious than she thought. The girls led MIna up to Lily's room.

Doris pulled Mina to her normal spot, while Lily grabbed the letters, hiding them behind her back. Purposely blanking their expressions, Lily and Doris boxed Mina against the desk.

Mina glanced between Lily and Doris. "Ok, I'm assuming either something has gone horribly wrong with Fred, or you two are pulling my leg and nothing's wrong."

Doris broke first. Unable to hide her wide grin or snicker. "I can't, I can't." Doris waved her hands in front of her. "Lily, we have to tell her!"

Before Mina could ask, Lily rolled her eyes, glaring at Doris. "See, I knew you would break first. You need to work on your acting, Doris." Lily grinned as she pulled the letters out from behind her back. "We found them, Mina. Fred and Dorothy's love letters!" Lily danced around the room, holding the letters above her head like a trophy she had just won. "We found them! We found all of Dorothy's letters." Both girls burst into a giggling fit, when Mina's face lit with a huge grin.

"You found the letters? Quit hogging them, already." Mina missed when she tried to grab for the letters in Lily's hand.

Lily held the letters higher, out of Mina's reach. "Hey, watch it. These letters are very delicate-- you have to be careful." Lily lectured her sister, before gently placing the letters in Mina's outstretched hand.

"*Woah*--I can smell her perfume. Holy smokes, these letters were well preserved. I can't believe her perfume still smells so strong." With nimble fingers, Mina opened them one at a time. "So Lily, this means Fred is free and you can go back to acting normal again--or as normal as you get. I bet that feels amazing?" Lily's grin disappeared. "Wait, he did leave, didn't he? I thought the letters were the key you were missing to free Fred? What happened?"

Lily pushed the rest of the letters toward Mina. "First read all the letters. There's someone important you need to meet. Once you read through the letters, we'll explain everything."

A few silent minutes passed while Mina read each letter. After she folded the last letter, Lily quickly explained how they found the letters.

Doris jumped in, cutting Lily off. She was skipping the best part--*Lily's epic fall*. "You should have been there, Mina. Lily wiped out. Falling right off the trunk. Her petticoat was all you could see except the trunk. *It was epic!*"

Laughter filled the room when Doris recalled Lily's dramatic fall in great detail. Lily tried hiding her flaming, red cheeks behind her pillow.

Daring anyone to laugh again, Lily finished relating the rest of their morning's discovery.

Mina released a long, tired sigh, finally relaxing into the chair. "Ahh, that is a wholesome reminder, that even when all hope seems lost, you can still make things right. Matthew saved Fred and Dorothy--saved them from dying with regret and anger. And might I add, Dorothy prayed for him. Maybe her prayers are what brought Fred's spirit to you to free Lily."

Doris flopped on the bed throwing her hands up toward the ceiling. "Isn't it romantic? Fred and Dorothy were going to be separated forever, then this knight-in-shining-armor came to their rescue. Love prevails once again." Doris' face took on a dreamy look, as she imagined their heart-wrenching final scene.

Mina interrupted Doris' happy thoughts. "You know what I want to know now? I mean, besides why is Fred still here?" The girls turned to Mina. "What happened to Matt? There's no way he was allowed to do what he did. Someone must have found out eventually. Did he lose his job? He did go against the family wishes, so I'll bet they would press charges for what he did."

Doris jolted upright, her eyebrows veed so deep, they almost touched. "What do you mean? Even if someone found out, why would they snitch on him? Matt made the right choice. Helping reunite two lovers before they died. Why would anyone hate on Matt for that? That's just wrong, in my opinion." Doris huffed, daring anybody to argue with her.

Mina stretched as she explained. "There are several reasons someone should report Matt's disobedience to his supervisor. If..." Mina held up her index finger. "...they did. Let's see, first Matt was Fred's nurse and worked for the home. If his supervisor found out he went against a family's wishes, the home itself could be sued. Resulting in charges, with Matt being fired as part of the settlement."

Lily thought before responding. "I didn't think about it like that. Matt might have gotten fired for helping Fred and Dorothy. Court fines or getting fired, that's not so romantic."

"Are you nuts?" Doris yelled, bouncing to her feet on the bed. With one hand on her hip, Doris argued, pointing at Lily. "That makes it even more romantic! Matt believed in their love! He risked his job and his freedom to help bring them together, one last time. Matt showed the world that love is more important than rules. True love prevails every time!"

"Someone's been watching way too many princess movies." Mina chuckled. "Although, I guess that's not such a bad thing."

Doris flopped back down next to Lily. "Hey, don't mock the power of love, Mina. Just because you've turned into a grumpy adult."

"Oh, have I got news for you. Out of all my grumpy adult friends, I am the fun one. So there. I'm not grumpy." Mina stuck her tongue out at Doris, who immediately returned the favor.

Lily chuckled. "She's not lying, Doris. Mina is the fun one... that's why she brought *chips*!" Lily pounced on Mina's bookbag pulling out the brand new bag of chips. She gave Mina her best anime-eye, pouting 'please'.

Mina was immune to Lily's charm, yanking the chips from her grip. "Girls, repeat after me, Mina is the best and most funnest adult ever." Both girls raised their left hand and repeated Mina's mantra. "Now, remember that." Mina opened the bag and removed a handful of chips for herself before passing the bag to Lily and Doris.

After finishing her snack, Lily spoke. " Another way Matt

could have gotten into trouble, now that I think about it, was taking Fred out in public. Fred was a bitter man when he arrived at the home. If Matt had been wrong about Fred, something much worse could have happened. It's possible Fred would attack Dorothy or even Matt. I mean, people lie and trick you into believing they have changed all the time. Sometimes, you think you know someone, but they are deceiving you the entire time. I'm glad that didn't happen but how could Matt take such a huge risk?"

Mina studied her sister. "You're right. That could have easily happened. Matt's decision could have gone south in a second, leaving Dorothy and Matt vulnerable if Fred turned violent and attacked them."

Doris sighed dramatically, drawing Lily and Mina's attention. "Man, can you both just stop. Stop killing all my joy? Yes, that *could* have happened, but it didn't. At least not according to the letters. The worst that is possible was Matt lost his job." Doris pointed out. "Lily. You better be careful--you're turning into a grumpy adult, too."

Lily tapped the chip against her lips. "No I'm not grumpy, I'm realistic. Fred was violent. What if he became violent while they were meeting? Matt wouldn't have been prepared for it. That's what I'm pointing out. Matt's plan turned out ok, thankfully, granting Dorothy's last wish. But, there are always consequences. That's all I'm saying."

"Ok, fair enough, but things turned out perfectly for Fred and Dorothy. So, let's not focus on the possible bad endings that never happened. Just live in the moment! Things worked out for the best and they were happy at the end." Doris argued.

"You're right. Matt chose to help them and things ended well. They loved each other until the very end." Mina straightened the pile of letters, as Doris wove her own version of Fred and Dorothy's love story. Mina wondered if she would make the same choice Matt did to help Fred and Dorothy. Especially if her job was at stake. She opened the top letter, re-reading it.

Dear Mrs. Cummens and Family,

I am sorry to inform you that your husband, Fredrick Cummens, passed away this morning, around 5am.

We found these letters, along with strict orders, to forward them to you.

The night-shift nurse wanted to relay Fredrick's last words.

"Tell Dorothy that I love her. Tell my children that I am sorry for everything and I love them."

We have enclosed all necessary paperwork with this letter.

Our deepest sympathy and prayers for you and the entire Cummens family.

Sincerely,

Howard Clinn, Supervisor

Valley Hills Care Home

Mina raised the letter to her nose, smelling the lilac scent, still faintly clinging to it. *Without Matt, none of these letters would exist. He did make the right choice. I wonder what happened to him after that day?* Mina wrote the question on a sticky note:

Matthew Geno, what happened to him?

After tucking the note into her book bag, Mina joined the girls' animated conversation, which lasted until Doris went home.

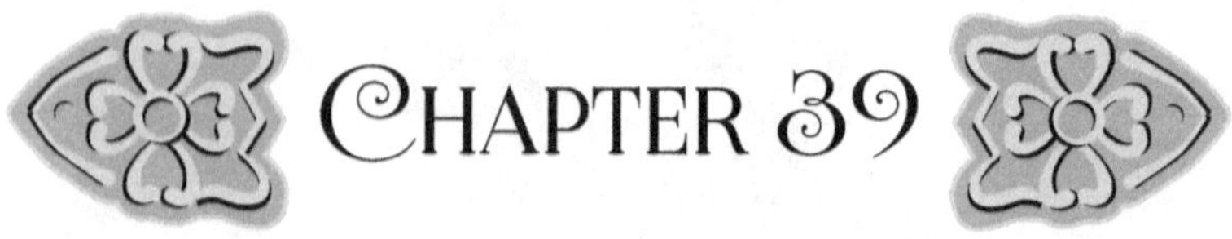

Chapter 39

Sunday, after the 11 o'clock mass, Lily mapped out a plan to free Fred. She felt like returning everything was all that was left for her to try.

Take all of Fred and Dorothy's things back to the Cummens.

Let them read everything.

Hopefully that will free Fred.

Monday was coming sooner than she realized, while Sunday flew by.

Lily took a sip of water. "Fred, I know you're frustrated, but please keep the headache-inducing drama to yourself...it would be nice to enjoy the rest of my weekend, headache-free." Lily had been planning how to approach Mrs. Brookes for a few hours now. Packing up her book bag, Lily grabbed her memory-collecting kit, then headed outside for the rest of her Sunday.

Monday morning seemed to ride the slow motion train the second Lily sat down in her Math class. She watched the clock, praying the time would move faster. Lily glanced over her shoulder toward Doris, who was busy, adding hearts in her notebook. Each heart had the initials 'D+D' in the middle.

The clock had barely moved one minute. Lily signed, catching the teacher's attention. They shared eye contact, while Lily pretended she was writing down the Math problem. Looking back at the clock, only two more minutes had passed. Lily wanted to scream in frustration..

By ten o'clock, Lily's notebook was full of scribbles, while her eraser tips were mangled with teeth marks. She made a note to ask Doris for her notes, since Lily wasn't paying attention.

What if my plan to free Fred doesn't work? What if I am stuck with Fred?

Fred, is there anything else you can tell me about that trunk, or the letters?

Lily was glad Fred was calm today. She felt his frustration flare only slightly since last night. Just like on Saturday, he seemed calmer when Lily was figuring out how to free him or writing his story.

Lily groaned, flattening against her desk during a 5-minute class change. "It's only 10:45 in the morning...today is taking for flippin ever."

Doris patted Lily's head softly. "Were you able to convince your Dad to get your pictures printed?"

Lily mumbled around her face pressed against the desktop. "Yep, it took some begging, but he said he would stop and get them printed today."

Doris poked Lily's side. "Thank goodness. I'm dying to hear what Mrs. Brookes thinks. Are you sure you can't stick around to find out? Speaking of, how is Fred today?"

Lily lazily pushed away Doris' hand. "He's doing surprisingly well. Yesterday, he gave me a lovely headache, but today he's playing nice and has calmed down. Almost like he is really looking forward to my visit with his granddaughter."

Doris smiled. "Good, I hope this works for both of you. You need a break from all these spirits hijacking your life, plus Fred needs to be free and move on." Each girl nodded their agreement. Doris slid back to her chair when the bell rang.

§

The minute the lunch bell rang, Lily grabbed Doris, and ran outside to eat their lunch on the grassy hill.

Doris opened her lunch box, disappointed to see a green mixed salad, once again. "So, explain to me, how do you know when a spirit has left? Like, moved on, for good. Do all of the spirits literally wait until the very end? After all your attempts to solve their story, before leaving?" She stabbed one cherry tomato with her fork.

Lily chuckled at Doris' expression of disgust as she ate the tomato. "You know, if you broil those, with salt and pepper, and throw some mozzarella cheese on top, they taste much better."

Doris chewed quickly, washing the awful taste down with tea. "Yeah, this salad is my punishment for asking Mom to help me eat healthier. I kinda meant it as a joke, but Mom being the supportive person she is, took it to heart, and it's been salads, salads, salads for weeks now...if I tell her I think I'm healthy enough, do you think she will make sandwiches again?" Doris picked dejectedly through the wilted salad. "Didn't that magazine have some healthy lunch ideas or something?"

Lily giggled. "I think it did. We should re-read the magazine again. Now that I will hopefully have more time to focus on other stuff here soon. Good luck with your mom making you sandwiches again. You gave up all claim to the lovely white bread when you invoked 'healthier' with an adult. Mmmm, this grilled ham and cheese sandwich is so yummy. What's that? Extra cheese and mayo? Yes, please." Lily bit her sandwich while Doris shot death glares her way. "Well, anywho, back to your spirit inquiry. I really can't describe it, but when the spirit is ready to move on I can sense their feeling of peace. Once I get that peaceful vibe, the spirit just disappears. Usually, that comes right after I write their entire story. Just like how a movie ends, with 'the end', my spirits leave when I reach 'The end'." Lily handed Doris half of her sandwich. "You can give me a kidney later."

Doris fiddled with her salad again. Shaking her head. "I can do this. It's only grass and veggies." She spiked another tomato. Taking a bite she chewed three times then spat it out in her napkin. "I lied...this is so gross..." Lily nudged the sandwich closer to Doris. "...organ donation it is." Doris grabbed the sandwich, chopping into it. "Thanks. Oh yummy bread, I've missed you."

Lily grabbed a few spinach leaves from Doris' salad, tucking them between her ham and cheese. "So what's with the healthy kick? I mean, good for you and all that, but I know there's something else going on, too." Lily added, nudging Doris.

Doris took a smaller bite, replying slowly. "Because...I saw Derek with this cute, skinny girl yesterday." Doris thought back on what should have been a happy moment for her. "There I was, wearing my soccer tee shirt, cheering on my brother. Looking cute and sporty for Derek. Then after the game, I saw Derek and went over to talk to him. Then **she** showed up." Doris gritted her teeth as she spoke. "This rando-chick came out of nowhere, and hugged Derek! She hugged him from behind!" Doris dramatically retold her painful story. "Like *she* was *his* girlfriend. Derek laughed and smiled at this rando-chick like he was totally in love. I. Almost. Died. I'm not kidding, Lily. There's no way Derek would go for a girl like me if she's around...she was super skinny. The perfect twig. Gorgeous hair, skinny, wearing a cute skirt and heels! Who the heck wears heels to a soccer game?"

Doris and Lily eyed the sad looking salad in silence while Doris continued. "So, I decided that in order to have a chance with Derek, I need to cut the snacks and junk out of my diet. After all, my mom says it's not exactly about what you eat, it's the balance. But, I think she forgot the balance part--or adding something not green." Doris huffed, then went back to eating her miserable salad.

Lily dug through her lunch box. "Ahh...so would the salad balance with a couple of donuts?" She asked, pulling out four small donuts.

Doris gobbled the rest of her salad. "You are the best, Lily! Oh my gosh, *donuts*." Diving for the last two donuts, Doris wept over her dessert. "You're the best, best friend ever."

Lily finished one donut. "You don't need to diet. If you want to slim down then yes, eat healthier foods and exercise. Just remember, everyone's body is different, and sometimes you have to find out what your body needs. You might eat enough greens, but you may need more exercise."

Doris grinned while she savored the donut. "Sounds like you've been taking health classes with Mina or something."

"I do sound like that, don't I. Actually, it's all from the Vintage Teen Magazine, I remember reading that part in there." Lily closed the lunch box and stretched her arms toward the sky.

Doris packed up her own lunch box, before laying back using her sweater as a pillow. "Oh nice, sounds like we will have to re-read it again here soon. Sounds like we missed a lot. Thanks, for encouraging me with my diet. My brother and Dad said I was looking pudgy, the other day, and that sure as heck didn't help my self-esteem."

Lily laughed. "Yeah, brothers are no help in the self-esteem department. Unless you're talking about fighting skills."

Doris scoffed. "Yeah, I don't need Danny to teach me any fighting skills."

Lily replied. "Yeah, no kidding. I've seen you hip throw your brother before, and girl you can take him any day...but, when it comes to compliments, brothers are the worst."

Their giggles turned into resigned sighs when they heard the bell ring.

Lily cheered. "It's only a few more hours. Can we do this?"

Doris cheered back with all the sarcasm of a teenager. "Yes, we can."

The girls headed inside, counting down to the final bell, so they could go home.

Unfortunately for Lily, the rest of the day dragged on, slower than ever. The ensuing hours resulted in more chewed up pencils and pen caps. *Go figure,* Lily sighed to herself. She had something to do after school. Something that will hopefully bring one family, in particular, a trunk full of happiness. Lily chuckled, *seeing Mina'a rolling her eyes at Lily's sad pun.* But the day decided to move as slowly as it could.

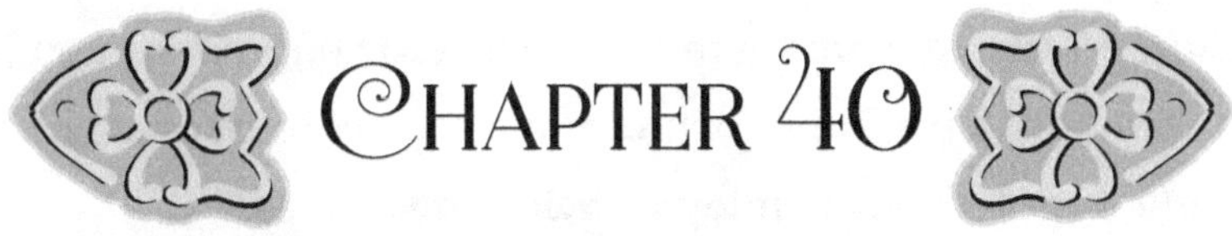

When the final bell rang, loud and clear, Lily's book bag was packed and ready to go. Slinging the bag over her shoulder, Lily ran to the family van.

The moment Lily arrived home, she started searching for Mr. Shels. "Is Dad home, yet?" Lily ran through the house searching for him. "Mom, have you seen Dad?"

Mrs. Shels dropped her purse onto the kitchen counter as Lily rushed through the door. "Sweetie, your Dad won't be home at his usual time because he had to make that special stop for you. You'll have to be patient."

Lily sat down with her bookbag on her lap. "Fine…" She pouted, pulling out her homework. Thirty minutes later, Lily was still tapping the pen against the side of the math book. Not a single problem done, just a few scribbles here and there. *Dad should be home any minute now.* The mantra repeated in Lily's head.

Lily couldn't concentrate on her homework, but she could calculate, with extreme accuracy, how long it *should* take her Dad to drive home. If Mr. Shels left work on time, It takes ten minutes to drive from there to the store. Then, maybe another ten minutes to print the pictures, and ten more to drive home. *Viola!* Roughly 30 to 40 minutes before he arrives.

But when Lily looked at the clock an hour had passed, and Mr. Shels was still not home. *What if something happened? What if Dad got hit by a car or had trouble at work? This is all my fault. I'll never forgive myself if anything happens to him.*

Panic spread, slowly creeping through Lily's body. A loud noise came from the front door. Lily sprang out of her seat, dashing through the house to see if her Dad was home. When she reached the entrance he was standing by the front door.

"Dad. Dad. Dad! Did you get my pictures printed?" Lily ran up to Mr. Shels.

Mr. Shels teetered from side to side when he tried to take off his shoes. "Lily, give me a second to get in the house. Lily, Stop it!" Mr. Shels set his shoes by the front door, as Lily reached into the plastic bag he had wrapped around his wrist. "Lily, enough already." Mr. Shels stumbled over Lily, falling to the floor.

"Sorry, Dad." Lily stepped back as Mr. Shels stood up, still gripping the plastic bag. Fluttering lashes, and painting on an innocent smile, Lily had perfected the 'innocent Angel' act.

Mr. Shels blinked once, shook his head and handed Lily the bag. "Take it, before you trip me again. That hurt."

"Thanks Dad! Sorry about tripping you. I love you!" Lily

zoomed away to her room upstairs. By the time Mr. Shels blinked again, Lily was gone.

Once in her room, Lily dumped the pictures on her bed. Sorting into three piles--one for herself; one for Doris; and last but not least, one for Mrs. Brookes. She would add those to a very special brown box, tied with string.

Flip-flip-flip. The three piles grew as Lily separated the pictures. After she finished, Lily placed them into three envelopes, marking each for herself, Doris, and Mrs. Brookes. Snagging her purse, Lily stuffed the envelopes inside, then headed downstairs.

Rushing into the parlor, Lily found Mrs. Shels relaxing on the couch. "Mom! Can we go to Mrs. Brookes now, please? Everything is ready to go. The trunk is super light and waiting by the front door." Lily pleaded, holding up the elegantly wrapped box for her mom to see. "*Please*....I promise I'll come straight home and do my homework...and chores, no complaints! Not a single one."

Mrs. Shel chuckled as she looked up from her tablet. "Well, only if you give me 50 bucks, then I'll see what I can do."

Lily smiled brightly, even she knew that meant *yes*. Lily gave her mom the hardest high-five smack as she could, which in the Shels house meant agreeing on how much money was owed. *Mrs. Shels-50 bucks.*

Mrs. Shels set her tablet aside, scooting off the couch. "I'm actually excited for you, Lily. It's not everyday that you find love letters in an old trunk. It sounds almost magical,...like a romance novel!" Mrs. Shels grabbed her wallet and keys. Lily followed her to the front door.

Lily continued. "Yeah, it is pretty cool, I always knew something cool like that would be hiding in antiques. I told you they always have a story."

Mrs. Shels pointed to one end of the trunk, as she picked up the other end. "When you and Doris showed me those letters after we came home, I couldn't believe they had been kept secret all this time. And that the letters were still readable. Then, when you said you wanted to return them to Mrs. Brookes, I thought it was the sweetest idea. Are you ready?"

"Heck yeah I am." Mrs. Shels and Lily lifted the trunk into the van, then headed out. "So, how was your day, Mom?"

Mrs. Shels scoffed.

Lily glanced at her Mom, catching her frown. "Rough day?"

Mrs. Shels nodded. "You could say that. Let's see, first the washing machine broke, then water sprayed everywhere. I had to use all the clean towels to mop up the mess, which means I not only have to get a new washer, I have at least 5 loads of towels sopping wet on my floor. And, that's just the beginning." Mrs. Shels sighed, shrinking down into her seat. Feeling like the weight of the world was on her shoulders. "I tried repotting plants to relax, but ended up dropping my favorite pot on my foot, before it broke. I think I prayed to all the saints for strength, because *that hurt like hell*. Then to top it all off, I burned my toast when I noticed I had broken about half of my fingernails, cleaning up the broken pot. It just really is not my day. How was your day? I know it was better than mine."

Lily's heart was instantly filled with concern and guilt.

"I'm sorry, Mom. Sounds like you had a rough day. My day was pretty good. Much better than yours, for sure." Lily knew she had been busy with Fred and the spirit stuff, but she shouldn't be too busy to ask her Mom how she was doing. *Am I really that selfish?*

Mrs. Shels offered Lily a sympathetic look. "Don't worry, Lily. It's not your fault--or anyone else's. Things like this happen. Trials, here and there. But because of you my day is going to finish with a great ending. Do you plan to stay, or just hand over the box of letters and leave?"

Lily smiled. "I did think about asking to stay, but at the same time I think it is best if I don't stay. The letters will probably bring up a trunk-load of emotions for the family." Lily giggled.

Lily recalled how excited she and Doris were when they found the letters inside the trunk lid. It felt magical. Like a movie scene, coming to life right before their eyes. She looked down to double check that she had everything.

One box with letters.

One small envelope with her photoshoot pictures

Plus a letter to Mrs. Brookes explaining the letters inside.

Lily smirked as she held the box tighter. "I think Mrs. Brookes will be pleasantly surprised."

Mrs. Shels parked in the Brookes' driveway. Lily hopped out, grabbing her end of the trunk, carrying it to the front door. Mrs. Shels headed back to the van, while Lily waited for someone to answer the door. She could hear footsteps right before the front door opened.

"Hello Sir. I'm Lily Shels, I borrowed the antique travel trunk from your Mom." Lily wanted to offer her hand to shake, but she was balancing the box and envelope on top. "ummm, Is Mrs. Brookes home?" Lily added her most angelic smile.

Carter Brookes grimaced. "Sorry, My uh...Mrs. Brookes isn't home right now. Can I help you?" He eyed the box in Lily's hands.

Lily bit her lip, thinking quickly. "Oh ok. Yes, can you take these?" Lily handed the box and envelope to Carter. "And, of course, the trunk. Please be sure Mrs. Brookes reads *this* letter first." Lily tapped the letter on top of the box. "Then, the rest will make sense. Please give it to her, the minute she comes home. *It's very important.*"

Carter had a confused and slightly amused look, as he looked down at the box in his hands.

Lily smiled brighter. "Just tell Mrs. Brookes, 'Lily dropped everything off'. We've talked before, so she'll understand that."

"Ok then, I'll be sure to let her know when she comes home. Thank you." Carter took the box inside, returning a few seconds later to grab the trunk.

"Thank you so much!" Lily waved goodbye, then hopped in the van.

"Thank you for bringing me, Mom. Especially after your bad day. *You're the best.*" Lily hugged her Mom.

"You're welcome, honey. You're so sweet. You'll have to let me know if you hear back from Mrs. Brookes about the trunk and letters." Mrs. Shels replied.

"Will do. I really wish she was here, so I could give everything to her myself. But, as long as she gets it, that's all that matters." Lily let the silence hang, as she dove into her own thoughts.

On the way home, Lily worried. *Will Carter give Mrs. Brookes everything? What if he throws it away? Or even worse, what if Mrs. Brookes is sick or in the hospital and she never gets to see the letters????*

Lily's heart sank when she realized all the bad things that could happen. *Fred...Fred please go make sure your granddaughter gets those letters!* Sending Fred to the Brookes house, with a prayer, Lily tried to focus on a positive outcome for everyone.

They arrive home and Lily heads off to finish her homework, and chores as she promised. Lily ended her day with a feeling of accomplishment. She had delivered the trunk and letters, finished her homework and completed her chores. Feeling exhausted, Lily flopped into bed following her nightly prayers.

After her prayers Lily lay snuggled in her warm blankets. *Why do we even say morning and night prayers? Am I praying for someone or just for my sleep to be good? Hmmm. I'm pretty sure my religion teacher would be very disappointed that I don't know the answer, especially since we read all about prayer and stuff from those catechism books.* She scoffed, turning over to check her alarm clock. *11PM, even the night is taking forever.*

Lily tossed around until she finally relaxed long enough to fall into deep slumber.

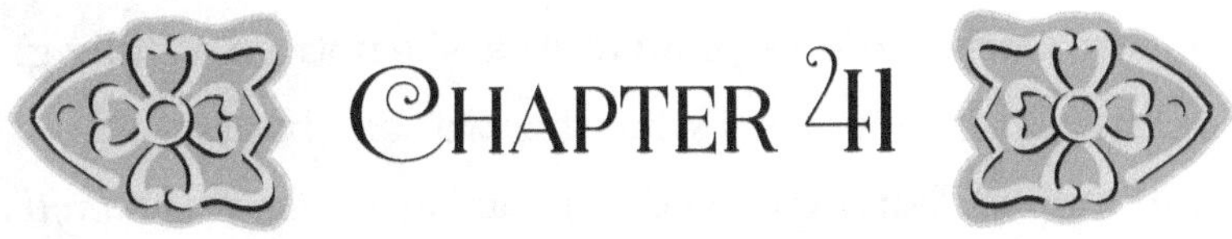

CHAPTER 41

Tuesday morning, Doris practically attacked Lily with questions the second she arrived in her classroom.

Doris' eyes sparkled with excitement as she drilled Lily for information. "So, how did it go? What did she say? Was Mrs. Brookes overcome with happiness? Did she cry? C'mon, spill the beans, what *happened*?" Doris slammed her hands on Lily's desk, grinning ear to ear as she waited for Lily's reply.

Lily quickly clapped one hand over Doris' mouth, trying to stem the flow of questions. Some of their classmates had turned to stare at them. Lily felt exposed and uncomfortable. One classmate approached Lily and Doris. She was tall--elegant with silky black long hair. Ava was smart, great at everything and to the surprise of many had a sweet disposition. She was very popular with everyone who knew her.

Ava approached Lily's desk, smiling. "Hmmm? What are you up to, Doris? Sounds like something exciting is going on."

Now what does Ava want? That fake smile, it's so sugary sweet, it makes my teeth ache.

Before Doris could respond to Ava, she noticed a chilly glare from Lily. Doris wondered what that was all about.

Lily hoped Doris received her message, *Don't say anything about Fred, Doris,* loud and clear. Lily shook her head slightly at Doris, before grinning in a lightning speed transformation, when Ava looked in her direction.

Doris' smile thinned when she caught Lily's message. She ignored it to answer Ava. "Oh, nothing really. Just gossiping, You know, girl stuff, family drama." Doris swallowed. Giving Lily a curious glance.

Ava pressed on, ignoring Lily's not so subtle 'go away vibe'. "Really? You sounded pretty excited. Anything you want to share?"

Lily interrupted before Doris could reply this time. "Really Ava, it's nothing. Doris was just excited that I finally finished a short story I was writing." Lily could already hear her Mother giving her 'the speak the truth at all times' lecture. "That's all it was. Nothing important." Lily tilted her head, smiling at Ava. *Mom would be proud. I didn't exactly lie to Ava. Told her the edited truth. Maybe this will get Ava off my back for a while.* Her sudden interest in me is weird. Ava never comes over to talk to us. *I wonder if Ava remembers all the drama that happened last semester-- with Isaac?*

Ava eyed Lily's notebook "You write, Lily? I didn't know

that." Ava stepped closer to Doris, turning up her charming smile. "Are Lily's stories any good, Doris?"

Doris ignored Lily's previous glare, happily answered Ava. "Yeah, Lily's really good, in my opinion. In fact, she's written several already." Doris' grin froze when she saw Lily's glowering look. "Errrrr...I mean it's nothing really. Lily is kind of protective of her writing. You know artists--authors--when they are working can get really touchy." Doris shrugged.

"Oh, I see. Sorry Lily, I didn't mean to pry. Well gotta go anyway. See ya." Seconds later, Ava walked back to her desk where a swarm of students surrounded her.

Doris waved until Ava was out of earshot. Turning back to Lily, she rolled her eyes and sighed. Then hissed through her teeth. "What the heck is your problem, Lily? Is Fred's temper flaring. Or is something else going on?"

Lily leaned in, trying to remain calm. "Doris. My *stories* aren't something I want *anyone* to know about. Especially Ava, ok?"

Doris knew there was more to this than Lily was telling her. "What do you have against Ava? She's super sweet and even though she's *Miss-Popular* she's never done anything to either one of us." Leaning in, Doris gritted out. "Unless you're not telling me something?"

Lily's gaze dropped to her desk and she started fiddling with her pencil. " It's nothing, really. I just don't want anyone reading my stories, that's all. So, please keep it down when we talk about them." Lily hoped Doris wouldn't push her to explain further. She knew she had to tell Doris the full story about Isaac, but not right now. After all, Lily was still dealing with Fred Cummens.

One spirit story at a time, that's my motto. Lily tried to send Doris another telepathic message. *I'll tell you everything one day, Doris. Just wait until I am spirit free.* Lily sniffed, *which should be any day now...hopefully.*

Doris knew the second Lily dropped eye contact, something was seriously up. Lily was keeping secrets again. But, Doris decided to wait and give Lily time to explain. "Oh sorry. I didn't realize I was being so loud. I was just super excited." Doris raised three fingers on her right hand. "I promise I won't tell a soul about your stories." Doris exhaled, staring at Lily, who was still avoiding looking at her. Doris chewed on a fingernail, frustrated by Lily's sudden concern about who was listening.

Lily stared at the wall clock. Time seemed to have frozen. "Look, from now on if you could be a little less excited, at least in school..." Lily paused, knowing she wasn't making any sense. Taking a deep breath, she continued. "I think for right now, we need to keep these stories absolutely secret. Maybe even to the point where we only talk about them outside of school."

Rolling her eyes again. Doris sucked in a deep breath, holding back her temper. "Ok fine. I won't say anything about these stories, and only talk about them *after school* with you. Any other rules, Warden?"

Lily's eyebrows shot up into her hairline. But before she could reply, the school bell rang. Doris quickly ran back to her desk, and ignored Lily for the rest of the school day.

The walk home was awkward and silent until Doris couldn't stand the cold treatment anymore. "Ok Lily. Spill it. What on earth happened between you and Ava? I'm not dumb, I know that glare well." Doris gripped her lunch box tighter and waited to see if Lily would answer her or not.

"Nothing happened. I just don't feel comfortable with others knowing about this spirit stuff I'm working through." Lily knew Doris was not accepting her sad excuse when she rolled her eyes. *Not yet, Doris. Please wait just a few more days.* Lily was worried about Mrs. Brookes. *Fred, any updates with your granddaughter yet?*

Doris swung her lunch box over her shoulder, giving Lily a side-eyed glare. "Sure. Try again. I know that's a lie. Why are you keeping secrets from me, again? Didn't you promise to tell me everything? Or was that a lie too?"

Lily stopped to stare at Doris for the first time during their walk home. "No, it's not like that at all! Look, I haven't heard anything from Mrs. Brookes. Fred hasn't left yet either, but I also haven't heard from him since yesterday. I'm on edge right now, that's all." Lily scratched her arm studying the sidewalk. "And yes, something did happen with Ava, but I don't have the energy right now to explain it to you. Once Fred is officially free, then I will sit down with you and explain everything--even about Isaac, in full detail. So, please, until Fred is free, don't ask about either of them. I'm too tired and frustrated today." Lily felt like crying. Instead, she sighed and looked at her best friend--praying she would understand. " I'm sorry about today...I just-"

Doris shook her head and smiled, cutting Lily off. "I forgive you! I didn't realize you and Ava had history between you. So of course I'll stay clear of her and not tell a single soul about the stories, unless you give me permission. Cross my heart. And I won't ask about anything else--about the spirits, or anyone, until Fred is gone."

"Thank you so much! I won't be visiting any antique stores for a while, after Fred. Which means, we will have plenty of time to catch up on all the past spirit cases."

Doris grabbed Lily's hand and squeezed it. "I got your back now. So tell me when you're ready, and I'll listen."

"Thank you, Doris!" Lily could finally take a deep breath. For the first time since Mina forced her to talk about the spirits, Lily could relax without having to hide things. With these two on her team, Lily knew her sanity was safe. She felt an overwhelming peace settle around her.

"Don't expect me to forget, even after Fred is gone. I'll wait a few weeks before reminding you. But that's it." Doris winked. Causing the girls to erupt in giggles.

The two girls updated each other on their latest Derek drama, and Patrick stalking, the rest of the way home.

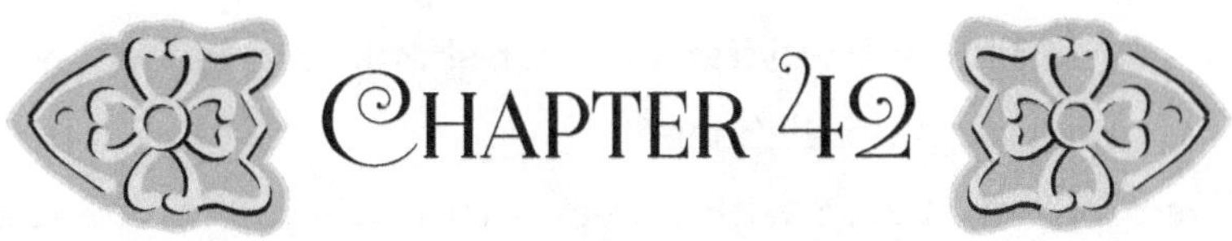

CHAPTER 42

Meanwhile, back at St. Catherine High School, Ava followed Lily and Doris as they left the school.

A student snuck up behind Ava peeking around a corner. "Ava, what are you doing? Who are you spying on?" Jen whispered.

"Sheesh, you scared me half to death. *Don't do that!*" Ava had to catch her breath after that shocking heart attack.

"So, who are you spying on, and why?" Jen peered around the corner, finding no one interesting in sight.

Ava brushed the hair out of her face. "*Spying*? Who said I was spying on anyone? I was just leaving when I thought I saw one of my ex's, that's all." Pasting a smile on to reassure Jen, she peeked around the corner again. *Dang, I lost them.*

Jen sighed dramatically, leaning against the building.

"Boy, must be nice--having an ex-boyfriend, or at least one to avoid." Jen flipped her hair. "How do you always get all those boyfriends? I can't even get one guy to talk to me after Mass."

"*Try wearing makeup*...ummm, I could help you." Ava adjusted her book bag straps on her shoulders. "Soooo...what do you know about Lily Shels?"

Jen looked at Ava with one eyebrow raised. "Lily? I don't know. She's about my age, black curly hair, green eyes--"

Ava interrupted the description. "That's not what I meant, Jen." Ava chuckled. "I mean, is there anything unusual or weird?" Ave walked down the sidewalk beside Jen as they continued.

Jen thought for a moment. "Generally no, not really...unless... you're talking about last semester? Lily was acting pretty weird."

"Yeah, I heard about that? Does anyone know if the rumors are true then? I was in the bathroom at the time when it happened." Ava plucked a few leaves from a nearby bush while she considered what Jen knew? And whether Ava could dig it out of her.

Jen copied Ava, plucking a few leaves herself. "Yeah, it was the strangest thing. If I remember correctly, Lily disappeared shortly after lunch, and didn't come back for a few days. I heard some of the teachers say they found her on the roof and it was a possible..." Jen lowered her voice, almost afraid to say the words out loud. "...a possible *suicide attempt*." Jen looked around, feeling exposed. "It was pretty scary. Especially for someone attending this school."

Ava ripped the leaves apart, piece by piece, as they whispered, in low serious voices. "That is scary...*terrifying*, actually." Ava dropped torn leaf pieces, leaving a green jigsaw trail. "Was the attempt confirmed? I mean, that's a pretty big thing to happen, yet no one knows what really went on that day with Lily." Ava stopped, turning toward Jen. "Plus, Lily came back to school a few days later as if nothing happened. What *else* do you know?" Ava noticed Jen's curious glance down at her feet.

Jen asked without looking up. "What's going on?" Jen felt uncomfortable with Ava's questions. "Why are you digging up stuff on Lily?"

Ava had already anticipated this question. "I just want to find out how she got through depression so quickly. *If she was* dealing with depression, at all?" She looked ahead, seeing the crosswalk coming up. "Sorry if I'm asking too many questions, Jen. It doesn"t mean anything. Just curious, is all."

Jen smiled, gently squeezing Ava's hand. "How is your therapy going, anyway? Is it getting easier?"

Ava sighed. *And this was the 2nd question I was expecting from Jen.*

Jen pulled Ava into a warm hug. Clearly she didn't want to talk about it.

Ava wiped her eyes on her sweater sleeve. "Thanks Jen, you're a great friend, you know that right?"

Jen nudged Ava's shoulder as they continued their walk home. "Of course I do. Just tell me when you need a hug or someone to talk to, ok? I'm here for you, Ava."

Ava smiled. "Thank-you Jen. If you need a hug or someone to talk to you just let me know, too. We can have a sleepover or something. Maybe even try out my new acrylic nail set. Or, I can show you how to get that perfect cat-eye look. Maybe that will intrigue the guys."

The two girls giggled and continued their walk home.

Carter greeted his Mom as she drove into the garage. "Hey Mom. Welcome back." Carter took the suitcase. "How was your weekend?"

Mrs. Brookes hugged her son. "Thank you, Carter. I loved it--just what the doctor ordered." She followed Carter into the living room. Sitting down, she continued describing her weekend. "Everyday, the girls and I went out to explore the town. We checked out a few new restaurants, plus, I bought a new dress. The spa facilities were wonderful. It's been years since I have had a day being pampered."

"That's everything we did, I think. I'm exhausted. I'm going to go upack before I end up falling asleep, right here." Mrs. Brookes walked into her bedroom followed by Carter, carrying her bulging suitcase.

"Man, Mom. What did you buy? This thing weighs a ton." He heaved the suitcase onto the bed with a mighty groan.

Mrs. Brookes set her purse on the dresser, noticing the new box and letter waiting for her. "What's this?" She grabbed them and sat down next to the suitcase.

Carter leaned against the bedpost. "That was left for you by some girl--the same one who borrowed the trunk from the antique store."

"Lily? Lily left this for me? I wonder why?" Dorothy gently lifted the box, inspecting the narrow box. "Lily said she was going to send me pictures from the photoshoot with the trunk, but this box is oversized for a few pictures." Mrs. Brookes shook the box, trying to guess what else was inside.

"Oh yeah. The girl also brought the trunk back. She said something about *'read the letter, then everything will make sense'*." Carter shrugged, then gave Mrs. Brookes a hug before leaving the bedroom.

Mrs. Brookes set the box aside, picking up the letter. Opening the envelope and taking out the letter, Dorothy read.

Dear Mrs. Brookes,

Hi again, it's me, Lily Shels.

I left you a surprise. And...I might have broken your trunk lid.

I would apologize, but something amazing came out that I think you and your family will find invaluable. Something exciting about your Grandfather, Fredrick Cummens.

After you finish this letter, please open the box.

God bless

Sincerely Lily Shels

Mrs. Brookes picked up the box and peeled off the brown paper wrapping. Opening the box. Dorothy gasped as she pulled out one of the fragile envelopes. Carefully unfolding the lilac scented paper, taking a deep breath she began to read.

§

Knock-knock-knock Carter rapped on the door to his Mom's bedroom.

"Mom? Did you want some coffee or something to eat?" Silence greeted Carter.

Sniffing loudly, Mrs. Brookes spoke through the door. "Carter, where is the trunk? Can you please bring it to the living room?"

"It's in the garage." Carter looked up, praying for patience. "Sure. I'll go grab it. By the way, the lid has a new hole in it. I don't know how, but thought I'd let you know. Anything else?" Carter asked, as he leaned against the door.

"Yes, ask your sister, Joanne, to come over this evening. I discovered something you should both know."

"Sure thing, Mom. I'll text Joanne to see if she can come over for dinner." Carter turned toward the garage, then remembered why he was there to begin with. "Are you sure you are ok? Want coffee or something to eat?" Carter asked, feeling the door handle turn under his palm. It was not locked. His shoulders dropped in relief.

"Just the trunk, and asking your sister to come over. That's all."

Puzzled by his Mom's response, he went to get the trunk. Carter texted his sister, then his wife, Megan, letting her know, company was coming for dinner. To his surprise, Joanne arrived early to help prepare dinner.

During dinner, Mrs. Brookes refused to reveal why she wanted to talk to them together.

Joanne put her napkin down, smiling. "Ok, Mom. We have waited until dinner is done, why don't you tell us what this is about?"

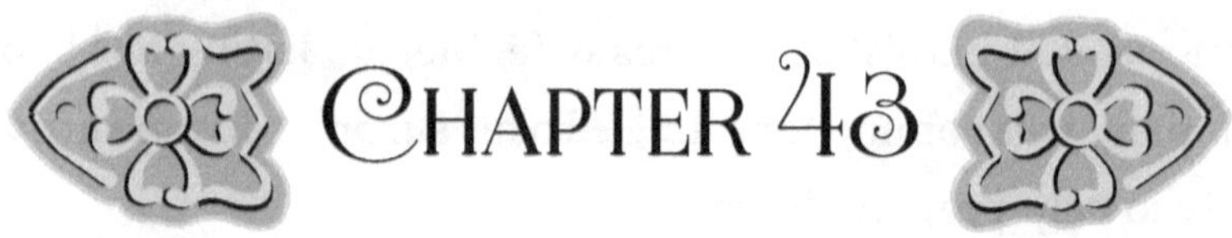

CHAPTER 43

Mrs. Brookes folded her hands. "Very well. If you'll join me in the living room. I'll explain."

The four of them moved to the living room, Mrs. Brookes, Joanne, and Megan waited while Carter moved the trunk in front of Mrs. Brookes.

Mrs. Brookes opened the trunk, revealing the rectangular cardboard box inside. "Carter, Joanne, Megan. Do you remember anything about your Great-Grandfather and Great-Grandmother?"

Joanne answered first. "I only remember being told that Great Grandpa went blind, ruined his marriage, then died in a nursing home somewhere all alone. Why? Is something missing?"

Carter responded next. "Yeah, that's all I know too. Grandma used to tell us that her Mom, Dorothy, had dementia, and would make up stories about visiting her Dad, Frederick, and writing letters to him."

Mrs. Brookes opened the cardboard box, then pulled out a single envelope. "I'm glad you remember at least that much. It'll make it easier to explain these letters. They prove that your Great-Grandma wasn't crazy or making up stories, after all. In fact, these are the very letters she talked about." She passed Lily's letter around for them all to see. "Apparently, the girl who borrowed the trunk accidentally broke the lid, and found Great-Grandma's letters inside. That's why Lily returned the trunk."

Carter opened a letter from the cardboard box. "Are these for real? I don't mean to be cynical, but Great-Grandma could have written all these herself." Carter avoided his sister's dark glance. He continued after clearing his throat. "She did have dementia, so it's possible she forgot that she wrote them and thought they were from her husband. Stop rolling your eyes, Joanne, it could have happened."

Joanne sighed dramatically. "Carter, always the little ray of sunshine, aren't you?"

Megan disguised her snicker with a cough. "Of course, if your theory is true, Carter dear. All the envelopes and letters would be written with the same handwriting. The address and signatures would be the same, as well. So, let's just read them and find out." Megan knew all too well that Carter and Joanne didn't see eye to eye.

Mrs. Brookes gestured to Carter to hand the first letter back. "Yes, let's start reading them. I would give each of you one, but they won't make sense unless we read them in order. Joanne, I'll start with you, since you're closest. Then pass it to your left and I'll give you the next one." Without further delay, Mrs. Brookes initiated the letter parade.

Before long, the four members of the Brookes family were silently reading. Halfway through the letters, Joane and Megan reached for the tissue box. The room stayed quiet, except for the sniffling tears.

Joanne's voice cracked. "I don't know what to say. It's really amazing after all these years to find out how things ended for Fredrick and Dorothy. Since the letters were hidden all these years, our grandparents never knew the truth. They lived the rest of their lives, hating their Dad and ignoring their Mom's stories. That's tragic."

Mrs. Brookes pulled a small diary from the trunk and a single piece of paper. "I can tell you now that your grandparents, my Mom and Uncle David, regretted everything but eventually found peace." Mrs. Brookes shifted, moving so everyone could see the diary and letter.

Carter reached across the table for the letter. "What's this?"

"This diary was my Mom's. This letter is from my Uncle David to Mom. They both have one regret in common, their father, Mr. Frederick Cummens." Mrs. Brookes passed the diary to Joanne. "Uncle David had the same vision issues as his Dad. At first, his family handled everything well. Soon after, David lost sight in one eye and things changed. His outbursts became worse. Thankfully, they found a good therapist. In her diary you'll read how Louise and David spent hours talking about their parents and how their Dad destroyed everyone's life."

Megan cleared her throat, holding the letter that she stole from Carter. "Sorry to interrupt, Mom. But this letter, from Uncle David, reads more as though he's apologizing for all those years he hated his Dad." Megan looked up from the letter. "Was there a reconciliation between David and Fred?" Megan bit her lower lip, checking the date on the letter. "Nope it can't be that, his Dad died years before this letter was written. So, why is David apologizing to his sister?"

Joanne flipped through a few pages of the diary. "I think I get what's going on here." She tucked a tissue between the pages to mark her spot. "Did Uncle David and Aunt Louise work through everything in the end? If you look here toward the end, Aunt Louise writes about attending therapy, too. She mentions her brother's loss of eyesight as a generic thing. Her therapist told her, their Dad would have had similar struggles, and worse since he lost sight in both eyes." Joanne pointed to a line of text in the diary. "Read this part,

Joanne waited until everyone read the paragraph, then continued. "Aunt Louise realized, a little too late, that her Dad's behavior was not exactly by choice, but the consequence of everything happening to him. I can't imagine how much regret Grandma Louise felt after realizing that."

Mrs. Brookes smiled, laying a hand on Joanne's shoulder. "She did regret it...for years. But eventually, both my Mom and Uncle came to terms with the anger toward their Dad, before they too died. The letter and diary were given to me after Mom passed. When I read it..." Mrs. Brookes wiped away a few tears that pooled in her eyes. "...when I read through the diary and my Uncle's letter, I still didn't understand the connection, until now."

Carter handed out more tissues, while asking. "What connection are you talking about? The fact that they both hated their Dad or that they regretted it in the end?"

Mrs. Brookes shook her head. "No, not exactly. The real connection wasn't apparent even to me until I received these letters from Lily. Both my Mom and Uncle were told about the letters their Mom wrote to their Dad. But, since Grandma had dementia, they simply didn't believe her, plus they never found any letters." Mrs.Brookes blew her nose. "After reading Fred and Dorothy's letters, I realized that even though Mom and Uncle David held a grudge against their Dad, they would have forgiven him. These letters were not a fantasy or part of their Mom's dementia, as they always believed. My Mom mentioned that she searched the attic and her Mom's possession, trying to find any trace of Fred and Dorothy's correspondence."

Megan tapped Uncle David's letter. "He mentions the letters too." Clearing her throat quickly Megan read aloud.

" 'Our Mom often spoke about her fantasy letters, saying

her and Dad made amends and were happy once more. I wish the letters actually existed. At least then, our family might have been able to weather the storm and recall happier times.'

Megan folded the letter. "David wanted the letters to exist and mend his family."

Joanne sniffed as she grabbed another tissue. "I can't imagine wanting something to exist all that time, and finally, here they are. They were so close to finding them. Maybe their Mom forgot where she hid them exactly, only remembering they were somewhere."

Carter examined the trunk lid while the three women speculated about what really happened, re-reading the letters over and over.

Joanne noticed the mountain of tissues and whisked them away. "I wish we knew where to find Matthew Geno. Granny and Uncle may not have known his name or the good he did for our family, but we do. If he's still alive, we could still thank him for reuniting our Great-Grandparents before they died."

Carter examining the outer part of the lid. "You can do what you want, but I think looking for a nurse named, Matthew Geno after 50 years, is like looking for a needle in a haystack." Carter didn't see Joanne coming up behind him.

"That's why I'm doing the research, and not you." Joanne spotted the diary and grabbed from the table to land a solid *whack* on her brother's head.

Carter yelped, rubbing the sore spot. "Dam--dang-nabit, gosh darn it all." Carter's swearing was cut short and edited after his mother's curt glare.

Joanne smirked, with her hands on her hips. "It doesn't matter how long it's been, I would like to thank Matthew for his help. Whether that is a handshake or a thank-you card. Or even prayers at his gravesite. It's important to acknowledge and thank this person for their kindness."

Mrs. Brookes collected the letters, diary and David's apology, putting them neatly back into the trunk. "If you do find him, Joanne. Please let me know too. I would like to say thank-you to Matthew, myself."

Joanne winked at her Mom, before heading into the kitchen to get something to drink.

The four Brookes' continued their conversation late into the evening. Talking about family, childhood memories, and all the times they were forced to eat their least favorite foods, which always ended with laughter and teasing. *Children never forget anything, it seems.* Mrs. Brookes chuckled to herself as she listened to her children's stories.

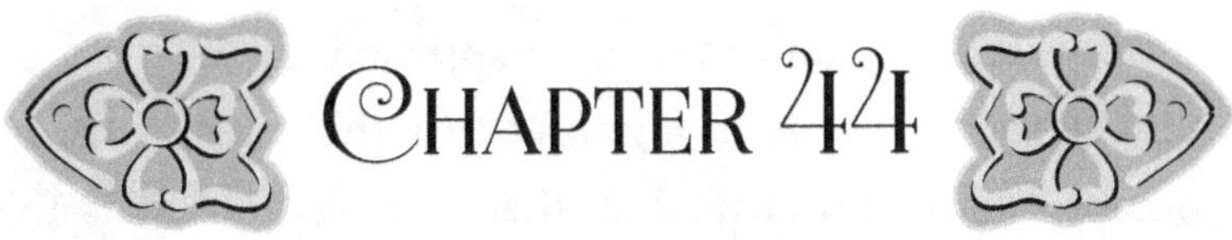

CHAPTER 44

Lily gently rubbed her stomach, then her head. Placing her pen next to her Math notebook. She stared at the last sentence she wrote.

"The end."

Written in the basic blue ink, Lily felt oddly bereft. Not sick, just a little sad. Then, a familiar sense of peace flooded her entire body. Lily's mind released the dopamine, as if celebrating her new found freedom.

Lily folded her hands in prayer, speaking softly. "Congratulations, Fred. You're finally free. God bless and please, please...don't come back." She followed that with a silent "Eternal Rest" prayer for the dead. Ironically, one of the prayers she uses quite often, thanks to her spirit stalkers.

Closing another notebook, Lily relaxed on her bed and

breathed a loud sigh. "Le sighhh." The euphoric feeling when a spirit leaves is something Lily won't ever get used to. It always seems unreal. She was struggling to free a trapped antique spirit for several weeks, then suddenly they're gone. Freed now, her part always felt like none of it ever happened.

Lily closed, her eyes trying to picture the spirit of Fredrick Cummens. She couldn't at first, then suddenly he was there, again.

Crystal clear in her thoughts, nodding his head slowly, he said *"Thank you, Lily"*.

Within seconds Fred was nothing more than a blurry memory, fading away like mist. A few tears streaked along Lily's temples. *You're welcome, Fred.*

Thank you

She let the tears fall, allowing this last memory to fade. Lily was happy for Fred.

Fred's story ended happily. He could not have left until his family received the letters, and forgiven him. I bet that moment was amazing for Fred. A long, hard, pain-in-the-butt spirit case--solved at last. And who knows maybe all those prayers did work.

Lily's heart and mind felt light, almost elated. She laid still for a few moments, listening to her own thoughts. It was weird getting used to her thoughts being the only ones inside her head. Pride and joy filled her to the very brim. Smiling, Lily high fived her own hand. "Well done, me!" *Thank you Mina and Doris. It was wonderful having people to share my problems with.*

Lily straightened into an upright position, before sliding off the bed. "Now, I can finally give Doris the completed story to read and review." She tucked the notebook into her book bag. Another wave of relief washed over her. "Doris, I can tell her everything. No secrets. Or lies. Mina will be so happy to hear the good news too." Lily pulled out her wallet from her desk, checking her cash inside. *I'll get Mina a coffee and donut as a thank-you for all her help. Where would I be without my sister.* Zipping her book bag, Lily set it by her door, ready for school the next day. "Note to self. No more antique stores, or garage sales or touching anything old, for at least a month." Turning off the bedroom light, Lily headed downstairs to join her family for snacks and game night.

Her next school day promised to be good. Lily felt as if a whole new life had opened up for her. She was finally free from her spirit stalker, and only had one last task to complete--Doris reading Fred's story.

As Lily entered the school at St. Catherines, she realized she could see past her classmates' immediate reactions, to the truth underneath. Everyone had their own cross to bear, and tended to hide behind core emotions as a defense. Exactly like Lily did with Doris--lying and redirecting the truth about her new abilities. Or, like Ava, who was hiding her grief about her lost sister with a smile and an overwhelming need to be needed. Or, Mina, becoming a nurse just to help others, or trying to fill a void?

Once Lily put her phone down, she could see that social media wasn't as important to her life as she once thought, family and real connections offered her so much more. A life filled with love, security, support, and unending possibilities.

Lily marched up to Doris, who was sitting at her usual desk. "Here you go. Finished Fred's story at last." Lily almost forgot she needed to be discreet. Laying the notebook on the desk, she winked, then walked away before Doris could respond.

Doris acted casually. *Nothing special going on here.* She picked up the notebook, opened it to the story and read. Goosebumps rose as she saw the title.

"Letters to free the soul.

A biography of Fredrick Cummens."

Doris snatched every second, between classes, in the hallway almost mowing her classmates down, and while her Biology teacher droned on and on about grasshoppers, to read Fred's story. Her morning flew by with her eyes glued to the story. When Doris turned the last page, she sighed. Thankfully, the-not-so-quiet sigh was ignored due to another student's cough. Doris felt an immediate urge to cheer, hoot, and holler for Fred. He was free at last, and his family had forgiven him. Doris loved happy endings and barely managed to contain her glee. Doris waited impatiently for lunch to share her excitement with Lily.

The other 9th graders in their class packed up their bags, grabbed their lunches, and headed down to the cafeteria. Not even the gloomy and wet day could dampen Lily and Doris's joy, even having to eat inside. They linked arms, skipping and singing all the way down the hall.

Doris sat across from Lily at one of the secluded corner tables. Trying to give themselves space and privacy. Doris pulled out Lily's notebook, sliding it across the table.

Doris deepened her voice to her best critique persona, calmly stating. "After reading Fred's story, I had to think long, and hard about my review…" Doris paused, rubbing her chin. "I'd give it…a minimum 6 star review!" Doris held onto her stern face for as long as she could, but a smirk broke it at the end. Grinning brightly, she gave Lily two thumbs up and continued her review. "The ending was perfect, making the whole story come alive. We have *Drama*!" Doris held her fingers up one at a time and listed different aspects of the story. "We have *Romance*. We have *Division*, destroying all hope! Then the *Wedge* between families, mended with help from an unexpected *Hero*! Plus the *Mystery* of the missing love letters, to keep readers on edge. Yes, Lily, this is your best story to date." Proudly Doris nodded her head, showing Lily that she was extremely impressed. "Ahh, I love it! *Love stories*. Especially when they look hopeless and it turns into a happily-ever-after ending."

Shaking her head, Lily couldn't help but laugh out loud. "Doris, you're such a hopeless romantic."

"I know." She practically swooned the response, pressing one hand against her forehead dramatically, like one of her favorite Victorian characters.

The two girls talked through lunch, almost forgetting to actually eat. Five minutes before the bell rang, they shoved as much food as they could into their mouths.

The rest of the day passed peacefully, for once. The entire school seemed to be lulled to a peaceful hum. School ended, releasing the students to their after-school activities.

Lily waved at Mr. Casdy, when they approached his vehicle.

Doris hugged Lily and said. "See you tomorrow!" Doris ran to the family car.

Shortly after Doris left, Lily's Mom pulled into the school parking lot.

§

Lily was home before she realized it. Her entire day felt as if Lily had been granted an unusually average day. Fred was free, the teachers assigned no homework, and she could finally share the excitement of releasing another spirit with her sister and her best friend. So many things to be grateful for, Lily was about to head up to her room when she heard her Mom call out.

"Lily, come here for a minute please." Mrs. Shel's voice came from inside the kitchen.

"Sure thing, Mom." Lily dropped her book bag by the stairs, then hurried to the kitchen.

"A letter came for you today." Mrs. Shels smiled, pointing to the letter. "It looks like it's from your Mrs. Brookes. If it's good news, can you share it?"

Lily rushed to the counter, grabbing the letter. She squealed with excitement. "It's from her!" Lily carefully ripped the paper envelope open. Scanning the letter quickly before reading it aloud.

Dear Lily,

I want to say, on behalf of my entire family, Thank you for everything.

These letters have given our family the peace and healing that we desperately needed. You did a huge favor for all of us, and we appreciate you returning everything after you found the letters.

I love the pictures you gave me from the photoshoot. They look fabulous. Well done!

Thank you, my dear.

Sincerely, Mrs. Brookes

P.S. We decided to keep the trunk!

Mrs. Shels hugged Lily tightly. "Oh honey, I am so proud of you! And I'm very happy to hear the Brookes have found some peace."

Lily danced around the kitchen with her Mom. "I'm so happy, too! Mrs. Brookes sounds so happy." While Lily hopped around, she tried to reach out to Fred. *We did it Fred! We did it.* After the impromptu dance party ended, Lily hugged her Mom again. Holding the hug for a few more seconds.

"Thanks again for that magazine and all your trips to the cummens for me. I love you!"

Mrs. Shels hugged Lily squishing the I love you out of her. "I LOVE YOU TOO BABY!!"

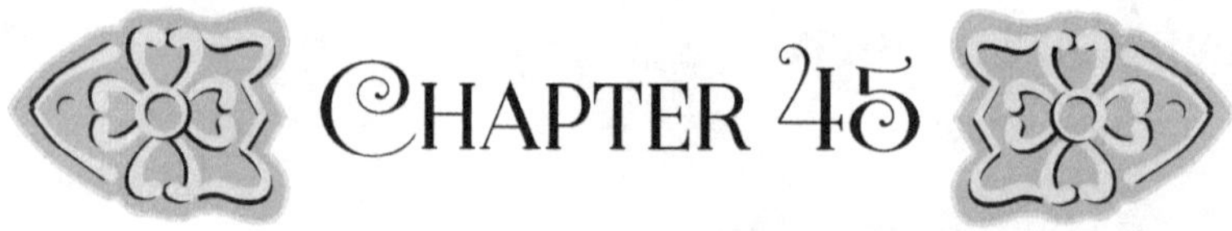

Chapter 45

Once she had closed her bedroom door, Lily scanned her empty bedroom, imagining blurry, new spirit stalkers surrounding her, drawing straws to see whose story is next. "Now listen here, spirits. Give me at least a month to recover, before sending another mission my way...*Please!* Trust me, if you have any hope of being freed, my brain needs time to heal and rest." A wry grin crossed her face, as Lily heard her crazy demand drift around the room. "No spirits present, and I'm still talking to myself, and negotiating with my imagination."

Lily rummaged through her closet. Pulling out the dress she wore for the photoshoot. "I should plan another photoshoot with Doris. We had so much fun." Nodding to herself, Lily unruffled the skirt. "You know this whole vintage vibe was kind of fun. Maybe that should become a brand or something for my social media. I mean, I already started a collection of vintage antiques."

The cellphone on Lily's desk rumbled. A text from Mina.

Mina: House sitting for friends. See you Saturday.

Grabbing her cell, Lily replied while swapping her uniform for comfy clothes.

Lily: Can you video chat tonight?

Mina: Around 7pm? Why?

Lily: Fred update. 7pm it is!

She updated Mina on Fred's spirit mission via text. Saving the letter from Mrs. Brookes for their video chat. Of course this would be the week Mina spent housesitting. Lily wanted to talk to Mina on video chat, especially after she received the letter from Mrs. Brookes. She had so many different things she wanted to share with Mina.

Checking the clock, Lily counted down the hours until her video call with Mina. "3 hours." Three hours before Mina was free for some spirit talk.

Mina had been working harder than usual. Working extra shifts, plus fitting in extra classes at college, when she could.

College.

Lily's thoughts wandered. *College? What would I major in?* She enjoyed writing, art, and helping people. *Or should I say ghosts?* After all, Fred's story helped reunite a family and heal the regret of a lost spirit. Lily created that reality–helped a family reconnect. How many other families are torn apart by cancer, disease or illness? For a second, Lily wished she could help mend every broken marriage or help heal more families like Fred's. Could she follow in her sister's footsteps –go to college to become a therapist.

That thought brought a smile to Lily's face, for a few seconds. Until she considered how exhausted she was after helping Fred, then imagining how many patients she would have to see everyday, plus her spirit stalker missions, Lily didn't think she could handle the emotional strain of both. Maybe, if the spirit stalkers left her alone, she could think about becoming a therapist. *But, will they stop coming?* Lily paused, standing in the middle of her room contemplating her choices. *I hope they stop...it would make my life so much easier. I'm not sure how much more of this double life I can take where my sanity is pushed to the brink.* But, at the same time. Maybe, this was guiding her toward something more. Maybe God has more plans for me that involve these spirits for some reason.

Lily giggled, shaking her head. "No way. Listening to people whine all day can't be what I do for a living. There's no way it would be a sane career choice. I don't know why I'm thinking about this now. I'm still in high school. I have plenty of time."

Heading downstairs, Lily walked through the noisy Shels household. Her brothers Max and Theo were fighting over video games in the parlor. Her Dad, sitting on the couch, was trying to ignore his bickering sons by turning up the volume on his phone. Once Lily was in the kitchen, she heard her Mom on the phone, making plans to meet her Aunt for lunch. Lily listened as she refilled her water bottle at the sink. Blocking out the sound of her Dad yelling at the boys. The sudden silence from Theo and Max, meant they were one squeak away from losing their video games.

Loud, noisy, and sometimes extremely overwhelming. Lily

smiled brightly, realizing she had so much to be grateful for-including her boisterous and obnoxious family. Rummaging through the cupboards, Lily grabbed a granola bar and some snacks packs, stuffing them into her skirt pockets.

Lily snuck a hug around her Mom, then darted upstairs, waiting for Mina to call. Another family member Lily was beginning to appreciate it more and more. These past 2 semesters had been extra stressful for Lily with Isaiac and Fred, taking so much of her time and emotions. She hoped and prayed that next semester would be peaceful, without any spirit stalkers interrupting her social calendar. That would give her plenty of time to capture Patrick's attention, tell Doris more about the last few stories, <u>and stay as far away from antique stores as possible</u>!

Sounded like a solid plan to Lily. *Ava…*

Lily added Ava to her mental list. *Avoid Ava as much as possible.*

Maybe Doris will help, once she finds out what happened that day with Ava, last semester regarding Isaac.

Lily grabbed her phone stand for Mina's video call. With less than two hours to go, she set up her snack center, water bottle and pillow seat. The excitement swelled as Lily waited. She had so much amazing news to tell Mina.

Fiddling with Mrs. Brooke's letter, Lily's eyes wandered to her closet.

What cute outfit should I wear in my next post? Maybe I should change my account name to Vintage something. Ohh maybe I'll get a thousand followers and become a Vintage Teen Magazine ambassador?

THE END

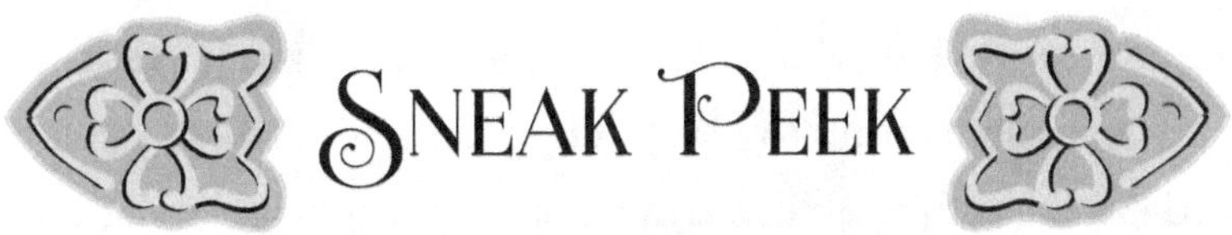

SNEAK PEEK

BOOK 2, FRAMED IN TIME

CHAPTER 1

After the 3 hour video chat with Mina, Lily said her prayers and passed out. With no spirit thoughts invading her mind, the silence gave way to the first peaceful sleep she had in months. Without the anxiety from the trapped spirits, nothing interrupted her deep, peaceful sleep.

§

Ava sat in her bedroom. Posters from her favorite artists hung on the walls. Her social media paraphernalia was in its usual corner, collecting dust. She hadn't worked on any posts or updates in months. A notebook, covered in scribbles, lay flat on her vanity table. Empty–the entire room, her house, and her world felt so empty without Yuki.

Ava's phone buzzed softly against her pillow, the flash lighting up her dark room. Picking up her phone, Ava checked the messages. Jen and a few of her friends were going out to dinner tonight. Ava's parents were both working late, and her sister...Yuki was still dead. It had been three months now, but it felt like hell. The days blurred together. Everything blurred into an unrecognizable shadow of life...at least until she ran into Lily Shels.

Ava's phone buzzed again, pulling her back from her morbid thoughts. It was Jen again.

Jen: I can pick you up at 5:30. So be ready when I pull up.

Ava replied with her usual 'K, with a kissy face emoji'. She flipped on the bright lights on her vanity desk. Squinting as she pulled away, shielding her eyes from the glare. "Holy shhhhhhh...man that's bright." Once Ava's eyes adjusted, she flipped to a fresh page in her notebook. Her thoughts returned to Lily Shels and how they "met" last semester. *Three weeks after Yuki died.*

Met? That's not exactly what happened, but no matter. Ava's mission was clear. She had to uncover what strange secret Lily was hiding. And who is Isaac? Ava had already been asking some of their classmates about Lily and her weirdness . Most of them gave the same answers as Jen. Lily was nice, and the only thing odd about her was whatever happened last semester, after we met, *Five weeks after Yuki died.*

No one seemed to know what really happened, either. It was a big mystery, and from what Ava found out, Lily and her were the only two who knew what actually happened that day. On that school roof. *Lily j–*

No, I won't think about that. Ava tossed her phone to the bed. Opening her notebook.

What is Lily Shels' secret? And why did she ruin my chance to talk to Yuki?

Ava circled the questions, her pen digging into the paper, ripping into the pages underneath. She stopped, laying her pen aside. Her hands shook as concentrated on slowing her breathing. Just like the therapist said. *"When you find yourself feeling overwhelmed, stop what you are doing and focus on deep breaths."*

Ava blinked away the angry tears. *Will I ever feel happy again? Truly happy?* Three months since Yukie died–was not enough time to work through her pain.

Ava wondered if her Mom and Dad dealt with the same pain? *Was that why they worked so much?* They didn't used to work everyday, late into the evening. But, since Yuki's death, they both worked longer hours, spending less and less time at home. The house felt like a nice, shiny seashell. Beautiful on the outside, but empty and cold inside.

Ava's phone buzzed again, scaring her. Walking over to her bed, she read Jen's latest text. She would be there in 5 minutes. Ava rushed around, putting on a new tee shirt, then patted down her mini skirt, smoothing out the wrinkles as best she could. Grabbing her eyeliner and lipstick, Ava quickly freshened her makeup. Practicing a smile in the vanity mirror, until a car horn honked--Jen was here. Ava grabbed her house keys, wallet and phone. Shoving them into her purse as she ran out the door.

Hopping into the car, Ava waved at Jen's brother, who was driving.

"Hey, Jen and Robbie! Thanks for picking me up." Ava smiled brightly.

Jen hugged Ava as she hopped into the backseat. "Yeah, no problem. I know it helps to get out of the house."

Ava's smile tilted. Jen knew all about her depression, that's why she didn't ask if Ava needed to be picked up anymore.

After 10 no-shows from Ava, Jen caught on that something was seriously wrong. Everyone in their friend group only knew Ava as a social butterfly. She continued to fake it, hoping someday soon it would be true, again.

Jen caught a glimpse of Ava's frown while they drove along. "Don't worry Ava. As long as you keep trying, I'll be right here with you." Jen switched topics trying to lighten the mood. "So, Robbie said the burger place we are going to tonight has great milkshakes too. He has errands to run, so he'll just drop us off then pick us up when we are done."

"Sounds great. Thanks Robbie." Ava's charming smile was pasted back on her face when she thanked Robbie, hiding her lack of interest. He was Jen's older brother, graduating from High School, and the sweetest guy she ever met. Robbie volunteered to be Jen and Ava's driver since he got his driver's license.

Robbie pulled around to the restaurant's front doors. Ava and Jen got out and waved goodbye as he pulled away. Dashing inside, the girls met up with a few classmates.

Jen constantly monitored Ava's expressions. Trying to read what was under her painted smile. She was growing more concerned about Ava's fixation on Yuki's death, and this new focus on Lily Shels. Especially since Ava started cross examining their friends.

To be Continued in book 2, Framed In Time.

About the Author

Mary Cecilia Freeman, or Cecilia as she prefers to be called, started her author journey at a very young age. Her focus has always been sparking new adventures and sharing a small glimpse into how she sees the world. With her many nieces and nephews in mind, she tries to speak to kids of all ages, and explore real life issues with a little magic thrown in. Thanks to her large family of 13 brothers and sisters, her inspiration for magical adventures never ends.

Even though she has been writing short stories for awhile, Cecilia ventured into YA for the first time with this new series. She first discovered Lily while strolling through an antique store, and realized immediately that there was a story waiting to be told. Her newest character, Lily and her story immediately sprang to life. Together Cecilia and Lily embarked on an exciting adventure: Cecilia working in a new genre and full length novel, *Lily's Guide to Releasing Antique Spirits.*

The author lives in Kansas with her family and one cat. So

far she hasn't made contact with any trapped spirits like Fred, even though she continues to visit multiple antique stores. But, she'll keep us posted in her blogs.

Read Cecilia's Blog here: https://writewithcecilia.com/

Be sure to check out my website for the latest blog and book updates!

https://writewithcecilia.com/

Subscribe and enjoy!

Follow and connect on social media:
Pinterest: https://www.pinterest.com/ceciliawrite/
Website: https://writewithcecilia.com/
instagram: https://www.instagram.com/writewithcecilia
Linkedin: https://www.linkedin.com/maryceciliafreeman

Support the Author!
Review the Book on Amazon here:
amazon.com/author/mcfreeman

First, dress up. Because, why not?

Go early on a Saturday morning, most places open by 10am so it's not that early.

Grab a coffee and snack on the way. Exploring is 100x's more fun when you've brought along something to sip on as you browse.

Take your time, look around. Antique stores can be very overwhelming with the abundance of stuff everywhere. Give yourself plenty of time to explore.

Don't be afraid to look in the crowded corners and have fun!

You never know what treasures you'll find! Happy Antiquing!